A Lesson in

Passion

Jennifer Connors

A Lesson in Passion

Published by J Connors Publishing, LLC
Gilbert, Arizona

ISBN 978-0-9824655-0-9

www.jenniferconnors.net

This book is dedicated to my husband, Darren. Without his encouragement, which bordered on annoying at times, this book would never have been printed. I love you dearly.

A Lesson in Passion

❖ Chapter 1 ❖

Men. The bane of every woman's existence. What did they say? Can't live with them, can't live without them. Or was that what men said about women? Did it matter?

Ginny kept contemplating her latest failure in the dating department as she drove to work. Eric was at the bottom of a long list of men she considered her "failures." Perhaps she was too picky, as some of her friends kept telling her. Of course, they wouldn't have to live with Eric's constant need to quibble every thing she said, so she didn't care what her friends thought.

She had become the "Three Date Wonder." Ginny was adept at knowing a man was completely wrong for her within three dates. Actually, she could tell after one date, but she was always willing to give him the benefit of the doubt. After all, maybe they were just nervous.

And so, like Eric, there were a string of men with a string of reasons why they were totally wrong for her. John picked his teeth at the dinner table in a restaurant. Mike was a bad tipper and a little too forthcoming about his politics. Murray spoke a little too fondly about his mother. Altogether, they were probably really good guys, but Ginny just couldn't cultivate any feeling about them. She was beginning to think of her love life as one big *Seinfeld* episode.

Ginny never considered that she had high standards. A good job, self-sufficiency and a decent sense of humor topped her list. Some compatibility would be good, but she loved to listen to a different point of view. She certainly didn't want a lap dog, needy and begging. It wasn't the perfect man she needed, just the perfect man for her.

No one would call her beautiful, but certainly not plain or ugly.

No horrible disfigurements, no huge scars across her body. She was tall for a girl at 5 ft 9 in, with a medium build and decent size breasts. Ginny would often remark on how she planned on losing those last ten pounds, but the lure of the vending machine in the late afternoon was often too great. Her brown hair had blond highlights since the early part of the century and was currently cut in a stylish A-line, like Posh Spice.

And yet, here she was, thirty and alone. Some of her friends, her married friends, would say she had no one to blame but herself. Her only non-married friend, Lisa, would say that all men are evil and to not waste her time anyway. Of course, her being a lesbian, it was not wholly unexpected. So who was right? Ginny didn't think it mattered... because she was unhappy.

Ginny pulled into her usual parking spot at Tinesdale Emergency Hospital in Mesa, Arizona. The hospital was named after Dr. Albert Tinesdale, founder and long time resident of Mesa. In his wisdom, he developed the glorified urgent care to alleviate real hospitals from having to deal with those smaller problems plaguing society, such as minor stitches and phlegmy colds. The hospital also saw it's share of larger problems: broken bones, concussions and an occasional birth.

She was a physician's assistant and worked most of her day stitching and wiping. Her parents couldn't understand why she didn't go to medical school and be a real doctor. Her mother was always fond of emphasizing the "assistant" part of her job title. Ginny was quite content in her choice of careers. She had the fun without the responsibility. Well, not quite, but at least she didn't have to pretend to be God.

Ginny walked into the lobby and made her way past the reception desk. Holly, good friend and receptionist, winked at her while she answered one of the never ending questions of the hospital's clientèle. Behind the last exam room was a door leading to the staff lunch and locker rooms. Ginny went into the locker room and bumped into Dr. Fielding. He was her mentor and favorite co-worker. He always had a kind word and wanted desperately to make everyone feel better. Today was no exception.

"You're looking very pretty today, dear," Dr. Fielding said with enormous smile.

"And you are looking quite handsome yourself, Dr. Fielding," Ginny replied. Dr. Fielding was old school, before political correctness would allow such a statement to be uttered. Ginny never minded, since she considered it a genuine compliment. Dr. Fielding was both happily married for over forty years and more grandfatherly than man. Of course, many of her other co-workers would receive a tart reply were they to give her the same compliment.

"Only a few days left before the big vacation, huh?" Dr. Fielding asked as he walked out of the locker room. He started singing the Beach Boys song *Kokomo* in honor of her upcoming vacation in the Caribbean.

Ginny started her day, which was much the same as every other day. A baby with a bad cough, a man who had taken a bad fall at work, an elderly woman with open sore from her diabetes. She always tried to make everyone feel better, much like her mentor did. Her mind just kept wandering back to her pathetic love life and her "old maid" status.

During a rare break, Ginny met Holly in the lunchroom. Holly was happily married to her high school sweetheart. They lived in a beautiful home in Gilbert with their 2 beautiful children. Holly was what Ginny would describe as "pert and perky." She was short, only reaching Ginny's shoulder and had a blond pixie cut. She had big brown eyes that when applied with makeup were smoky and alluring. Her husband, a real estate agent, was pure schmooze and someone Ginny could see cheating on Holly, who would probably be none the wiser.

"I have something for you," Holly said handing a large plastic grocery bag to Ginny.

"Oh, you shouldn't have," Ginny said. Then she looked in the bag. "Really, you shouldn't have," Ginny remarked sarcastically.

"Come on. You're going on a beach vacation. You'll need something to read."

Ginny began removing the paperback books, one at a time. *Desire in the Highlands, Lover's Cove, The One Perfect Love.* There must have been at least fifteen romance novels in the bag. Ginny quickly put the books back in the bag before someone came in and saw them. How embarrassing would that be?

"Not my thing, Holly, but thank you for thinking of me," Ginny said trying to hand her back the bag.

"You are not going on a nice vacation, sitting on the beach reading work stuff. You're going to have a fun, relaxing time. These books are perfect." There was that word again: perfect.

"I've never really been into romance novels. I would much prefer history or biography or better yet, gory serial killer stuff."

"I can't understand why you don't have a boyfriend," Holly said with her own measure of sarcasm. "Consider these books instructional. How to be a damsel to catch the perfect husband," Holly smiled.

Dear God, Ginny thought. *Is she kidding? Romance novels instructional?* Ginny began to consider that maybe Holly was a serial killer on the side. No one could actually believe that the "romance" in romance novels ever happens in real life. She was going to become part of some adventure where a bare chested mega hunk would sweep her off her feet and beg for her hand in marriage? Ginny didn't think so.

"This is one of my favorites," Holly said as she pulled out one of the books. "The heroine is saved by her one true love. Oh, it's so romantic. And the sex parts are really hot!"

"You know what these are, don't you?" Ginny asked jokingly. "These books are girl porn, pure and simple."

"Ewwww. What are you talking about? They are romantic and fun and elegant. They are set a long time ago when life was simpler. They're about aristocracy and lords and ladies. How is that 'porn'?"

"It's well documented that men are visual while women are emotional. These books feed the female imagination with ideas of far off lands and singularly perfect men. Regular porn shows men boobs. It's the same thing but appealing to a different audience."

"You really are insane, Ginny!" Holly looked close to slapping Ginny. "These books show you that life can be as wonderful as you hope."

Ginny stared at Holly intently. For the first time, she considered the possibility that maybe Holly's life wasn't as perfect as she led everyone to believe. Maybe Holly needed the escape that these books provided, because her life was as tedious as the rest of theirs.

"Take them with you. You'll see they're easy to read and enjoyable. I know you won't be disappointed," Holly said as she left

4

the lunch room.

Ginny would be polite, bring them home and forget about them. Holly would only hear that "Oh no, I forgot to bring them." She took a few out and stared at the covers. Do men like this really exist? Not the Fabio types who pose for the covers. She wondered if any of these guys ever quibbled about every little thing you said.

Ginny was always a stickler when it came to packing. She loved to travel, so she had gotten quite good at packing over the years. This trip was an easy one, just a week at a beach resort in Jamaica. She was going with her best friend Lisa. The best part of going on vacation with a lesbian was they never fought over the same love interest. If anything, Ginny was often jealous with how easily Lisa found love interests. Lisa got to pick the locale this time, since Ginny had dragged her up to Machu Picchu last year and was still listening to Lisa complain about it. Make a girl climb one mountain and it was bitch, bitch, bitch.

She rechecked her bags to make sure she had everything she needed. The essentials were all there: bathing suits, razor and sunscreen. Was there anything she forgot? Oh yeah, reading material. Ginny went to her pile of books, but realized she had read everything there. *Crap*, she thought. She didn't have time to stop at the bookstore or library.

She could pick up some books at the airport, but Ginny was notoriously cheap and hated paying a premium for reading materials. Suddenly, she was staring at the pile of books given to her by Holly. She didn't have time to get anything else and these were free. They were also small paperbacks, so they wouldn't take up that much space in her carry-on.

Ginny grabbed the bunch and stuffed them into her beach bag. She thought about what Holly had said about the books being "instructional." She started to look forward to ripping them apart. "Oh, Gerald, could our life be anymore perfect?" "No, my darling, it couldn't!" Should be a blast!

Just then, a car honked in her driveway. Lisa was usually late, but Ginny had gotten into the habit of always telling her to be at her house a half hour earlier than necessary. Worked like a charm, Lisa was on time. Lisa was what Ginny would call "the pretty lesbian." She was almost as tall as Ginny, but much more buff. Hours at the gym had defined every muscle on Lisa's body to perfection. Her hair was long and the most beautiful shade of chestnut, natural of course. She had pretty blue eyes and a heart shaped face. Most guys tripped over her when she walked into a room. Lisa loved taunting men... it was her favorite game at parties.

The drive to the airport was uneventful. With the 202 clear straight to their exit, it only took minutes to get there. They decided to park off site since Ginny had a coupon. Lisa was always amused by Ginny's cheapness. Lisa liked to live in the moment, where Ginny was a planner and saver. Again, it was a wonder they were such good friends, but they shared some pretty hairy moments growing up that cemented their relationship.

On the shuttle to the airport, Lisa kept talking about her latest failure in the romance department. It was always refreshing to know that Ginny wasn't the only one who couldn't hold onto a lover for very long.

"She was so clingy. And she always insisted on making the bed. Who gives a crap if the bed is made or not. I'm just going to mess it up later that night anyway!"

"I don't know what to tell you and I'm certainly not the one to go to for advice on love. Oh, and I never make my bed either," Ginny said.

"Good for you. Let's make a vow, right here and now to never make our beds!" Lisa stated triumphantly while holding her hand over heart.

"Here, here! To never making our beds and to not settling for crappy relationships!" Ginny dutifully placed her hand over her heart as well.

"Let's just try to see how many times we can get laid in one week while on vacation. Do you remember your special name?" Lisa asked referring to their secret identities for lustful one night stands. Not that Ginny had ever had the chance to use the name, nor could she even remember the last time she'd had sex.

"Was it Lola?" Ginny asked.

"I was Lola because it was close to Lisa. You were Penny," Lisa said.

"I don't like Penny. I want something new and exotic. How about Sheila?" Ginny asked, trying to keep a straight face.

"Sheila, huh? You kind of look like a Sheila," Lisa stated matter-of-factly.

"What exactly does a 'Sheila' look like?" Ginny wondered aloud.

They arrived at the airport and checked in their luggage, then waited for twenty-five minutes in the Post 9/11 TSA party zone. Ginny always worried that Lisa would do something to get them pulled aside and strip searched. Once she asked Lisa if she would request a male officer to search her so she wouldn't get turned on during the search.

After arriving at the gate with thirty minutes to spare, Lisa went off to buy some magazines and a snack. Ginny gave her money for a bottle of water. While Lisa is gone, Ginny pulled out one of the novels Holly gave her.

Desire in the Highlands was the first one she grabbed. She was reading it as Lisa walked back with her booty.

"What... the hell... is that?" she asked, spotting the overly sexy couple on the cover.

"Holly's idea of relationship advice. She thinks that these will cure my desire to be alone. I will never again find something wrong with any man," Ginny replied tartly.

Lisa just stared at her. Ginny knew she had a litany of things to say on the subject of Holly and the "perfect marriage," but decided that it was better to refrain. She knew that Holly was a close friend of Ginny's, although she couldn't figure out why.

"I understand why Holly reads those, but I never took you for a 'romance novel' type."

"I forgot to pick up something else and these were free," Ginny knew what was coming next.

"You make a good salary, Gin, you can pluck down ten dollars for a goddamn book that won't embarrass me on this trip."

"These embarrass you? Oh, well, now I'm going to read the whole lot while basking on the beach next to you," Ginny was really enjoying this. "Anyone who asks is going to hear that you authored them."

"You suck so bad!" Lisa was not someone you wanted as an enemy. Her ability to humiliate and shock was way out Ginny's league.

Not long after, the airline announced boarding. Off to the perfect beach vacation. Ginny couldn't wait!

❖ Chapter 2 ❖

Ginny had never been to Jamaica before and Lisa swore that the resort was both beautiful and boasted the best nightlife. They arrived at Montego Bay without any issues only to be carted onto a bus for their resort in Negril. This was probably one of the most harrowing bus rides in her life. Much of the road was along a high cliff above beautiful crystal blue water. Unfortunately, some of this same road was practically one lane, so the bus driver would honk to let any other traffic know he was coming. Ginny wondered what would happen if the other traffic didn't hear their warning.

It took nearly three hours to reach their resort. The ride could be both breathtaking and heartbreaking. The views of the ocean and high cliffs were incredible, a real testament to God. That was overshadowed by the extreme poverty of some of the small towns along the way. When the bus would stop for a red light, people would crowd the bus to sell their wares or children would beg for money. Ginny, always the champion of the underdog, immediately would buy something and turn around and give some change to the kids.

Lisa could never understand how Ginny would fight over being overcharged fifty cents at the grocery store, but then turn around and give anything she had to anyone who would ask. Lisa had to admit it was one of the things she loved best about her friend, even if she didn't get it.

Finally at the resort, Ginny and Lisa were ready for a shower and dinner. It was an all-inclusive resort, including unlimited alcohol. They both had plans to let their hair down and meet as many interesting individuals as possible.

The resort was impressive. The lobby was filled with all Caribbean colonial furniture, dark woods, elaborately ornate with colorful cushions. A large counter, located on the left side of the lobby, was staffed with three hotel workers waiting to assist the large bus load of passengers. Ginny and Lisa walked over in the hopes of securing their room key as soon as possible.

Brenda, the first available front desk employee they reached, was a dark skinned beauty with her hair pulled severely back in a bun.

Both Lisa and Ginny were admiring her smooth, flawless skin and incredible white teeth, although for different reasons. She kept stealing glances at Lisa and Ginny began to wonder if after only five minutes at the resort, Lisa already had a love interest.

With key in hand, they followed the detailed directions to their room.

"Damn, you work fast," Ginny said with both annoyance and admiration.

"What are you talking about? I was just admiring her beauty. Don't tell me you've never admired a pretty boy face before."

"Of course I have. But I never seem to have a shot of 'admiring' said face up close and personal," Ginny laughed.

"What can I say: when you got it, you got it!" Lisa said with her usual smirk.

The room was the usual, with a lot of Caribbean flare. The beds were covered in brightly colored and flowered bed spreads, and floral prints adorned every wall. The bathroom was utilitarian, with one of those underpowered hairdryers and small vanity that would barely accommodate one girl's stuff, let alone two. The best part was the balcony overlooking the ocean. It cost them extra, but waking up and being able to hear the ocean and enjoy the view seemed worth it.

Ginny stepped out and inhaled the salty air and listened to a steel drum band playing in the distance. She really needed this vacation. She had been putting in extra hours and covering for some of the other PA's lately and needed to deflate. Ginny was scanning the beach for some potential love interests when a banner caught her eye: Welcome Gay and Lesbian Alliance Members.

Ginny had been to many resorts that were hosting conferences for certain groups. She began to wonder how many non-gay vacationers would be around. Lisa joined her on the balcony, wearing a towel from her quick shower.

"Lisa, this resort isn't only hosting the Gay and Lesbian Alliance, is it?" Ginny could care less about a person's sexual orientation, but would like to meet guys who liked boobs.

"Of course not." Lisa said. "My friend Ted told me about this and said that he only knew a handful of people coming."

Ginny covered her head in her hands. "Does Ted know every gay man and woman who like vacationing in the Caribbean?"

"Relax... I'm sure there will be plenty of straight available guys around. You'll be even more sought after with all the unavailable women around," Lisa said with a smile.

Well, as it turns out, the entire resort was hosting the Gay and Lesbian Alliance. As Ginny and Lisa walked by the beach to check out the party, there wasn't a straight vacationer to be seen. Lisa, who is quite adept at picking straight from gay, couldn't find one single heterosexual male in the crowd. While Lisa was gone checking with the hotel management, Ginny went to the bar and ordered a beer.

Ginny wasn't really that disappointed. After all, she was at a beautiful resort, with unlimited alcohol and incredible views. She didn't really expect to meet anyone special anyway. Ginny could make the best of it and still have a good time dancing and partying and sunning herself.

"Well, I checked with management. It seems that the entire resort was booked by the GLA. I'm so sorry, Gin. I really had no idea," Lisa was clearly upset.

"Don't sweat it, Lisa. There are worse places to be and not have any available men around. I can still party and drink and lay on the beach," Ginny put on her best "who gives a damn" smile.

"Gin, you're the best. If you want, I'll pretend we're together and we can both be celibate this week."

"No way. At the very least, I intend to rip apart your choice in mate. Don't take that away from me!" Ginny said looking around at the potential.

"You may want to do a little experimenting this week. You never know what lurks in your psyche," Lisa was always jokingly trying to recruit Ginny to play for the other team, but alas, you can't chose your sexual orientation.

"Thanks, but no thanks. I'll stick with the stick," Ginny said eliciting a face from Lisa.

"How do you deal with that thing!"

The night was, from Ginny's point of view, very interesting. There were people from all over the US and the world. Ginny was talking to a group of guys from Portugal. They were very excited not to be judged and to let their hair down. They found it very funny that Ginny was not gay and spending the week at the resort.

Dinner was quite an affair. There was a huge buffet set up in the main dining room. Long tables with everything from fish to chicken to goat were laid out in huge chafing dishes. There were rice and pasta dishes as well as an enormous array of desserts. Cakes, pudding, cookies, and fruit tarts were arranged on the last table in the line. Ginny realized that she would have to work very hard not to gain an enormous amount of weight.

Ginny filled up her plate and sat next to Lisa at a big round table that seated ten. Immediately, Lisa introduced Ginny as her "straight" friend who was very understanding. Ginny smiled embarrassingly as the others at the table said how great she was to be such a good friend.

The table was mostly women, with one male couple to balance the estrogen. The conversation mostly revolved around their real lives, occupations and hobbies. One woman, who was drop dead gorgeous with long blond hair and clear blue eyes, was telling the group about her work with troubled teenagers. Ginny watched her as she spoke. The woman was clearly exaggerating her perfection, so it was easy not to like her. It was even easier not to like her if she wasn't exaggerating. Ginny just sat and listened as she ate her dinner.

Ginny dug into her buffet feast. She decided that if she couldn't suck face with someone she would either later forget or want to forget, she could at least try some of the local cuisine. She chose "some kind of stew" with meat that she couldn't identify. It was actually quite tasty and not at all gamey. She finished it up, along with various side dishes and two desserts.

After dinner, Lisa and Ginny went to the dance club. The alcohol was flowing and the music was blaring. Ginny could feel herself beginning to unwind as she got up often to dance to her "favorite song." In other words, anything with a beat. Lisa was already mingling heavily, but would often join Ginny to dance. Ginny had always loved music. Her parents brought her up in Classic Rock, her older siblings had her grooving to all things 80's, and she had recently acquired a taste for alternative. One thing she couldn't stomach was anything by those lip syncing artists: Brittany Spears, Christina Aguillera, those annoying boy bands and especially any singer chosen on American Idol.

Of course, after several shots of "whatever," one could dance to anything, look foolish, and still have a great time. Ginny was getting funky to some kind of rap, when a couple of guys began sandwiching her in between them. Ginny hardly noticed and cared even less. She could not be stopped. She finally had to sit down or fall down.

"You okay?" Lisa looked at Ginny with some concern. "You look a little pale."

"I think so. I'm think I'm just jet lagged," Ginny replied even though she had never felt like this before on the way to a destination. Sure she would feel tired and sick coming home, but never at the beginning of a vacation.

"I'm going to bed. I bet I feel better tomorrow." Ginny started to head back to the room. About halfway there, she realized that she was going to throw up and very soon. Looking around, she noticed some tall bushes and ran around them just as she hurled. It took several minutes to recover long enough to make it back to her room. She was forced to smell the sweet cloying scent of some exotic plant. Usually, it would have been soothing, but when forced to vomit in the bushes, it became very nauseating.

She finally returned to the room, only to have to vomit again and again and again. *Dear God,* Ginny thought, *what is going on?*

Ginny's first thought was maybe she drank more than she could handle. As she lay on the bathroom floor, thanking the tile for being so cool against her face, she thought about how much she had drank. Yes, she had several shots, but that was about it. She wasn't mixing and she only had water with dinner. Then she started to think about dinner. Mystery Stew. *What the hell kind of meat was that any way,* Ginny thought grimly. *Oh God, please don't let this be food poisoning!*

As a physician's assistant, Ginny knew what the recovery time for food poisoning was: at least two days from the onset and that is just to start feeling somewhat normal again. *This could be a real vacation killer,* thought Ginny. *I'm sure it's just jet lag combined with alcohol. I'll be fine by tomorrow.*

Lisa didn't return to the room until the middle of the night. She found Ginny still lying on the floor in front of the toilet.

"Geez, Gin, what's wrong?" Lisa looked so concerned despite her drunkenness. Her slurred words were almost comical to Ginny, who had little to find amusing in the past few hours.

"I don't know. I've been calling Ralph on the porcelain phone since I left you in the club. I'm hoping it's just too much alcohol and not the mystery stew from dinner," Ginny said in the most pathetic voice. She looked up at Lisa and knew immediately that she had met someone already. "Can you please help me to bed and then you can tell me about your new friend."

Lisa was amazed by how each of them knew when the other had gotten lucky. It was like some kind of badge they wore, but only the other could see it. Lisa tried to be gentle when getting Ginny off the floor, but being inebriated herself made the whole scene comical. She dropped Ginny a couple of times and then Ginny had to help her stay up on the way back to their beds.

Ginny threw off her bedspread and climbed into bed with her clothes on. She was just happy to lie on something soft. Lisa was raving about her "new" friend. She was a photographer from New York and she lived in a loft and went to great bars and lived like a gay version of *Sex and the City*. As Ginny half listened to her best friend of many years, she wondered how drunk she was to buy that load of bullshit. If her "new" friend truly lived like she said, Ginny was a secret agent with the CIA.

Ginny's last thought before going to sleep was how much fun it would be to make fun of her friend over being so gullible when she's drunk.

Any hopes of feeling better the next morning were quashed. Ginny managed to sleep occasionally between exhausting bouts of vomiting. Lisa woke the next morning to find Ginny back on the bathroom floor and not able to move. She quickly got Ginny's pillow and a blanket to try to make her more comfortable. Ginny looked so pathetic that Lisa's heart just dropped. After the mix up with the resort being "all gay" and now she couldn't even get out of the bathroom. How much more could her dear friend take?

❖ Chapter 3 ❖

Ginny spent the first few days of her vacation in bed in her room. Her only consolation was being able to see the ocean and listen to its soothing, gentle waves crash on the beach she couldn't bring herself to sit on. Lisa was constantly checking on her and bringing her toast or water. No one could ask for a better friend.

Ginny's only other friend was the pile of romance novels Holly had given her. During the long hours of lying in bed, unable to move or risk a new vomiting session, Ginny would lie reading book after book. When she wasn't sleeping, she was reading about all the people who had love lives and got to have earth shattering orgasmic sex, even when it was their "first" time. She read about past lives in worlds that seemed to be perfect despite a lack of decent health care, running water, solid roads, or technology of any kind.

Well, Ginny thought morosely, *Holly was right about one thing: the sex parts are pretty hot.* Not that it would do Ginny any good, even if she did feel better, with an extreme lack of potential partners. And so, when not sleeping or sitting on the toilet so the offending food could escape in other ways, Ginny was either lying in bed or sitting on the balcony. To keep entertained, she became engrossed in past lives and ridiculous problems.

Why doesn't she just stand up for herself, Ginny would think while reading a particular passage. She shook her head in disgust that women would ever allow themselves to be so subjugated by men. Ginny was not so naïve to realize their predicament, but at the very least, they could withhold sex until their "perfect" man came to his senses.

On the third day, Ginny started to feel better enough to go and sit on the beach. She was still extremely shaky about eating in the dining room though. She'd often make Lisa go and get her some bread and water. "At least I won't gain a bunch of weight on this vacation," she told Lisa when she returned with the food.

"If anything, I'm pretty sure you've lost some weight," Lisa retorted. "You know, the gaunt, stick figure thing is so in for all the models."

"Something tells me that no one will mistake me for Kate Moss," Ginny smiled back. "And that's okay with me, since I like having boobs."

The morning was spent in a lounge chair on the beach, reading more about the incredible lives of fictional characters. There was a nice breeze blowing and the ocean was calm and glass like. Ginny was content to watch the other guests frolicking in the water or participating in the unlimited water sports available at the resort.

Around noon, Lisa came by with some more bread and a little ginger ale to sooth any remaining discomfort. Ginny noticed that the sky was getting dark. "Are we in for a storm?" she asked Lisa, who had taken the chair next to hers.

Lisa surveyed the landscape. "Looks like it. They have those storms all the time. You know, the ones that only last a few minutes, then it goes back to blue and beautiful."

"It would cool things down for tonight," Ginny replied. "I love to listen to the rain when I'm sleeping. The only bad part is that I usually have to get up to pee."

"Nice," Lisa said with a laugh.

As it turned out, it wasn't one of those storms that ends after a few minutes. It was an unbelievably violent storm that tears everything up. Ginny got her wish, to listen to rain as she tried to sleep. Unfortunately, the sounds of lounge chairs hitting the side of the hotel and trees being thrown back and forth was enough to keep her up all night waiting for something to come crashing through their balcony door.

Lisa and Ginny were sitting together watching the carnage outdoors. "Is it only me, or does this ring of the 'worst vacation ever'?" Ginny asked while watching some sign fly past the window.

"You're not dead, so technically, it could be worse," Lisa replied.

Ginny turned and stared at her friend. "Are you trying to jinx me? Haven't I been through enough?"

Together they laughed over the irony of it. Two minutes later, the lights went out and the two friends were left in the dark. "Great, just great!"

"Do me a favor," Ginny asked Lisa, "Don't miss the toilet when you have to go in the dark!"

"Agreed!"

They tried as best they could to sleep, since they had nothing else to do. Lisa wondered if anyone was at the dance club when they lost power. She could imagine them all huddled there, too scared to walk back to their rooms. Lying awake in the dark, she started to envy them.

In the morning, the worst of the wind was over, but the rain continued. Lisa went over to the lobby to see if they would ever get the power back, while Ginny continued to sit in the room, reading yet more romance novels. She began to stare out the balcony door and wonder how she managed to get it so wrong.

I've traveled all over the world. I've met people from dozens of countries. I've seen wonders of the world. Where did I go wrong on a crummy beach vacation! She thought to herself. *No men, not feeling well, no power, no sunshine... I don't want to think how it can get worse!*

With that thought, in popped Lisa, wet from head to toe and looking extremely unhappy. She was carrying a box with their hotel room number on it.

"Good news or bad news," was all she said as she sat on a chair by the bed.

"Good news, please," Ginny replied.

"I got this box of necessary supplies to survive the rest of the week if we wish to stay. It has candles, matches, a couple bottles of water and some sort of protein bars."

Ginny did not look amused. "And the bad news..."

"If we leave and head back to Montego Bay, our chances of getting a hotel room are nil. The airport is shut down until clean up can be completed and the resort will not refund any money because it was an act of God."

"So, there won't be any food provided?" Ginny wasn't all that disappointed.

"They will have the kitchens up by tonight, but most of the food will be packaged. This is to get through today."

"Well, it seems we have no choice but to stay here a few more days."

"My thoughts exactly," Lisa did not look amused. "I bumped into some of my new friends in the lobby and they are planning on having a party in their room tonight. We, of course, are invited."

Ginny didn't know if she was up for a night of "girl" talk. She hadn't slept, she'd barely eaten and now she was sitting in a hotel room, with no air conditioning and no power. At the moment, she felt a little defeated. "I'll pass. Besides, I have all these books to read. How will I get by if I don't find out what happens to the pirate and his new girlfriend?"

"I'm sure this goes without saying, but next time you totally get to pick where we go!"

Ginny couldn't help laughing at this. Truth was, she almost always picked and Lisa willingly went along. She followed Ginny to the pyramids in Egypt, the Great Barrier Reef in Australia and to Machu Picchu in Peru. Ginny knew she had a great friend and wouldn't trade her in for anything, even for a better week in Jamaica!

By the end of the week, Ginny and Lisa were done with a capital D. Although they still had water in their room, they had no hot water. They never got the power back in their room, although the dining room and lobby had power from a generator. It rained most of the time, so they couldn't sun themselves on the beach as a consolation.

Ginny spent most of each day, sitting on their covered balcony, reading her collection of romance novels. Lisa would often venture out to meet up with her "new" friends and begged Ginny to come along. Ginny just didn't have the energy after her food poisoning. She felt bad ditching Lisa, but knew she would just be a drag on the group.

When the bus came to pick them up to return them to Montego Bay, both Ginny and Lisa had to admit that they couldn't wait. "The potential of a hot shower, along with food that doesn't scare the crap out of me to eat, makes this homecoming especially welcome," Ginny stated the obvious.

"Since reading those books, you started talking funny," Lisa commented back.

"Why, Lisa, whatever do you mean? I'm simply expanding my

vocabulary to include a wider range of words to describe simple things."

"Whatever. Although I agree with your current assessment that the situation warrants our immediate withdrawal," Lisa said with a smile to show Ginny that years in the business world could produce a similarly ridiculous vocabulary.

"Should we leverage our synergies and be more proactive towards solutions?" Ginny spent a lot of time with Lisa and read a lot of Dilbert, so she'd learned the business jargon.

After another harrowing bus ride, they arrived back at the airport to find that it had been cleared and that most flights were finally back on schedule. They were so ecstatic to get on the plane home that even the mostly drunk crew of college guys couldn't dampen their spirits. *I get to take a shower in my own bathroom, get to sleep in my own bed and eat food I know won't make me gag,* Ginny thought as she reclined back in her seat after take-off. Never had she been so happy to go home.

They arrived on time at Sky Harbor and made their way to the luggage carousel. Lisa looked sullen and wasn't very talkative on the flight. "What's wrong with you? You can't tell me your not happy to be home," Ginny said as they watched each piece of luggage pass by.

"I feel awful about how this vacation turned out. We spent all that money and you sat around and read a bunch of half-assed books."

"Every vacation has its problems. Remember when we went to Germany and they lost my luggage? I was wearing the same outfit for a week," both Ginny and Lisa smiled fondly. Lisa spotted her bag and grabbed it.

"Yeah, it was a very unflattering outfit, if I remember correctly. Which reminds me, have you ever worn it again?"

"After a solid week of it, no. It got burned when I got home." Ginny collected her bag and they walked outside to catch their shuttle back to the parking lot. "Oh, God, remember when that greasy Italian guy wouldn't leave you alone in Egypt. He latched onto you like a puppy."

And so it went, story after story got both Ginny and Lisa howling with laughter. They arrived at the lot and got into Lisa's car. Both girls kept coming up with one amusing anecdote after another. "Remember the smell in our hotel room in Spain? It smelled like dead fish and sewage. Remember how the front desk said it was just the restaurant on the first floor? We never did eat there, did we?"

"How about the shark scare in Australia. That woman made everyone freak out over a tuna or something. I wonder if she still feels bad about that?"

Lisa pulled onto the 202 heading east. The stories kept coming since Ginny and Lisa had been vacationing together for over ten years, since they graduated from high school and went to Rocky Point in Mexico. Their friendship had lasted past the easy times of childhood and through the difficult times of high school, especially since they were both too different to be popular. And now, they were occasionally mature women with different lives, but still, the best of friends.

Both girls were having a great time, probably the best time they'd had all week. It was no wonder that neither of them saw the pick-up truck before it hit them.

❖ Chapter 4 ❖

Ginny felt a strange pounding in her head. She was vaguely aware of her surroundings, but in a detached sort of way. She heard sounds but couldn't identify them, she felt a strange movement and she smelled the most God awful smell. *What's going on?* she thought to herself as the pounding continued.

Taking a deep breath, Ginny tried to sort it out. She could be very analytical about things, which served her well in her job. The last thing Ginny could remember was driving home from the airport. *Did Lisa and I get in an accident? Are we okay? Am I dead?*

Ginny began to panic. She opened her eyes but everything was dark. She tried to move, but couldn't seem to move her limbs. Ginny had never been so scared. She couldn't move, couldn't see and there was that smell again. *Surely this couldn't be heaven, not with that smell,* Ginny thought. *Of course, this could be hell and I may have overestimated God's forgiveness.*

Ginny's head began to clear and she realized that she was slumped over something, with her butt in the air. She knew that no EMT or paramedic would transport her to the hospital in such a position. Taking a deep breath, despite the foul odor of animal and outrageous body odor, she willed her mind to clear.

Okay, where could I be? I'm not in heaven, no St. Peter, no pearly gates, massive headache. This could be a cruel introduction to hell, but I don't believe in hell. She decided to take an inventory of everything she did know.

She couldn't see. Why? Was she blind? No, there was something on her head. Ginny tried to reach up to touch the cloth covering her head, but then realized that her hands were tied together. *Dear God, why am I tied up?*

Slowly she began to realize that she was moving. Or, more to the point, the thing she was slumped over was moving. *A horse,* Ginny smiled to herself as she put it together. She was on the back of a horse. *Why am I on the back of a horse,* she wondered.

Ginny began to think of any possibility for her situation. Was she in some warped Stephen King novel where a deranged nurse was taking Ginny back to her house to make her write the perfect novel? Did she get kidnapped by some Deliverance types who were going to take her back to their lair and make her their wife?

As Ginny kept coming up with the most outrageous ideas, she began to hear men talking and laughing. Ginny listened closely, but couldn't understand them. *What is that language?* She tried to place it, but it was completely unfamiliar. Ginny's confusion turned to fear. *What have I gotten myself into?*

All of a sudden, the horse stopped and Ginny heard a large group of people begin to cheer. *Oh, great, this can't be good*, she thought as she was manhandled off the horse. A quick assessment told her that she was not permanently damaged, no broken bones. She realized that her feet were also tied together.

The cloth over her head was viciously ripped off and for a moment, Ginny still couldn't see. The sunshine was so bright, it overwhelmed her after the darkness. As her vision returned, she squinted to look around. She was in the center of a large group of men, standing on a wooden stage. The men were dressed strangely and looked quite deranged. Ginny's head swam as she tried to take in the situation. *Is this some kind of movie set? Is this a period piece from the Middle Ages?* Then suddenly, she realized something else. *Am I shorter?*

Could I be dreaming? Ginny grasped onto that possibility. *Maybe I was in an accident and am in a coma, and this is some elaborate dream I'm having. But why do I not feel like me?*

Ginny began to look around in earnest. The men, mostly big, brawny types were wearing a variety of animal skins and tunics. There were plaid colored kilts as well. They were very dirty, with matted down hair and brown streaks on their exposed arms and legs. They were also the hairiest group of men Ginny had ever seen. *Wait*, she thought to herself, *this is just like the book I read about the Highlands in Scotland. Dear God, is my dream based on a romance novel?*

It occurred to Ginny that if this was indeed a dream, she should be able to do whatever she wanted with no consequences. Ginny eyes lit up with the possibilities. She would, of course, be saved by some mega-hunk who would then want to marry her. The sex would be incredible, especially after her celibate week in the Caribbean (not that she was all that sexually active beforehand). And

22

she bet she would be able to do things in her dream that she would never do in real life, like fight her way past all these sick, smelly men.

The biggest, hairiest and smelliest of the group stood in front of Ginny, speaking in the same language Ginny had heard earlier, but couldn't understand. For some reason, she could now pick out a few words here and there. *Gaelic,* she thought to herself. *He's speaking Gaelic and for some reason, I know some of the words.*

Ginny listened intently and managed to understand a little of what he told the large group of men. She heard something about a new mistress, since the old one was worn out. *Could that be right?* The men are laughing and leering at her. *Uh-oh, am I the new mistress?* There were no words in Ginny's mind to describe how foul and disgusting that possibility was. Ginny's face must have demonstrated how she was feeling, because big, hairy, smelly guy started laughing at her.

Ginny began to look around for her escape. She was surrounded on all sides by walls or buildings. The courtyard walls were at least ten feet tall, with ladders intermittently dispersed and a wooden ledge that spanned the walls. At the one end was a large door, or maybe a drawbridge, she couldn't tell. Between her and any wall was at least twenty men, none of which looked at all sympathetic to her plight. Ginny started to fidget when she felt something on her leg.

Something was wrapped around her right calf. Ginny started to fidget to try and determine what it is. *Could be a sheathed knife,* she thought hopefully. Then Ginny realized that one small knife would get her to the first row of men before she was disarmed. Staring at the large wooden door at the one end of the courtyard, she noticed that a man, dressed in a plaid kilt, was trying to climb over the wall. He obviously did not want to call attention to himself.

What's he doing?, Ginny wondered. All of sudden it occurred to her that the kilted man was going to open the gate. *I bet there's a bunch of men on the other side waiting to come in here and rescue me.* Ginny needed to make a grand diversion and fast.

She was considering her possibilities. If she could get to the knife, she could use it to cut her ropes. *Wait,* she considered, *maybe I can get to the knife with a diversion for her rescuers.*

She paused only briefing to consider how humiliating the next few minutes would be. *A girl's got to do what a girl's got to do, especially if she doesn't want to be raped by a large group of dirty, smelly men.*

23

With that, Ginny threw herself to her knees and began wailing as loudly as she could. She made an outstanding spectacle of herself, Oscar-worthy indeed.

"Please, dear men, please don't hurt me!" she screamed. "Have mercy on me!"

Curling herself into a ball, she reached under her skirt and found the knife in its sheath. Next came the delicate operation of trying to saw through her ropes. Trying to concentrate on not slashing herself, Ginny managed to cut through enough of the rope to pull free. All the while, she continued to beg for mercy and listen to the crowd laugh at her. *Hope you're enjoying the show, boys.*

The ropes around the her wrists were easy compared to her ankles. Ginny was bent in half, reaching under her skirt, to try to cut through her ankle restraints. She seemed to have plenty of time, since the gross men were practically doubled over in laughter at her display.

Fortunately, during her tirade, the kilted man had made it over the wall and was ready to open the gate. He looked as though he needed one more big diversion to complete the job. *Okay*, thought Ginny, *here we go.*

Ginny stood up and faced biggest, dirtiest and smelliest. He stopped laughing and stared back at her, trying to intimidate her. Smiling and looking him in the eye, Ginny shouted loud enough for everyone to hear, "Hell would be too good for you, asshole."

He raised his hand as if to strike her, when Ginny pulled out the knife and threw it. Having no experience at all with knife throwing, even Ginny was amazed when the knife not only hit the mark, but embedded right into his eye. The giant dropped like a stone to the ground, kicking up dust and making the stage shake.

For a moment, the crowd was silent. They were clearly stunned at what Ginny did, but not nearly as much as she was. *Wow, didn't know I could do that!*

There was a loud crash as the doors were thrown open. The men in the courtyard, still stunned at the killing of their leader, turned to see about thirty kilted warriors at the entrance to their keep. Ginny stared at the group, aware that a bloodbath would soon follow. The man in the front of the warriors was huge, bigger than even the head smelly guy. He was also stunning, with wavy reddish, brown hair and muscles big enough to be seen from space.

He's got to be my mega-hunk, Ginny thought. *Oh, the sex should be spectacular!*

With a roar of animal proportions, the head warrior raised his sword and started running into the keep. All the men behind him raised their swords as well and began screaming. Most of the men inside the keep were not prepared for the battle that was about to begin and many of those closest to the gate doors were mowed down in no time. Not wanting to be in the middle of the action, Ginny turned around trying to find someplace to hide.

Jumping off the stage, she ran to the nearest ladder and began climbing it. About half way up someone grabbed her ankle. Ginny turned to see one of the smelly guys trying to pull her down. "What the hell?" she asked to no one in particular.

Turning on the ladder, Ginny used her other leg to kick the dirty guy in the face. He dropped for a moment, giving Ginny just enough to time to scale the ladder. He climbed up after her, but didn't realize that there were several heavy objects at the top of the wall. Ginny began throwing buckets and sacks of grain until he finally fell to the ground.

Ginny turned to see who was winning, although she was fairly certain who was on top. She looked around to find something she could use to help, but there wasn't much. Twenty feet along the wooden pathway, she spotted what she was looking for: a bow and arrows. Ginny had never used a bow before and it stood nearly as tall as she was, but she picked it up and started to string an arrow into it. As she got the arrow loaded and ready to fire, she looked down and noticed that her boobs were smaller. *Who am I?* Before she could consider the possibilities, Ginny turned to the mayhem and carefully aimed at a bad guy.

Suddenly, a bad guy went down, with an arrow stuck out of the back of his head. "Whoa, did you see that?" Ginny screamed at no one in particular. She was beginning to like this dream. It was becoming like a video game, with the killing unreal and detached. If necessary, she could reason it as justifiable, since these same men wanted so badly to violate her in unimaginable ways.

Ginny picked up another arrow and started shooting at a different bad guy. She felt like she was contributing to the battle, not just standing around to be rescued. *Now that ladies, is how it's done,* she thought happily, not wanting to fall into the romance novel, saved from the villain, damsel in distress crap that she had read over and over again.

She noticed that the her mega-hunk was watching her and not paying particular attention to the battle. For a brief moment, their eyes locked and Ginny could feel something between them. Electricity, maybe? She didn't know, but it was palpable. Ginny also noticed that a bad guy was about to come up behind him and make him into mincemeat. Before she could think about it, she picked up another arrow and fired it at the bad guy, only to notice that mega-hunk knew he was there all along. With a loud clash, mega-hunk raised his sword up in time to thwart the blow from behind, at the same time Ginny's arrow met its mark by embedding in the guy's chest. Mega-hunk slowly turned to look at her, not looking at all pleased.

Searching around her, Ginny realized she had no more arrows. With nothing else she could do, Ginny ran along the wooden ledge toward the building that was directly across from the gate. Just as she reached the next ladder, she remembered something the big, smelly guy had said. *The old mistress is worn out,* Ginny thought for a moment. *Where is that poor girl?*

Ginny climbed down the ladder and made her way to the building. Without a doubt, she knew she needed to find and save that girl.

❖ Chapter 5 ❖

The building was menacing, made of large, gray stones, slick with humidity. Men were being slaughtered around her, but Ginny cared little about them. After all, they had asked for it. However, there was some poor woman somewhere who needed help. She raced into the building and started to panic. *Where could she be?* she wondered. *What if I can't find her and these new guys are up to no good as well?*

With that, Ginny stopped herself, took a deep breath and tried to calm her nerves. *First, this has got to be a dream, so just go with the flow. Second, think logically... where would they keep a prisoner? Wasn't it always in some underground dungeon? Find a door that leads down!* Getting it together, Ginny started her search.

After a few minutes she found the door. There were stone steps, quite steep that led down into shadowed darkness. The steps were damp and slippery, so Ginny took her time to avoid falling. The torches on the wall cast only enough light to see a few steps ahead. The smell was bad before, but now it was nearly overwhelming. *This must be what crushing terror smells like*, she thought to herself as she finally reached the bottom. The floor was covered with hay and there were many non-human inhabitants watching her as she walked by. Tiny feet scurried in every direction as she passed. Ginny didn't know if she could take much more of this place so she hurried along the cells to find what she was looking for.

Luckily, there wasn't anyone around to get in her way. She looked in each cell and didn't find anyone. Panic started to set in again. For whatever reason, Ginny had to find this girl and help her. She had never been so compelled before in her life. The thought of having dodged the bullet this woman had endured for who knows how long was driving her to search each cell carefully. In the last cell, Ginny almost missed a small form in the corner. "Hello, are you okay?" *Wow, is that my voice*, she thought. It didn't sound like her at all. Ginny noticed some movement, then saw a pair of eyes shine from the light of the nearest torch. "I'm not going to hurt you. I want to help. Can you tell me where the keys are?" Every time she spoke, she listened to herself. It was like listening to a recording of your voice, only this was someone else's voice.

"You're English?" was all the woman said.

"Huh... what... oh, yeah, sure, I'm English. Listen, I don't know how much time we have. Do you know where the keys are?" Ginny was speaking in a panic and sounded somewhat annoyed. She could reason it was a dream, but right now, it felt real and she wanted to get this woman out before someone came along. Ginny was angry, angrier than she'd been in a long time. The kind of anger you feel when you watch the news story about the abused small child left for dead by the boyfriend of his mother. And she knew that she could and maybe even wanted to hurt someone. She also knew, and this was the greatest source of her anger, that she hadn't the ability to inflict the kind of harm that people who would do this deserved. Those warriors were doing it for her, but she didn't know their intent, so she had to do this on her own.

"By the chair," came a weak and defeated voice.

Ginny turned around and spotted them. She grabbed the keys and went about unlocking the ancient cell door. As she entered the cell, Ginny was struck by the conditions this fragile looking woman had so far survived. The cell had no bathroom and reeked of urine and feces. There was some straw for her to bed down on, but there were also insects and rats. The inhumanity of it reminded Ginny of a novel she'd read about Nazi concentration camps. *This is what happens when we surrender our humanity*, she thought, disgusted to share her species with the likes of these men.

The woman sat up and continued to stare at Ginny, as if wondering if she were a dream. Her face was gaunt, her eyes lifeless, and her hair was dirty and hanging in strings around her face. Again, Ginny was reminded of the pictures of the Jewish prisoners during World War II.

"My name is Ginny and I want to try to rescue you," Ginny said knowing not to get her hopes up. "Can you walk or do you need me to carry you?"

"Could you carry me?" The woman was obviously used to disappointment.

"Right now, I think I could carry you in one hand," trying to sound courageous, Ginny just sounded pathetic.

28

The woman nodded her head and took Ginny's outstretched hand. As she stood up, her face contorted with pain. "Lean against me... that's good. We'll take it one step at a time. When we get out of here, I'll examine you and treat your wounds. That's it... oh, what's your name?" Ginny was rambling, trying to keep her cool despite her fear.

"Aileana... from the clan McKenna. How did you get here?"

"I was kidnapped. I was taken here to replace you."

"A profession I would not recommend," Aileana said with a smile that didn't reach her eyes. Ginny's heart was breaking for this woman. Despite the horrors she'd endured, she was trying to calm Ginny's fears and help in their escape.

Climbing the slippery steps was taking a long time. By the time they reached the top, Ginny was out of breath from half carrying Aileana up. Despite her emaciated form, the woman still had enough bulk to make it a challenge to assist her. Ginny wasn't sure which way to go, being in the dark dungeon had muddled her mind. She stared in one direction, then the other, trying to determine which way she had come.

All of a sudden, she heard a loud crash to her right. Heavy footfalls were coming in their direction, so Ginny looked around for a weapon. There, standing against the wall, was a short sword. She quickly leaned Aileana against the wall and reached for the sword. Just as she picked it up, men came running around the corner. Ginny put her body in front of Aileana and made her stand by raising the sword. It was heavy and Ginny struggled to keep it up.

Three men were standing in front of her, staring at her incredulously. They had far bigger swords and were covered in blood. Ginny recognized them as the intruders, with the one in the middle her mega-hunk. Ginny was unable to speak, breathing heavily from helping Aileana and from trying to keep the sword up. She was shaking from fear and her eyes were wide. She wasn't sure what she was supposed to do. It was quite obvious who would win this match.

Ian couldn't believe what he was seeing. This slip of a woman was trying to ward off three men with a tiny sword that she couldn't even hold up. A smile formed on his lips at her audacity. He knew that she must fear them. They were a ferocious sight, especially after a battle. *Truthfully, it wasn't much of a battle*, Ian thought to himself.

Cowards never put up much of a fight. Still, this girl is willing to stand up to us. How refreshing.

Ginny saw the leader smile and it scared the hell out of her. Summoning up what little courage she had left, she said, "Please, just let us go... I just want to help this woman... you have no beef with us, we've done nothing to you." *Stop rambling, you idiot!*

Suddenly, the man on the left saw the woman behind Ginny. "Aileana, is that you?"

"Alec? Aye, 'tis me," was all Aileana got out before sobs racked her. Ginny threw the sword down to turn and help her. Before she could complete her turn, the man on the left, Alec, had pushed past her and knocked her into the wall. Before Ginny could fall down completely, her mega-hunk grabbed her and pulled her aside.

"Who are ya?" Ian asked abruptly. He had Ginny by the arm and was pulling her away from Aileana.

"Aileana, are you alright? You know these guys, right? They aren't here to hurt you, are they?" Ginny looked back with concern.

"Fear not, Ginny, they are here for me," Aileana said as she put her hands to Alec's face. She looked like she was in a dream, one that she would never had allowed herself to have. After so much pain and despair, she was feeling some peace.

"Please," Ginny pleaded to mega-hunk. "Let me help her. She's been hurt and I can help her."

"Are ya a healer then?"

Ginny noticed the soft cadence of his Scottish burr. It was almost hypnotic. His eyes are the deepest blue she'd ever seen. He had a chiseled face, a perfect jawline, on a square head that reminded her of her Norwegian ancestry. He had a reddish five o'clock shadow, which matched his hair. *My God*, she thought grimly, *I really am in a romance novel!* The unreality of the situation pulled her back to his question.

"Yes, I'm a healer," *sure, whatever you say,* "Can I please examine her now?"

"Nay," Ian turned and walked away while still dragging her by her upper arm.

"What the hell is wrong with you?!" Ginny screamed while ripping her arm from his grip. *This is getting a little too surreal*, Ginny thought. She was in a medieval castle, with a Greek god inspired

Highlander, having no way of knowing how or why she was here. One thing she did know, with absolute certainty, was that she was no pushover.

"Who the hell do you think you are? I want... to... help... her. Capiche?" Ginny was standing toe to toe with the giant. "Do... you... understand... me?" Speaking deliberately slow, she hoped she made her point. All the while making him feel like the ass he was acting like.

Ian closed his eyes for a moment and prayed for patience. When his eyes opened again, he glared at the Englishwoman. No one would dare speak to Ian McKenna like this. It just wasn't done. Ian was the Chieftain of one of the most feared clans in the Highlands. He made his reputation in battle and had the scars to prove it. There were many who would die of fright just to stand as close as this woman was standing to him right now. And yet, she wasn't backing down.

"My name is Ian McKenna and ya'll never speak to me like that again."

There was that burr again. Ginny was always a sucker for any accent to come out of Great Britain. That, coupled with him being one of the best looking guys she'd ever seen this close up, was making her a bit frazzled. Regardless, she had to stick to her guns. She knew that Aileana was hurt and she wanted only to help her. Ginny decided that a different tact was needed.

"Ian McKenna, I..."

"Ya'll refer to him as Laird McKenna," came a booming voice behind her. Ginny turned to see the man who had been standing to Ian's right. He had one, big ugly scowl on his face. He looked absolutely primeval, wearing nothing but a kilt, smeared with blood. He was bigger than Ian and by far the scariest man to walk the planet.

Ginny was not about to hedge her bets on pissing this guy off. Turning back to Ian, she said, "I'm sorry, Laird McKenna. Aileana may need medical attention immediately. You went to a lot of trouble to rescue her, wouldn't it be meaningless to let her suffer more now."

The scary man began to spout off to Ian in Gaelic. Again, Ginny picked up a few words, enough to get the gist of the conversation. Scary man felt that Ginny was not to be trusted and the clan should just leave now. Ginny watched Ian's face during the speech. Ian never took his eyes off her while scary man was speaking. Scary man finished his diatribe and Ian turned and spoke to Alec.

31

"She's yar wife. Do ya want the Englishwoman to heal her?"

It was Aileana who spoke first. "She came to rescue me. I dinna think she means me any harm." Alec began to shake his head, but Aileana turned to him and said, "You can stay with us if ya want. She is a good person, Alec. Trust her."

With a long sigh, Alec consented to the exam. "Not here. I willnae have ya stay in this place a minute longer. Do ya have yar potions with ya?" Ginny had no idea what he was talking about.

"I don't have anything. I was kidnapped and brought here just before you guys arrived," Ginny waited to hear their reply. It was obvious that they had little trust for her and felt they had even less use for her.

It was Ian who spoke first. "Broderick, look around this keep for a healer's den and grab whatever ya find. Alec and I will bring the women out. Once ya're done, have Alistair and Callen help ya with burning this vile place to the ground. We will meet ya on the ridge beyond. Aye?"

"Aye, Laird," was all Broderick said in return. A moment later, he was gone. Ian then turned his face to Ginny, "Ya'll come with us. Ya'll help with Aileana." *Isn't that what I said I'd do*, Ginny thought nauseatingly, rolling her eyes like a teenager.

With that, Ian grabbed Ginny's arm again and started pulling her out. "You don't need to pull me along, I'm willing to come. You are welcome to help Alec with Aileana."

"My brother doesnae need my help with his wife." Ian suddenly turned Ginny to face him. "What were ya thinking by getting her on yar own?"

"You all seemed kind of busy, and I wanted to help," Ginny replied to the strange question.

Ian shook his head in disgust. This woman had no idea how insulting it was to not allow them the duty of rescuing one of their clan. The English, they never seem to get anything right. He was tempted to leave her behind with the burning keep, but she might prove useful. Ian would not admit that it was because she was quite beautiful and might prove useful in other ways.

"Where are ya from?" Ian asked, knowing that she would probably never see it again. Although this girl was innocent in the taking of his sister-in-law, Ian knew he had to come away with something. The disgusting band of men who made the mistake of stealing a member of his clan had paid the ultimate price, but still, he would take anything of value that he could. If the only thing this keep offered was a young Englishwoman, he would take her.

Ginny thought for a moment about Ian's question. Just as she thought she would have to make something up, it all came to her in a flash. Ginny wasn't Ginny anymore, she was Lady Genevieve Chatham, daughter of the late Lord Royce Chatham. No siblings, no family, just her now dead father. Her mother died in childbirth, her family land stolen by traitors. She knew some Gaelic because they lived so near the lowlands of Scotland. Ginny rolled her eyes at the soap opera-ish drama that was this girl's life. *Of all the bodies, in all the romance novels...*

At least she had something to tell him. "I'm Lady Genevieve Chatham. My father was murdered and his lands stolen. I was taken by this band of merry men as payment for their loyalty to those who orchestrated the plot against my father. You may call me Ginny," Ginny started talking like she was writing the novel now.

"Hmmm. I wonder if they will be lookin' for ya."

"Why would they look. They obviously wanted me dead anyway. I'm sure they'll assume as much when news of what happened here gets to them," Ginny wondered if Ian was looking for another fight. Curiosity won out, "Why do you care?"

In a low, whispered voice, he said, "When I take ya, I dinna want any trouble with anyone looking for ya."

"Ooookaaaay."

They continued to walk outside the keep. A young boy in a kilt walked a very large horse over to Ian. Ian climbed onto the horse with ease and looked down at Ginny. Ginny had no idea what he wanted her to do, so she started to walk in the direction of the other warriors. After just a few steps, Ian angled his horse in front of her, blocking her escape.

"What?" was all Ginny could say.

Ian, not one for words, reached his hand down to her. *Does he think I'm getting on that horse with him*, Ginny thought anxiously. The horse, a beauty by most standards, was at least two feet taller than the top of her head. It had a chestnut brown hide and big soulful brown eyes. Ginny could admire the horse's beauty, as long as it was far enough away.

Ian began to get impatient. He was trying to be a gentleman and offer her a ride. *Does she really want to walk to the ridge?* he thought. *Why must she make things difficult.*

"Did you want to give me a ride?" Ginny giggled nervously over the thought of riding on that thing. She was pretty sure where this story was going, but could she manage to hold onto some of her dignity. She began to walk away, toward the ridge with the other warriors, when all of sudden she was being lifted up on top of the horse. "Dear God, what are you doing?" was all she could ask before he plopped her on his lap and began to gallop away.

Ginny grabbed hold of Ian around his waist and buried her head in his shoulder. She was quite certain she was going to fall off and die. Or worse, be paralyzed, waiting to slowly die. Up, down, up, down, over and over again until Ginny was certain she would be sick. "Are we there yet?"

Ian chuckled to himself. It was quite amusing to see this poor girl so frightened over something so ridiculous. It was also a little insulting considering his skill. Did she really think he would drop her? Was this the same girl who stood up to him and his men? Ian reached the ridge and dropped Ginny to the ground. She landed on her butt and let out a few choice curses.

Ian raised his right eyebrow, listening to her unladylike litany. *She is quite a feisty thing*, he thought amusingly. *What am I ever going to do with her?* Ian's face turned dark thinking about her safety. Bringing her home would not guarantee she would be safe, since his clan would undoubtedly want to do her harm as well. He couldn't send her to her home just to be slaughtered. It seemed he had some thinking to do.

Ginny looked up at Ian with a murderous look. As she tried to get up, Ian reached down and lifted her up again. "Thanks," Ginny murmured before sending a few other whispered words his way. She turned around to see the warriors walking up the hill. On the other side of the ridge was where they had set themselves up for battle. There were horses and tents, some fires were burning as well.

"This way," Ian sounded surly. He brought her to a tent and opened the flap. Ginny ducked her head to enter and saw Aileana lying on some blankets on the one side. Ginny rushed to her side and asked if there was anything she could fetch. Alec, her husband, quickly got defensive. "I will tend to her needs, Englishwoman. Ya said ya could heal her. Now is the time."

"Of course," Ginny was not certain what his problem was, but didn't want to make anyone angry with her. This was a camp of very large men with very big swords. Not to mention, it would do little to help Aileana.

Ginny wanted to examine her, but both Ian and Alec still lingered in the tent. "May I speak to you both outside, please," she asked sweetly. Both men exchanged a glance that indicated that that wasn't an option. "Please, not in front of Aileana," she whispered.

Begrudgingly, both men left the tent, but would go no further than the very front. They stared at Ginny like this was beyond an inconvenience and to get on with it. "I need to examine your wife, from head to toe. Do you really want your brother standing there while she's undressed?" Ginny had dealt with abusive partners, worried parents and unreasonable patients, but his went above and beyond.

"Ya will not put my poor wife through any more humiliation," Alec stated.

Ginny could feel her patience wearing thin. "What, then, would you have me do for her?" she said making sure that her voice didn't carry into the tent.

Alec and Ian exchanged glances. They obviously had no idea what needed to be done. Ginny let out a sigh of exasperation. "Look, I'm trying to help. Your poor wife has been through a real trial, and I just want to try to ease any suffering. I will not harm her further, but I can't help her if I don't know the extent of her injuries."

Alec bowed his head. Without looking up, he said, "I know. I couldnae protect her. Do what ya must to help her. I willnae disturb ya." There was so much pain in his voice. He truly believed he'd failed her in the most important job he brought to his marriage and now he suffered along with her. He would never be able to atone for his mistake in letting her out of his sight, away from the village, but he could do something to help her now.

Ginny smiled a soft smile and re-entered the tent. As Ginny went about what ministrations she could provide, considering her lack of supplies, Aileana sat quietly and answered what questions she could. The examination took only a few minutes. Aileana had been raped repeatedly, by many different men, who cared little about her safety. Ginny never dealt with a rape victim before and didn't know what she could do for this woman now. She had no antibiotics to give her in case of venereal disease. She had no way to ease her discomfort with pain medications. So, in the end, she did what she could by gently washing Aileana from head to toe and soothing her with impotent words.

Calling out to Alec, Ginny ordered hot water and soap. When those things were brought in, she asked for a comb and scissors as well. The poor woman, above everything else, had lice. Ginny used a washcloth to wash off the filth the woman had been living in for weeks. Bowls of hot water needed to be replaced every few minutes, since it took no time to turn the water grayish-brown.

Hating to ask it of her, Ginny knew a good way to get rid of lice was by cutting her hair. Not being much of a history buff, she seemed to remember that long hair was important during this era. "I need to cut your hair, to help get rid of the lice. If you don't want me to, I'll do my best, but can't promise anything."

Aileana was silent for a moment. It seemed that she had lived through so much humiliation, what was one more thing. She had been growing her hair since childhood. Her golden brown tresses now reached to her backside and had waves of natural highlights. Alec loved her hair, loved the way it tickled his chest when she made love to him up top. For some reason, Aileana wanted it gone. She didn't feel beautiful anymore, so what did it matter. "Cut it," came her whispered answer.

Ginny chopped her hair and began using the comb to remove the nits. Having a horrible dislike for most bugs, this duty was nearly overwhelming her. After every few minutes, Ginny would wash her hands to prevent them from transferring to her. Still, she thought she could feel them crawling over her, making her tremble.

Ginny was trying to think of some of the natural cures for lice and remembered something about oils. She knew there were several that you could use together, like lavender and olive. Thinking about the time period, there were few choices. Eucalyptus was definitely out, rosemary was a likely choice. Olive oil was probably ridiculously expensive and not likely available. In the end, Ginny did her best and would check what the supplies that soldier brings back from the keep.

When complete, Ginny asked, "Do you want me to fetch your husband?"

"Will I die soon?"

"What?" Ginny gasped. "I don't think your injuries are so serious that you'll die."

"Would ya help me if I wanted to?" Her voice was desperate and tears filled her eyes. She knew that she would never be whole again and certainly didn't want her husband to live out his life with half a wife. Every night in that cell, she would pray for the end. Every morning she would be disappointed. Now, above all else, she wanted to sleep forever and let the pain finally disappear.

"I can't do that," Ginny said quietly. "I will do anything else for you, but I won't help you die."

"Then, yes, ya can fetch my husband for me."

Ginny hesitated and stared at the woman lying on the ground. Aileana would not meet her gaze, but stared at the wall of the tent instead. Where there was companionable silence during the examination, now there was tension. Ginny couldn't give her what she wanted, so now she planned on asking her husband the same request. Ginny barely knew Alec, but it was pretty obvious he adored his wife. This request, made out of desperation and grief, was likely to destroy the man.

Ginny left the tent, and Aileana's request, to search for her husband. She didn't have to look far, since he was never out of sight of the tent. He strode over to her, with purposeful strides, looking hopeful. Ginny had trouble meeting his gaze at first, but forced some courage into her system and looked up. Alec saw it immediately and was stopped short in his tracks.

"No," Alec whispered.

"Your wife will survive her injuries, I think." Ginny paused, trying to think of the right words, "But I don't think she wants to." The anguish that crossed Alec's face was like a body slam to Ginny. She felt all the air whoosh from her lungs and had trouble replacing it. It was one thing for someone to lose their battle against disease or injury, it was quite another for someone to give up. Aileana was giving up.

Alec looked confused. "What do ya mean? Will she live or no'?"

"Her injuries are superficial. The deeper wounds are things I can't heal. I think she's been praying for death for so long now that she's forgotten how to live." Ginny didn't think she was making much sense to the man, but these were the only words she had to describe it. Surprisingly, Alec nodded his head and went to the tent. Before he entered, Ginny said, "I had to cut her hair. 'Cause of the lice. Try not to look surprised."

He nodded back at her and entered the tent.

No sooner had he entered the tent, did Ian walk up behind Ginny. He moved so stealthily that she didn't hear him coming. When he spoke, Ginny jumped like a skittish cat. Ian grabbed her to keep her from falling on her face. With laughter in his voice, he asked, "Did I scare ya?"

Ginny was in no mood for games. She shook her head in disgust and asked, "Do any of your men require any healing? I've done all I can for Aileana."

Hearing the depression in her voice, Ian asked gently, "Will she no' live?"

Not in any mood to explain it to him, Ginny shook her head. "She'll survive... but I don't know if she'll live." With that, Ginny walked away trying to find someplace to be alone. From the moment she'd come to this place, she'd been going full tilt. Now, as exhaustion was closing in, she wanted a moment to be alone and breathe.

❖ Chapter 6 ❖

Everywhere she looked, there were warriors. They were preparing meals, tending to horses, tending to fires. There didn't seem to be two square inches for her to be by herself. On the far side of the camp, was a small stream that wound its way down from the ridge. She walked over and drank from the edge, using her cupped hand to hold the water.

Then she used the water to wash her face. Before she scooped up the water, Ginny saw her reflection and realized that she was in someone else's body. Her face was smaller, heart shaped with full lips and almond shaped eyes. She couldn't tell the color from her reflection. She had black hair, pulled back into a braid that ran the length of her back. Ginny had to admit that Lady Chatham was quite a beautiful girl. *Of course she is*, she thought, *this is a romance novel, right?* She'd already realized she was shorter, but seeing this was strange, overwhelming.

After the shock of realizing that she wasn't herself, Ginny used the water to wash off. The coolness of the water refreshed her again, but did nothing to soothe the ache in her heart for Aileana and Alec. As she stared at the beginning of the sunset, Ian approached her, making himself known early on so as to not scare her again.

"Some of my men could use yar skill. Minor injuries, but..." Ian stopped and just stared. He noticed that she was beautiful, but in the coming sunset, with the sun so bright on the horizon, she was breathtaking.

Ginny turned and looked at him. "Of course. Were you able to procure me any supplies from the keep?"

"Aye, Broderick found some things. I'll show ya the way."

Ginny followed as closely behind as her legs would allow. Ian's legs were long and his strides purposeful. He scarcely glanced back to make sure she was keeping up. *What a gentleman,* Ginny thought as she started to double time it so as not to get lost.

Beside the tent for Aileana was another tent. Ian lifted the flap and motioned for Ginny to enter. Inside, there was a pallet on the ground for a makeshift bed and a bunch of old jars and bottles lined up along the one side. Ginny began to open the jars to try to discover what items Broderick had found. Nothing was labeled, of course, so Ginny was using her other senses to figure out the contents. Her grandmother, God rest her soul, was a huge fan of herbal remedies. Grannie would grow her own plants and mix them into potions and poultices that she would use on her neighbors, many of whom had no insurance and were happy for the help. Grannie passed on her knowledge to Ginny, who appreciated the time spent with her grandmother, but ended up pursing modern medicine instead.

Ginny found a needle and fine thread, good enough for stitches. She found what she thought was an opium based poultice that could be rubbed on a wound. Ginny had to give these people credit. Although they were working with very little knowledge compared to Ginny's standards, they were very resourceful with their treatment methods. Of course, nothing could replace decent hygiene for eliminating many of the ails of the day.

Ginny poked her head out of the tent and asked Ian for a few more things, "I need some hot and cold water. Also, can I have boiling water to put a few things in to sterilize them?"

"Ya want to what?" Ian asked, looking confused. In the short time he'd known this woman, she'd spoken oddly, even for the English, but he attributed it to her youth. Now, she wasn't making any sense at all.

"I need to clean the needle and thread. Boiling water will do the best job. Please," Ginny looked at Ian hoping he would just do it and not ask a lot of questions.

"Aye," was all he said.

As Ginny continued to investigate her booty, her first patient walked into the tent. Ginny was taken back by how young he looked. The boy, no more than sixteen or seventeen years old, was a tall, gangly creature with bright red hair and freckles that covered every inch of his body. He looked reluctant to be there.

"Hi there. My name is Ginny. What seems to be the problem?" Ginny tried to sound as friendly as possible so this kid didn't think she was going to hurt him.

The boy kept looking at everything but her. He would open his mouth, then quickly close it again. Then he would shuffle his feet, clear his throat and rub his hands together. Ginny continued to stare at him, but was afraid to say anything more since he looked like he was about to bolt.

As softly as possible, she turned to the boy and said, "I can't help you if you don't talk to me. I mean you no harm and will be very gentle."

With that, the boy's head popped up and he looked angry. He spat out, "I am not afraid of ya. How dare ya think such a thing."

"Alright then... boy... what can I do for you?" Ginny emphasized the "boy," to show him that she was not afraid of him either.

He sneered and began to walk out of the tent, when he suddenly came back in, followed closely by Ian. The boy stood before the laird and bowed his head. He looked somewhat terrified of Ian, not that Ginny could blame him.

"Have ya been fixed already, Ronald? Ya were no' in here so long." A smile came across Ian's face like he was in on a joke that Ginny was not privy too. It did not take long for her to find out what was so funny.

"Ronald here slipped and fell during the battle. He needs some stitching done to his arse."

With the bright red hair and freckles, it was hard to believe that Ronald could get any redder. However, here the poor boy stood, practically glowing from the embarrassment. Ian looked quite proud of himself for discomfiting the young warrior. Like the army, you have to break them down, before building them back up. Obviously, Ian was still breaking this one down.

"Very well, please lie down on your stomach on the blanket and I'll take a look," Ginny went into professional mode. She'd seen every kind of naked body and it didn't faze her in the least. Of course, this boy didn't know that.

Ronald shot a pleading look at Ian, who continued to stare back at him. When Ronald didn't move, Ian raised one eyebrow as if to say, "Well." Ronald lowered himself to the floor and covered his face in his hands.

"I know ya willnae disgrace yarself or me, Ronald. I will stay here to make sure the lass does a good job." With that, Ian turned to Ginny and waved her to continue.

Ginny knelt beside the boy and lifted his kilt. He had a nasty slash across his right cheek. "What did you land on, Ronald?" Ginny would often make idle chitchat to comfort her patients. She found that if they were talking, they tended not to be as scared.

"A scythe," was the only answer he would give.

Ginny cleaned the wound as best she could, getting any debris out. She used the anesthetic she found to dull the pain of the needle. Then, as she'd done a thousand times before, under far better conditions, Ginny began to sew up the wound. She was surprised that the boy never flinched or cried out in pain. Ginny didn't think she would be so calm under the same circumstances.

When completed, she covered the wound as best as she could without any tape. "You need to clean the wound with soap and water at least three times a day. You need to keep it dry and covered until it's time to take the stitches out."

Ginny barely got the instructions out before the boy bolted from the tent. She stared at the tent opening and began to giggle over the situation. She honestly felt bad for the boy, but he was practically purple by the time she'd finished. To avoid looking at Ian, who would probably send her into grand fits of laughter, Ginny walked over to the water and carefully washed her hands. She didn't have any soap, but used some of the alcohol she found among the items Broderick brought back.

Once composed, Ginny turned to ask Ian if there would be any more patients. As she turned, she saw another man walk into the tent. "Hello, what can I do for you?" Ginny noticed a large number of warriors right outside the tent opening, all staring inside.

"I have been hurt, my lady," the warrior said, with a gleam in his eye.

"Okay, where have you been injured?"

"Why, on my dallywag, my lady," the warrior said with a big smile on his face.

Ginny had an idea where this was going. One of the first jobs she had out of school was an ER in downtown Phoenix. She'd treated her share of drunk college students who couldn't quite navigate a curb. Most would be all too proud to show off their goods, especially to the female staff. Ginny put on her game face and asked the obvious question, "And what, sir, is a dallywag?"

"This," the warrior screamed and lifted the front of his kilt, laughing uproariously with his comrades behind him. When he finally took a breath, Ginny looked unamused.

In a loud enough voice so all the gang could hear, she examined his private area and exclaimed, "I can see what the problem is... you obviously lost most of it during the battle!"

The laughter died in seconds, but suddenly, all the men outside the tent began to roar again with laughter. The warrior in the tent immediately dropped his kilt back down, turned a bright shade of red and snarled at her like an animal whose food was threatened. If he thought he could intimidate her, he was mistaken.

"I'm sorry, sir, but my skills are not that good. I'm afraid I can't help you," Ginny put on her sweet smile and turned her back on him. *Let him stew in that for while, arrogant bastard*, she thought to herself as she continued to inventory her supplies.

She felt him approach, before she heard him. As she turned, the warrior grabbed her by the arms and began to shake her. Ginny couldn't break free, since this guy was a good foot taller and weighed at least a hundred pounds more than her. So, she did the only thing she could do: she screamed.

A few seconds later, Ian walked into the tent. In a flash, Ginny was on the ground and the warrior was hurled out of the tent. Ian followed him out and began yelling in Gaelic. Ginny picked herself up and walked to the opening of the tent to watch. Ian said something about respect and protection. God, she hoped he meant for them to respect and protect her. The troublemaker began to speak to the laird quietly, while gesturing toward Ginny. She couldn't make out anything he said, but figured he was defending his actions because of Ginny's insult. She rolled her eyes in response.

Ian barked some orders at the men and they took off running. Then he turned to Ginny with fire in his eyes. *Great, what now*, Ginny thought glumly. She was in for something, that was for sure.

Ian walked over to the tent and grabbed Ginny's arm to drag her back in. When safely inside, Ian turned Ginny toward him and grabbed both arms as the other warrior had done. Ginny winced at the soreness that would be bruises by tomorrow. When Ian saw her grimace, he released her immediately.

"What were ya thinking? He coulda killed ya for yar insult."

Ginny's eyes widened. "Exactly what should I have done. He

comes in here to try to shock me. Was I supposed to run out of the tent and scream 'Penis, oh my God, a penis.'" Ginny finished her a brilliant "damsel in distress" voice.

It was Ian's turn to look shocked. It lasted only a moment before he regained his composure. "And what do ya know of men's bodies?" His voice was mocking her, like he already knew she was pure. What he didn't know was that this body was pure, but the mind was not.

"I have treated many men for many different reasons. I am not so easily shocked as you or your men might think. My behavior toward your man was in response to his behavior towards me. I certainly don't think insulting him was unreasonable," Ginny always thought she could have been a good lawyer.

Ian stared at Ginny blankly, but his jaw was tightening. *This woman has no idea what she is in for*, he thought to himself. However, he knew that if she was tough enough, she might just survive his clan. With a smile on his face, he said, "Aye, his behavior warranted an insult. And the one ya gave was... decent. However, ya must hold yar tongue. It will get ya in a heap of trouble if yar no' careful."

"I have little doubt of that," Ginny replied. This was a dangerous situation for her. Ginny often started to speak before thinking about what she was going to say. And currently, the people around her would be very unforgiving. Still, it was fun to play with them.

Ian stared at her for another minute, then turned and left the tent. Ginny followed close behind and asked, "I take it that there are no more of your men who will have me heal them."

Ian laughed a booming, hearty laugh. It made Ginny smile in response. "I've little doubt that ya willnae be attending any more of my men."

"That's a shame, cause I'm really good at what I do," Ginny said with a touch of arrogance in her voice. Ian was once again taken back. He'd never met any woman who would behave this way. He found it refreshing, but also disconcerting. *She willnae fit in*, he thought. His smile faded and he strode away from her as fast as he could.

❖ Chapter 7 ❖

Ian wanted to get going as soon as possible, but he had to consider Aileana. She had been through too much to force a long journey on her. He also had to consider everyone's safety. Ian had no way of knowing if any more of their enemies were around. The men who took Aileana were working on someone's orders. Even with all the confidence he had in his men, they could be easily outnumbered.

He needed to consult his brother, but didn't want to take him away from his wife just yet. As he stared at the last of the light, Broderick strode over. As usual, there was a scowl on his face. Ian knew his right hand man had something on his mind and he always wanted to encourage him to be honest. Broderick always wanted to show him proper respect, which could get in the way.

"What is it ya want, Broderick?" Ian asked, as he continued to stare at the sunset.

"When do ya plan to leave, Laird?" was his response.

"I wanted to discuss that with ya. I'm worried about Aileana, but I'm also worried about staying behind too long. What do ya think?"

"We should leave as soon as possible. Before sunrise, I think. Aileana will be safe with Alec. We canna be sure that our enemies arenae watching as we speak."

"Aye, true. There is another matter, as well. What should be done with the Englishwoman?" Ian knew Broderick's answer before he asked, but wanted to hear it from him.

"We should leave her behind. Someone will find her and take her in. She is of no use to us."

Ian raised an eyebrow to him, "Do ya think? She's a healer, and our clan has been without one since Gretchen."

"She is English and our clan will not take too kindly to her, no matter her skills," Broderick came off as surly, but Ian never took exception.

"Surely ya wouldnae just leave her here alone. She would be in danger and yar too much of a gentleman to leave a woman in danger."

Broderick harrumphed. No one referred to Broderick as a "gentleman." Of course, Ian was right. She might be English, but she

45

was still defenseless. Broderick was not the type of man who wouldn't come to the aid of a woman. Finally succumbing, he rolled his eyes. In one last ditch effort he said, "Maybe I could take her to the nearest keep and dump her off there."

Ian laughed. "Yar effort is relentless. We dinna know who her enemies are. I'm sure ya would agree that any manor lord would not be forthcoming if he was in league with her father's enemies."

"Fine," was all Broderick said. He'd known all along that Ian planned to keep her. It was plain as day that he found her attractive, although Broderick could not figure out why. She wasn't hard to look at, but she was English and there was no overcoming that. Broderick went off to prepare the men for their departure.

"Before sunrise, then, Laird?"

"Aye, before sunrise."

Ian went off to look for Ginny. He found her in Aileana's tent, talking softly to the woman. He walked into the tent and asked, "Where is Alec?"

Ginny jumped at the sound of his voice. *That man moves like a cat*, she thought again. "He went looking for you and asked that I stay with Aileana."

"We will be leaving before sunrise. Ya should get some rest. The journey to my keep can be strenuous." And with that, he was gone.

"He likes ya," Aileana stated. She'd barely said a word since Ginny came to sit with her. Ginny had been yammering on, but had to be careful about what topics she brought up. Aileana didn't need to hear about the future, so she pulled some of the memories she had from Lady Chatham. Unfortunately, Lady Chatham lived a sheltered and boring life, not much in the way of good stories to tell.

Ginny stared at Aileana incredulously. "Really. I think you read too much into it." Even as Ginny spoke the words, she knew Aileana was right. Isn't this the romance novel set up? The mega hunk hero can't resist the heroine and is forced to fall in love with her.

"Ian could use a good woman in his life."

"Probably. Do you really think I'm that good woman. I'm

English and he hates the English," Ginny said trying to play the part.

"Aye, ya could be. He and his brother are so different. Alec is tender, where Ian is... not," she said, wistfully.

"Alec... tender? Really? I haven't seen that side of him yet."

"Ya will. Indeed."

"We leave before sunrise. Ya need to do whatever to make yar wife ready," Ian was informing his younger brother.

"Aye, it would be best to leave this place, for everyone, especially Aileana," Alec was staring at the sky, not really in the conversation.

Ian regarded his brother with care. He knew the enormous guilt Alec shouldered. He allowed his wife to visit her family in the south. Alec had too many responsibilities to go with her, so he sent a few men to escort her. The ambush left all the men dead and Aileana missing. It took weeks to discover where she'd been taken, although they were never able to discover who was behind it. Ian had vowed to discover the perpetrators and mete out his own justice. Questioning and torturing a few of the lowlanders proved ineffective.

Now, his brother was not the same. He was distant and preoccupied. Since her disappearance, Alec had been on a rampage. Indeed, until the moment they found her with the Englishwoman, he was fierce and determined. Now, he was anything but. Ian waited to see if Alec would confide in him.

"Do ya know what she asked me?" Alec would not look at his brother when he spoke.

"Nay, what does she want?"

Alec turned to his brother with his eyes on fire. "She wants to die and she wants me to do it!"

Ian was stunned. He was not a fan of religion or the church, but he believed suicide was a sure pathway to Hell. And, as far as he was concerned, asking another to commit the act, didn't change what it was. He stared at this younger brother for a moment before responding. "What did ya tell her?"

That set Alec off like a roman candle. "What do ya mean? What do ya think I told her? Do ya think me capable of murdering my own wife?" Alec's face dropped. Soon after, he fell to his knees and covered his face in his hands. His punishment for allowing her to go to her family on her own was worse than he could imagine. And it did not come close to comparing to hers.

Ian was not accustomed to dealing with such feelings. As far as he was concerned, there were few emotions worth visiting. Fear and rage were his two top favorites, obviously with fear being the other man's problem. In battle, he would concentrate his rage to make him a powerful killing machine. Love and sadness were two emotions he avoided as much as possible. When Alec first met Aileana, he was so besotted that Ian could hardly avoid it. Eventually, he was able to turn a blind eye to it and Alec was able to continue as a skilled warrior.

Now, Alec was tortured over his guilt and Ian had little to offer to assuage it. He waited patiently for his brother to compose himself. The sun had completely set and the only light was from some fires and the moon. Soon enough, Alec stood back up and turned to his brother, "We will be ready." With that, he walked away.

Alec walked back into the tent to find his wife fast asleep and Lady Chatham snoring next to her. He didn't know what to do for his wife, but knew he needed to sleep next to her tonight. The time she was missing had burned his soul beyond repair. All he wanted was what time he had left, since his wife seemed content to give up and die.

Ian had set up the other tent for Ginny, so he went to pick her up and put her in it. Right before he could lift her, Ian's voice, menacing though just a whisper, came from behind. "What are ya doing with her?"

Alec turned around to look at Ian. "I was going to carry her to her own tent. I mean to sleep next to my wife tonight."

"Aye, I will do it. Be with yar wife."

Ian walked over and gently lifted the sleeping form from the ground. She weighed little more than a feather. When he had her securely in his arms, Ginny turned to him and began to cuddle closer to his body. Ian nearly dropped her. The wave of passion hit him so hard, he hardly recognized it for what it was. Lust, pure and simple.

He walked to the other tent and put her down on the makeshift bed. He found a blanket to cover her with, but soon she was shivering. Perplexed, he watched her try to get comfortable. Soon the shivering got worse and she looked as though she would wake up, so Ian did the only thing he could... he warmed her up. He laid down next to her and threw his enormous arm over her body. Still wrapped in the blanket, he hauled her body as close to his as he could without waking her. In her sleep, Ginny let out a small sigh of relief and fell back into a deep sleep. Ian, on the other hand, got more uncomfortable, due to his increasing erection. He had never slept this close to a woman who he didn't have sex with first. *This will be a long night*, he thought glumly, trying without success to get some sleep.

The next morning Ginny woke up with that uncomfortable feeling of wondering where she was. In this case, it was also when she was, but first things first. It was still dark, she was having a wonderful dream about being warm on the beach, when she was shaken awake. Opening her eyes, she immediately went on the defensive and started to yell. A giant hand covered her mouth and a disembodied voice stated, "Calm down, it is just me." The Scottish burr reminded her of all that had transpired in the less than twenty-four hours since she arrived here.

It was cold and damp outside as she slid from the tent. Her eyes could barely make out anything, since the moonlight was now covered over with clouds and there was a light drizzle coming down. It was a miserable feeling being cold and wet and half asleep. Add to that the fact that she was in a different time and strange place, and it was nearly unbearable. Ginny kept her hopes up for a better day.

"Ian, where can I... uh..." Ginny was at a loss for words. Obviously, there were no bathrooms, but as far as she could see, there wasn't anywhere she could go to be private. Although she barely drank anything, she needed to go badly.

"What is it?" Ian asked with no shortage of contempt.

"Where might I relieve myself?" she asked, embarrassment forgotten, when she heard his tone.

Suddenly, Ian felt bad. He knew he sounded surly, but after spending a sleepless night, frustrated and denied, he was bad company for anyone. Obviously, Lady Chatham was desperate. He endeavored to be more kind.

"Ya may go behind the tent. I will make sure that no one disturbs ya," he said as gently as possible.

Ginny sensed the change and was immediately leery. Ian had been almost entirely grumpy to her and now he sounded nice. She knew she shouldn't look a gift horse in the mouth, but she had to wonder what he was up to. Trying to remember the romance novel rules, she considered that maybe he was just in a bad mood, just like she was, and he was trying to behave better. Of course, she wouldn't take it that way, as the heroine, and it would lead to some misunderstanding. Better to just take it for what it was, a kindness.

"Thank you, Laird. I'll only be a few minutes." Ginny ducked behind the tent and went about trying to urinate while squatting on open ground. Truth was, Ginny was never a "pee in the woods" kind of girl. The few times she went camping she insisted on facilities. She could live without a shower for a couple of days, but did not like using the world as her toilet. Fortunately, she wasn't wearing any panties to get in the way. After a few frustrating minutes, and some near misses with her only clothing, she finally came out from behind the tent. Thankfully, she could not see Ian to tell how angry he was for her taking so long.

"Ya'll be riding with me today. Ya might want to get some water and a bit of something to eat before we leave," damn if he wasn't sounding surly again.

"Where can I get some food?" Ginny kept her voice even, since she wasn't in the mood for an argument.

Ian gave an exasperated sigh. *How much trouble would this girl be?* he thought to himself as he led her towards one of the fires. There, one of his men was making oat cakes. *This might be a first for her*, he thought more merrily than earlier.

The warrior, a man named Duncan, happily invited her to sit down with him. He handed her a cask to drink from, filled with weak ale. He was regaling her with stories of his life and skill. Duncan felt it necessary to tell her that he was unmarried and did not have the same prejudices against the English as the rest of his clan. Ginny could do nothing but smile. She thought he looked awfully young, but knew that she was probably pretty young looking too.

Ian noticed the two from across the camp, laughing and flirting. He felt his jaw clench at the sight. *What is that boy doing?* he thought as he walked back over to the fire.

Ginny had just taken her first bite of an oat cake and was surprised at how it tasted like nothing, no flavor at all. *Still*, she thought, *when in Rome, any port in a storm, beggars can't be choosers.*

When Ian came back, Ginny noticed that first, he looked downright pissed off and second, he was amazingly handsome in the firelight. The angular lines of his face were more pronounced and his hair looked like it was on fire. She could see the set line in his jaw and immediately wondered what she'd done this time. *Dear God, I was just sitting here*, she thought, closing her eyes and lifting her face to the sky.

"If yar ready to go, come wit' me," Ian said as he was walking away.

"Thank you for breakfast, Duncan. I hope to speak to you again sometime."

Ian was getting more perturbed. Surely she wasn't interested in Duncan. Why, the boy couldn't even fight that well and was skinny. "Now! Lady Chatham," he screamed at her to get her moving.

Ginny ran after him with a smile on her face. *Could the laird be jealous?* She certainly hoped so. It would probably be the brightest point in her day. As she followed behind Ian, she began to sing Do You Believe in Magic by the Loving Spoonful: *Do you believe in magic? In a young girl's heart, How the music can free her, Whenever it starts.*

As she continued to sing, Ian was rethinking taking her with him. *She's obviously daft or she wouldn't be singing to herself. What could I be thinking?*

❖ Chapter 8 ❖

Ginny began to realize that this dream may be some sort of purgatory. How else could you explain that she had not awoken to find herself in a hospital bed without any memory of the strange goings on she had experienced.

Also, how could you possibly explain that she could feel and smell and taste this "world" she found herself in. Is God just messing with her for being too picky about men, or is he punishing her for reading a handful of romance novels on her worst vacation ever?

Riding on Ian's lap for the better part of the day, Ginny was reminded why she always hated horses. Of course, they smell, but worse, they had minds of their own. Riding them made your ass hurt and there is always the fear they will start to gallop and pop your butt right on the ground. Ian was kind enough to balance her on his lap, but the lack of control was something Ginny had always hated relinquishing.

"Are we close to your home yet?" Ginny asked hoping for either a reprieve or a quick end to her suffering.

Ian continued to ride without comment. *Perhaps he didn't hear me*, she thought.

"Excuse me, Laird. I was wondering if we were close to your home or is it possible to take a short break?" Ginny asked again in a louder voice.

Still, Ian said nothing.

Now, perhaps girls during this century would have taken the hint and let it be. Ginny, however, was not from this century. She decided that his rudeness could be matched with her own. And so, she began to squirm and wiggle on his lap, trying to find a more comfortable position.

This isn't working, she thought. *Maybe if I hang my legs on the other side. That would relieve the pressure on the left side of my ass.*

Ginny began to shift so her legs were on the other side. First she maneuvered her right leg under Ian's arm holding the left rein. Now she was straddling the horse.

Wait, this is much more comfortable. Maybe I should ride like this for a while, she thought happily.

Ian couldn't believe what this girl was doing. First she started shaking her bottom back and forth against him in the most provocative manner. Now she was straddling the horse, butt up against his manhood. Ian was trying to control the erection she was causing him. This ride was going to be long indeed if she didn't stop moving around so much.

She shifted back so her ass was on the saddle. *Oh yes, much better indeed.*

Before she could enjoy it too long, Ian kicked his horse into a full gallop and headed for a grove of trees to the right. Ginny tried to reach behind her to hold onto Ian, but realized that she couldn't quite get a good grip. Just as she thought she was going to slip off, Ian wrapped his arm around her middle to keep her in place. This was definitely the part she hated about horses the most.

Once they reached the trees, Ian hopped off the horse and dragged Ginny into the woods. He was trying unsuccessfully to control his temper, but this was his last straw. He knew damn well that English girls did not ride astride. She was either trying to seduce him or she was truly simple minded. It made no difference, he wouldn't and couldn't take much more.

"Excuse me, Laird... am I to be afforded some time to refresh myself?" Ginny asked Ian's back as he dragged her further into the woods.

Suddenly, Ian turned around and glared at Ginny. "What were ya doing on my horse?" His question was full of anger, like he would hit her out of rage. His face was bright red and he was panting like an animal.

Ginny was shocked and her eyes were as big as saucers. She didn't understand why he was so angry. "I was uncomfortable and trying to shift to a better position," she stated matter-of-factly. For the first time since the battle, Ginny was truly afraid of the man before her. If he wanted, he could snap her neck and be done with it. Ginny knew she should placate him, but then again, she was never known to back down even if the odds were against her. Gearing up for a battle, she let her anger show.

"Why are you so angry? I tried to speak to you, but you

deemed it too beneath you to respond. So I decided to take matters into my own hands."

"Do ya think it twas appropriate to sit on a horse as ya did?" Ian was trying to control his anger. He knew he was scaring her, but he also knew that she needed to learn her place. How unseemly would it be to let his slip of a girl have any control over him. It would destroy his credibility and ruin him as Laird. Not to mention Ian would be damned before he let her take advantage.

"Do I care what you think is appropriate when my ass is numb from my knees to my neck?" Ginny asked, dripping sarcasm and using her hands to demonstrate where she's numb. *What am I doing? I need to shut up! Why can't I just be demure and suck it up until I can figure out my options?*

With the quickness of lightning, Ian reached out and grabbed Ginny by both arms and hauled her up to his face. His face was getting even more red and he was quickly losing control. Both of her feet were off the ground and she was dangling at his mercy.

"Ya'll do as I say, when I say it. There will be no compromise, there will be no alternative. Ya belong to me and my clan, and ya will act appropriately," Ian hissed and threw her to the ground. Ginny landed with a thump, nearly knocking the wind out of her. "Take a few minutes to refresh ya'self and meet me by my horse. Any more inappropriate behavior will be met with severe punishment." Ian stormed away quite proud of his restraint.

What the hell? Ginny thought as she watched him walk away out of sight. She didn't really think her behavior warranted such seething anger. Ginny had never dealt with such unreasonable rage before. Of course she's had her share of kooks and weirdos, who would rage against her and the hospital staff. At least that rage could be explained by their mental illness or a parent's worry. But this? This could only be crazy and dangerous and Ginny did not want to get back on that horse with him.

She also did not want to see what would happen to her if she disobeyed. She was in the middle of nowhere in a time and place she had little familiarity with and absolutely no resources to pull from. Ginny quickly tried to regain her composure. With shaking hands, she took care of her needs and walked back to the edge of the forest, almost half expecting Ian and his horse to be long gone. Keeping with her current streak of luck, there he stood, speaking to his second in command in harsh whispers.

Taking a deep breath, trying to calm her already frayed nerves, Ginny took a few steps beyond the safety of the trees. Ian turned and commanded, "Ya'll ride with Broderick." Then, without another word, he hopped back on his horse and rode off. Broderick looked like he'd rather sleep in a bed of snakes than undertake this duty. Ginny sighed with resignation, for there would surely be worse battles looming, if her situation was anything like the books she'd read.

Broderick climbed back onto his horse and held out a hand to help her. Ginny found herself sitting with her legs opposite from before, so at least her right cheek could take some abuse for awhile. Broderick, not known for his communication skills, kept silent the rest of the day. Ginny took the hint and said nothing as well.

Stopping for the night, Ginny was exhausted from sitting on top of the horse and not eating a damn thing. Her head pounded from having no water all day, her joints and back hurt and her disposition was bleak. They stopped to camp by a creek in an open field filled with flowers. The fragrance, which would normally be a comfort to Ginny, was now making her eyes water and her nose itch. Above everything else, she now had to suffer with allergies.

Ginny walked over to the creek and scooped up some of the water to drink. Many of the men joined her, slurping up great amounts of water. They filled their waterskins and then turned to water the horses. Returning to Broderick's horse, Ginny stood awaiting orders. There probably wasn't much she knew how to do, but she could do something.

Ian was watching her from a distance. When Ginny turned and noticed him staring at her, she walked over to him. The long day had reduced her anger and fear. Also, he was currently looking agreeable. "What can I do to help?" she asked, thinking she sounded helpful, but immediately noticed his head drop. She turned without another word and sat down on the edge of the camp. *What the hell does he want from me. I'm trying, aren't I?*

After a few moments of feeling sorry for herself, Ginny

wandered over to a copse of trees on the edge of the field. Scotland really was breathtaking. The hills and valleys were covered in green grass, which was stunning against the blue sky. Dotted throughout the landscape were groves of trees, adding to the green, and high, craggy mountains. Ginny had always wanted to visit and if she ever made it back, she definitely would.

After taking the time to once again "pee in the woods," Ginny began to gather sticks for firewood. Ian obviously wouldn't explain how she could help, so she would just do what she could. Returning to the camp, Ginny dropped the firewood by the nearest warrior who seemed to look like he needed it, then turned and walked back to the woods.

After gathering another handful, she again returned, dropping her load by another man. She repeated the process until she could no longer find any sticks to gather. She didn't have a hatchet, so she was limited to what was on the ground or easily broken from the trees. Once completed, Ginny looked around for Aileana and Alec. Perhaps they would be kind enough to invite her to dinner.

There were only two tents set up. She found the pair in the first tent, talking softly. Not wanting to disturb them, Ginny turned to walk away when she heard Alec call out to her. Alec walked out of the tent. "Can ya stay with Aileana for a while? I need to speak to my brother."

"Of course," Ginny said, knowing it was what she'd hoped for, a chance to talk to someone who didn't yell at her. Alec turned and strode off and Ginny entered the tent.

"How are you feeling? Was the ride too much for you?" Ginny asked, going immediately into medical mode.

"Nay, it was heaven being in Alec's arms again. I dinna think I ever would have the chance again." Aileana stared out the tent as if she could track her husband still.

"I'm glad it wasn't too taxing on you," Ginny wished she could say the same.

"I saw ya riding with Broderick. I would have thought you would be with Ian."

"Ian got mad at me, scared me half to death with his temper, then dumped me on Broderick. It was a great day," Ginny said sarcastically, with a big smile on her face to emphasize exactly how she didn't feel.

Ginny started to stretch out her back, leaning back as far as she could without falling. Then she went to work on her sore shoulders. Next would have been her backside, but she didn't think Aileana wanted to witness that. It seemed that every part of her body ached. Ginny remembered feeling this way only after she started yet another workout routine.

"Can I rub yar back for ya?" Aileana asked.

"What... no, no. That's kind of you, but it's not necessary. I just really want to eat something and go to bed."

For the first time that Ginny had seen, Aileana's face lit up. She got up and began to pull things from saddle bags her husband had used. She began to prepare some supper for her and Ginny immediately protested. "Let me help you."

"Nay. Ya saved my life. I can make ya a meal."

Ginny sat down on the pallet Alec had prepared for Aileana. "Thank you. I really appreciate it." Suddenly, a waterskin was handed to her and Ginny took a long pull of the weak ale. Ginny watched Aileana as she made a fire, prepared some tasteless oat cakes and fried them. Aileana was a different person when in her element and that was exactly where she was: cooking, preparing, taking care of someone else.

It looked to Ginny like it was doing her friend a world of good. Well, Ginny hoped they were friends, since she had no one else in this time period. Even her persona, Lady Chatham had no one. It made for a lonely existence.

Just as Aileana was finished removing the cakes from the pan, Ian and Alec walked to the tent. The look of fury on Ian's face was obvious. His eyes narrowed, his breathing quickened and the redness was back. Before anyone could ask what was wrong, Ian went into a rage. His voice was menacing, "What do ya think yar doing? Lying there waiting to be served by my clan."

Aileana was the first to speak up. "I asked to make her some supper."

"Ya willnae sit there like a queen. Ya should be serving Aileana for all we are doing for ya." Ginny stared at his face. Not a word would form on her lips. Silent and mute, Ginny was incredulous and... scared. Terrified to be more accurate. *This would be it*, she thought. *He will either kill me or leave me behind.*

Alec, being the voice of reason, could see where this was going. "Ian, my wife asked to prepare the meal. Ya need no' be so upset. We owe Ginny for what she did to aid us in Aileana's rescue."

"Nay!" he screamed with renewed vigor. There was no getting through to him. Staring Ginny in the eye and panting from his anger, Ian again spoke in his menacing tone, "Ya willnae be served. Any food ya eat, ya will prepare. Any place ya sleep, ya will build. Get to it, tis almost dark." With that, he stormed away.

"I will see what that is all about. Til then, Ginny, ya better go and find ya'self some food." Turning to his wife, he said, "I will be back soon to eat with ya." And then, he was gone as well.

Still speechless, Ginny rose and left the tent. She could hear Aileana crying and turned to her. "Maybe you could show me how to make those oat cakes?"

A smile came back to Aileana. "Aye. 'Tis easy. Come and I will show ya." Together, the two women prepared and cooked. As soon as it was done, Ginny had made her own tasteless dinner. Before she could sit down to eat it, Ian and Alec walked over. Once again, Ian was growling like a junkyard dog.

"Where did ya get those?"

"I made them myself. Aileana showed me how."

Grabbing the meager offering out of her hands, he said, "Now make yar own." With two bites, her dinner was gone. Ginny was already shaking with hunger and now she was also shaking with rage. She did what he asked and still, it wasn't good enough.

Before she could stop herself, she rose up, stepped right up to Ian and said in as equally menacing a voice, "What the hell is wrong with you? You wanted me to make it myself, so I did. Why would you do that?"

"I am the Laird. Ya owe me everything ya have. Cooking my dinner is expected," was all he said in reply, once again turning on his heel, he strode off.

Ginny could feel the tears in her eyes. She could feel the draining of her energy as she slipped into helplessness. Defeated was not the word. She was shattered.

Alec grabbed her by the shoulders and walked her into his tent. He handed her his dinner and told her to eat it quickly before Ian came back. He winked at her and left the tent. Ginny did eat the oat cake, while she cried huge tears that streaked down her cheeks. When she was done, she left the tent, made her way to the creek and washed her face.

The sun had nearly set, casting huge shadows across the camp. The bright red sky looked beautiful with the mountains in the foreground. Ginny laid down next to the stream, her head feeling heavy. She was lying on her side, using her arm as a pillow, watching the last of the light fade away. After it was gone, she moved to her back and looked up at the stars. Stars that had been there for millions of years, and were still there in her time. She realized that she just wanted to go home.

Once it became dark, Ginny rose and made her way back to the tent. Before reaching it, she saw Ian sitting outside the tents speaking with Broderick and Alec. Remembering what he said about finding her own accommodations, she looked around at the fires scattered about. She had no bedding, no blanket. She had no tent and no coat. Every fire was surrounded by men, with no room for her.

Ginny couldn't bring herself to beg Ian for anything. She was already feeling the sting of uselessness and weakness. Instead, she wandered back to the woods where she'd collected the firewood. Finding a soft spot among the pine needles, she made a bed for herself. Hating the idea of bugs crawling on her, but too exhausted to care, Ginny closed her eyes and fell asleep. She didn't expect it to last too long, since she was already cold, but wanted to get a few hours before it became impossible.

Ian had watched her make her way to the trees, figuring she was just taking care of her needs. When she didn't return, he went looking for her. He didn't know what had come over him. The anger, even for him, was unreasonable. He saw her sitting there, waiting to be served, and something in him snapped. After speaking to Aileana, more like Aileana screaming at him, he realized his mistake. He was waiting for her so he could apologize and offer her his tent.

He found her curled up on a bed of pine needles, looking so small and defenseless. It made him feel worse. Ian kept her to protect her, but there was no one to protect her from him. He knew he had to do a better job because if he didn't show that he accepted her, his clan never would. Bending over as quietly as possible, Ian picked up the sleeping form. Again, she curled into him, seeking his warmth.

Walking back to the tent, he gingerly placed her on the bed he'd made for her. He placed the kilt blanket over her and laid next to her to keep her warm. Ginny turned in her sleep to face him. He bent slowly down, placing soft kisses on her face and lips. Feeling himself getting excited, he stopped and closed his eyes. It would be another long night.

Ginny was having the most wonderful dream. She was warm and content, lying in her big bed under tons of covers. She sighed in her sleep, happy for the moment.

The moment didn't last. The next morning, Ian shook Ginny awake and told her to prepare to leave. It was still dark, with no dawn light in the horizon. As she was leaving the tent, Ginny stopped. *How did I get in the tent?* Ian must have found her and carried her in. But why? The man was incredibly confusing. Taking a deep breath, Ginny walked to the stream, drank heavily and washed her face.

By the time she had finished in the woods, it looked like everyone was already leaving. Ginny had no idea who she would ride with today, so she went to Broderick and asked him. "Am I to ride with you today?" She sounded so meek, so broken. So unlike her in real life. It bothered her that after only a couple of days she could feel this way.

"Aye," was all Broderick said before he climbed his horse and helped her up.

"Thank you," was the last thing she said for the rest of the day. Broderick was again not into conversation and neither was Ginny at this point. She sat as still as stone, trying to warm herself when possible. After half a day, they came to another stream, where the men got off and watered themselves and their horses.

Stretching herself as much as possible and drinking as much water as she could stand, Ginny began walking around the other warriors. After not moving for so long, she felt sore, like being on a long flight. Just wandering around was helping both her joints and her spirits. Finally, she went around some bushes and took care of her other business. When she popped back out, Ian was waiting for her.

"May I speak to ya?" he asked, like she had a choice.

"Sure," was all she said, afraid to say the wrong thing.

Ian looked at his boots and the sky and the bushes, everywhere but at her. He coughed and ran his fingers through his hair. Ginny waited, wondering what was going on.

"Last night was... I behaved... I feel... bad about how I treated ya," finally, he got it out. He stared into her eyes, looking as if he'd hit her if she made a big deal out of it. For the first time that day, Ginny smiled.

"I forgive you," her face serene. Maybe things wouldn't be so bad after all.

Ian hrumpfed and walked off. Ginny figured that was the best she could hope for. Shaking her head, she turned to seek out Aileana and see if she had anything to eat before she was forced to get back on a horse with Broderick.

❖ Chapter 9 ❖

After hours of silent riding, Broderick finally spoke. While pointing to a rock wall in the distance, he stated, "Our home."

His economy of words did nothing to quelch the joy Ginny was feeling over the prospect of getting off that damn horse and away from Frankenstein. During the hours of silence, Ginny began to assign nicknames to those of the clan she knew. Broderick was Frankenstein, for his big, brooding ugliness and lack of communication skills.

Ian was "the emperor." Do not speak unless spoken to, do not do unless told to and do not think unless you're a man. Charming to the end.

Alec was "the knight." He seemed the only one with an ounce of gentility. He was probably more like his brother than she had yet to see, but at least he could be accommodating.

Ginny's excitement was short lived since she came to realize that the wall was still miles away from where they were going. *Damn Frankenstein for getting my hopes up*, she thought to herself since she had no one else to talk to.

Ginny began to look around and admire the scenery. The chill in the air told her that they were pretty high up in altitude. The craggy mountains were covered in huge boulders, that Ginny imagined climbing. During these summer months, the hills were covered with sprays of color from all forms of wildflowers. She began to try to identify the species that might assist her in healing.

The longer they rode, the cooler it got. Even during the middle of the day, it was starting to feel more like winter in the Northeast US than the summer in Scotland. Ginny had always complained about the cold. Her blood had thinned after so many years in Arizona. She was used to a January that even if it was cold, you could count on warming up in the sun. The sun barely penetrated this place and she began to shiver. Then the shiver turned into chills. Her feet and hands had long ago gone numb.

She knew that Broderick would not appreciate her snuggling against him, but his skin, although mostly bare and exposed, was generating delicious heat. So, slowly, she moved against him. Closer and closer until she was practically inside his kilt. She put her hand on his chest, trying to be nonchalant and acting like she was steadying herself, but all the while enjoying the tingling feeling of warmth. Normally, she would sit on her hands to warm them up, but that was not an option.

Broderick would stiffen every time she moved closer. Ginny knew he didn't like her, which was actually an understatement of his true feelings for her and all English folk. He would try to lean further away from her as she would try to inch herself closer. Suddenly, Ian was at their side eying her suspiciously.

"Yes, Laird?" Ginny asked, knowing she was in for something.

Ian looked at Ginny, then looked at Broderick. The look on his face went from disgusted to sympathetic. As usual, the sympathy was not for Ginny. He let out a great sigh and had Broderick stop his horse. Ian reached over, and with little effort, grabbed Ginny and pulled her back onto his horse. Ginny had to admit that she was grateful for the change, but knew she was in for some lecture on decorum or proper behavior. It was almost laughable considering his behavior over the last few days.

Before she could say anything to explain herself, Ian put his arm around her and dragged her back against his body. As with Broderick, Ian was oozing heat from his pores. Ginny leaned her head against his shoulder and relished in the warmth of his body. She was reminded of the books she'd been reading on her vacation about hard, strong bodies. Ian definitely fit that bill, with broad shoulders, well defined chest muscles and a hard six pack. Ginny yawned against his chest and felt herself falling asleep. She didn't want to be rude, but figured Ian didn't want to speak to her anyway. In no time, she was dozing.

Ian looked down at the top of Ginny's head in wonder. *How could she be cold when it was so goddamn hot out.* She was nuzzled against him like a kitten on a windowsill on a sunny day. He found it hard to admit that it was quite erotic and even this was turning him on. Ian was well known for his discipline and he found himself losing it for this Englishwoman.

It would all change when they reached his keep. He loathed to admit that he had no idea what he was going to do with her. His people had good reason to distrust the English and would not accept her willingly. She was a great healer, so that might help smooth things over. They were without a decent healer since the elderly woman, Gretchen, had died last fall.

Ian leaned down and smelled her hair. It was fresh, like wildflowers. Being as disciplined as he was, this attraction was absurd. Ian had had women. Many would offer themselves up freely to him whenever he wanted. Lately, with all the extra responsibilities that came with being the chieftain, he thought little about his own needs and hadn't bedded a woman in months. That was the reason he was losing his mind around this girl so often. Once he got back, he reasoned, he would seek out some female attention and it would cure him of this crush. Then he could get back to business as usual.

❖ Chapter 10 ❖

Ian nudged Ginny awake as they began riding up the last hill to his village. She woke with a start and almost fell off his horse. Chuckling, he explained, "Ya see the keep on the hill? That's my home."

"Oh, we're here. Thank God. I will be grateful to get off this horse." Ginny wasn't kidding. Although she'd fallen asleep riding with Ian, she was stiff and uncomfortable. What she wouldn't give for a hot bath, a good meal and a chance to walk off her leg cramps.

The village that surrounded the keep was filled with small, utilitarian huts. As the warriors approached, many of the clan came out to greet them. Once inside the village, Ian helped Ginny to the ground and dismounted his horse. Pulling the reins, he began to walk the rest of the way to the keep, greeting his clan on the way. The villagers were happy to see them return, with many asking Ian about Aileana. He was polite, but evasive. It would be up to Alec to provide more answers if he was inclined.

Ginny walked behind Ian's horse and to the left. She was looking around and admiring the scenery that she didn't hear the first gasp, followed by several slurs aimed at her. When a small, older woman stopped her, Ginny was taken by surprise. The woman stared at her and asked, "Are ya English?"

"I was rescued by Ian at the keep where Aileana was being held," Ginny said, sensing that being English around here was not in her favor.

"Dear God," the woman said, crossing herself as if she were in the presence of the devil. "YAR not welcome here!" And with that, she picked up some mud on the ground and threw it in Ginny's face.

Shocked beyond belief, Ginny could only stand there. The woman began to spit on her until some other villagers came along and pulled her away. Ginny then recognized the litany of curses and slurs being directed at her. *What the hell have I done*, she thought as more of the villagers began to throw things at her.

Turning her body to protect her head, Ginny felt the rain of objects connecting with her body. It was a good thing she had turned, because a rock narrowly missed her head and hit her shoulder instead. Looking in every direction for a route to escape, Ginny realized she was surrounded and trapped. Her body went into preservation mode and she was about to start fighting back when Ian appeared at her side, picked her up and carried her off on his shoulder. He was screaming at the clan to stop their attack, but they were in a frenzy and would not be so easily put off.

Ginny could still feel rocks hitting her butt and legs, so she kept her arms over her head. Suddenly, there was a roar, much like the battle scream Ian gave before entering the keep in the south. This time, however, it was Broderick. It seemed that no one was going to cross the enormous warrior and the screams, slurs, taunts and rocks suddenly stopped.

Ian ignored his clan and kept going until he had Ginny safely inside the keep. He entered an enormous room and dropped her down. Ginny barely had time to steady herself. She was covered in mud and spit. The shock was starting to wear off and the anger began to set in. She was attacked, without provocation, and Ginny sensed that they would not have stopped until her head was on a pike. With the fear of that possibility, came more anger.

"WHAT the hell was THAT," she screamed at Ian. Although she knew logically that Ian had saved her, not just this time, but before with the men who kidnapped her, he was the only other person in the room to rail against. Her face was red, she was sweating from the anger and fear, and she needed to release the stress or go mad with it. Unfortunately, Ian didn't understand this.

"Don't yell at me, wench. I dinna spit or throw rocks at ya."

"No. You just forced me to come to this God awful place, where men throw rocks at women for no good reason. Where it's freakin' cold and smells and where I'm hated."

Ian looked shocked. Did she really think of his home at God awful? Could she really be mad at him for saving her from certain death if he'd left her behind? This girl needed to learn her place and fast. The sun was setting, so he knew it was time for her to go to bed and cool off before he dealt with her again.

"Ya will come with me, NOW!" he screamed at her, grabbing her arm and dragging her to a small room off the great room. He threw her inside and turned to say, "Ya will stay here until morning,

Lady Chatham," spitting her name out as if it disgusted him to say it. "We will talk in the morning." And with that, he closed the heavy wooden door and locked it.

Ginny looked around. The room was no bigger than her walk-in closet at home. There was a small window, situated high up the wall that provided little light. She could see some straw in the corner and a blanket on the only piece of furniture in the room, a wooden chair. The room had no bathroom, only a chamberpot in the corner and no where to wash off the spit and mud. This would be a grim night indeed.

Ripping off the bottom of her chemise, Ginny used it to wipe off her face and arms. It smelled so bad, like this room was used for animals. For all she knew, it probably was. Dogs, maybe. She sat on the chair, shaking from head to toe. If this was a romance novel, it was the worst ever. All the books she read did not have situations as awful as hers.

Looking over the blanket and straw, she couldn't see any fleas, but would she see them in the very little light she had? Ginny wrapped the blanket around herself and laid down on the straw. Exhaustion over took her and she feel asleep. Tossing and turning most of the night, the only sleep Ginny got was filled with nightmarish dreams about her head on a pike.

❖ Chapter 11 ❖

The next morning, after getting no sleep, Ginny was in the worst mood of her life. She couldn't remember feeling this bad when her beloved grandmother died. It was worse than defeated, it was utterly glum. She had heard the door being unlocked early in the morning, before there was even enough light to see the door.

Once the sun began to shine into the small window, she decided to venture out. The small room was beginning to feel more like a tomb, where she should have expired during the night. Unfortunately, that didn't happen.

Ginny was grumpy, thirsty, hungry and pissed. A bad combination for anyone to be around. She walked to the great hall of the keep, in search of some water. On the table, there was a pitcher and several goblets. Ginny walked over and smelled the contents of the pitcher. *Thank God*, she thought as she poured herself some water.

She drank several glasses and sat on the bench of the long table. She was too absorbed in her own thoughts to notice that Ian, Alec and Broderick had all walked into the room. She began to pour herself some more water when Ian scared the breath out her by speaking.

"What are ya doing?" he asked in his usual menacing voice.

Christ, I now have to ask permission to drink some damn water? How much more am I supposed to take? This is medieval! Oh wait, this really is medieval.

Ginny turned to face the men. "I was very thirsty. I found this pitcher with water and was drinking it," Ginny said in as sweet a voice as she could muster considering her circumstances, her position as a pariah, her lack of sleep, and her current state of uncleanliness.

Ian had about enough insolence from this wisp of a woman. Did she not understand anything of the way things were done. She was not a guest, she now belonged to him and would behave as such. "Who told ya that ya could drink the water?" Ian asked, obviously trying to control his unfounded anger, again.

Ginny stood up. "No one. I assumed it was here for anyone who was thirsty."

"Ya assumed incorrectly," Ian face was almost comical. Why would something so innocuous be such a source of contempt.

Ian had been laird only a short time, but had come to expect certain behavior from his clan. It was high time that this Englishwoman learn her place, which was extremely low in his estimation. His only problem was, he still needed to figure out where she would fit in. Now, as on other occasions, Ian realized that he had no idea where she would fit in. The reactions of his clan proved that she would never be accepted. Perhaps it was a bad idea to bring her here.

Ginny had enough. She was about to start freaking out, when all of a sudden, surprising everyone, including herself, she began to laugh. At first, just a giggle. Then it exploded into full blown fits of doubled over laughter. Tears were streaming from her eyes and she could barely breathe. The situation was so ridiculous, she had no choice. She needed to blow off steam and this was infinitely better than freaking out on three men twice her size.

Ian watched her in disbelief. He could feel Broderick stiffen and should do something to quash this rebellion right now before things got out of hand, but Ian was dumbfounded by her audacity. How could she not realize her danger? Could she be that addle-brained not to recognize the level of disrespect she was demonstrating?

Just as she was about to control herself, she looked up to see Broderick coming toward her. She looked him in the eye right before the blow sent her flying to the ground. It took a full fifteen seconds before Ginny realized what had happened. Frankenstein had back handed her. Pain shot through Ginny's face like fire. She couldn't see straight, except for the stars that wouldn't dissipate. A primal anger grew in Ginny's chest, unlike anything she'd ever experienced before in her life. It was one of those scary moments when you realize you could kill someone. Like when a parent sees someone harm her child and knows with absolute certainty that she could easily destroy another human being.

Ginny stood up slowly. She pulled herself to her full height and walked over to Broderick, who, for the first time since she met him, had a smile on his face. He spoke in his usual menacing tone, "Ya'll show respect to your laird."

"He's not my laird, you overgrown piece of crap." And before

Frankenstein could react, Ginny punched him square in the nuts. Not any punch... Ginny linked her hands together and shot upward with all her strength. Since he was not expecting it, she had a clear shot with no way for Broderick to protect himself.

Broderick was twice her size and easily three times her weight, but Ginny toppled him like shaky house of cards. When he hit the floor, the building shook. She had succeeded in knocking the breath out of him as well as eliminating his chances of bearing children. *Thank God there won't be any little Frankenstein's running around*, she thought merrily.

Ginny looked at the other two men standing there, gawking at her in amazement. Broderick still hadn't tried to get up. Ginny stepped over his massive frame and stood before Ian and Alec.

"You condone hitting defenseless women in your clan? What kind of beasts are you?"

Alec was the first to regain the ability to speak. "I'm not sure I would call ya defenseless, my lady."

Ginny turned and left the building, with Ian and Alec still trying to comprehend what had just occurred. Surely this tiny woman did not just bring down one of the biggest and strongest members of the McKenna clan.

Ginny walked down a small pathway to the lake at the bottom of the hill. She knew that the water would be extraordinarily cold, with their elevation and that was just what she needed. She kept her head high as she walked past the clansmen and women who made their disgust for her quite obvious the day before. Many smiled when they saw the budding bruise on her face.

She sat by the lake and pulled out a small handkerchief from her pocket. She dipped it in the icy water and applied it to her face. Ginny amazed herself by not crying. She began to think she was in a perpetual state of shock and couldn't muster the energy to cry anyway.

Ginny heard giggles behind her and turned to see a group of four girls, not more than fifteen in her estimation. They stared at her with open curiosity. One girl, a beauty with long red hair and striking green eyes began to walk toward her. The girl sat next to Ginny.

"What happened to ya?" the teenager asked innocently.

"I disrespected the Laird and he had his henchman deal with me," Ginny said as she continued to blot her bruise with the cool compress.

"Why would ya do that?" *A good question*, Ginny thought. *Why do I provoke him so much. I am obviously going to have to learn to live with the situation for the time being, so can't I muster some strength to act the way he wants.*

"What's your name?" Ginny asked.

"Maude," she said keeping her head down.

Damn, it may have been a good name to them, but only brought visions of bad 70's television to Ginny. Ginny smiled and said, "My name is Ginny. Lady Chatham. And I don't know why I did what I did."

Ginny realized that this girl didn't seem to suffer under the impression that she was there to destroy the clan or carried some fatal disease. Ginny didn't want the girl to suffer by being associated with her. The other clansmen made it quite clear how they felt.

"Maybe you should go, Maude. I wouldn't want you to get in trouble for speaking to the likes of me. Your parents would undoubtedly be displeased."

"I can see for myself yar not evil. We have good reason to distrust the English, but I dinna think ya alone are responsible for our troubles," *Maude had a good head on her shoulders and would make a good leader someday, if she weren't a woman*, Ginny thought grimly.

The other girls started calling Maude back to them. Ginny and Maude looked up in time to see Ian charging his way down the hill. *Great*, thought Ginny, *here it comes.*

Before either girl could escape, Ian was standing above them. "Maude, go home now."

"Yes, Laird." *Now why couldn't I be more like that*, Ginny thought. *Just obey, don't think! It would keep me from getting smacked.*

Ian crouched down next to Ginny. She could see his powerful thighs under his kilt. To buy some time before the inevitable confrontation, Ginny put her handkerchief back in the water and reapplied it to her cheek. Ginny noticed that Ian smelled good, compared to her surroundings and the other clansmen. He smelled like the outdoors, with a hint of musk. He wasn't hard on the eyes either. *Typical romance novel*, Ginny thought, *the hero smells clean while the rest wallow in filth.*

The silence carried on for a while. Ginny figured he was stalling from telling her that he would now have to kill her for her disrespect. Not to mention, it would gain him valuable points amongst the clan that so hated the English. Or was he using a tactic to try to earn a confession from her. Did Ian think that she couldn't withstand a long silence and would start spouting off like a prisoner in an interrogation room. *Damn unlikely*, she thought to herself.

"Do ya want to explain ya'self?" Ian tried to be gentle. He realized that he had been far too unfair to her. His behavior was unacceptable for a man of his position. Ian wanted to make this work, since Lady Chatham would be staying for a long while.

"Do you really want to hear what I have to say?" Ginny knew she should take another tact with Ian, but she was tired and fed up with all she had dealt with. Ginny's face was like stone, revealing nothing of the warring emotions she felt at the moment.

"I wouldnae have asked if I werenae willing to listen." Ian realized that this woman could very well be the death of him. He had the urge to pull her to him and kiss away the insolence. He smiled at the notion that would be so shocking to someone so innocent.

"I am trying, Laird. But in the time since our arrival, I've been yelled at, spit on, made into some kind of pariah, given nothing to eat or drink, made to sleep like an animal and beaten by a man twice my size. Every time I try to do something, you come along and tell me I've done something wrong. I don't know your ways and I don't see how I've done anything so horrible to deserve the treatment I've received from both you and your clan," Ginny could feel her composure breaking, but she would be damned before she cried in front of the likes of him.

"If you don't want me, can someone take me back to England and dump me off somewhere. I'll figure out what to do from there and you and your people will never have to deal with me again," Ginny was sincere, but she felt utterly empty. She knew she'd reached her limit.

Ian stared at her for a time. He was amazed that someone so young and small could be so brave. He also knew that she was his and he was unlikely to let her go. He felt such a strong need to keep her safe, and could not understand why he was trying so hard to push her away. Ian was not ready to admit how much he wanted to bed her. How just seeing her made him hard. He knew that was why he was so surly to her most of the time.

"Yar not going anywhere," Ian could see the disappointment in her face. "Ya will learn our ways and the clan will eventually accept ya."

Ginny made a noise that indicated that she did not believe that would ever happen. Of course, if this situation was like the romance novel, Ian should be seducing her soon and the clan will come to love her. As far as Ginny could remember, no women get back handed in the books she'd read, so maybe she'd already changed the storyline.

"And..." Ian spoke just above a whisper..."Ya must be punished."

Ginny had been waiting for the other shoe to fall. She lifted her face and met his eyes. She tried to maintain a stoic look. "How am I to be punished? I can't imagine how it could get worse." That was the wrong thing to say, as things can always get worse.

"Ya'll be paddled in front of the entire clan. It will be a demonstration that no disrespect will be tolerated," Ian stated.

"And what will be Frank..., I mean, Broderick's punishment?" Ian looked incredulous. Did she mean to indicate that Broderick had done something wrong? Surely he misheard her.

"Broderick has done nothing wrong," Ian said putting an end to the discussion. But, of course, Ginny could not let things lie.

"Done nothing wrong? He attacked me!" Ginny could feel her blood starting to boil. She was disgusted that he could think it perfectly alright for the big bully to beat up the defenseless. All of sudden, Ginny stopped. "What am I being punished for... exactly?"

"Ya laughed at my command. I take my leadership seriously, as ya should as well."

"So, Broderick hitting me..."

"You hit him back. It seems the matter has resolved itself."

Ginny was about to laugh, but didn't want to insult the laird again. She wondered if Ian actually admired how she handled the situation. She didn't go crying to him, but defended herself. She could see that he looked at her differently, perhaps with a little more respect than an hour ago. Somehow, it made the episode more tolerable.

"Very well... let's go and get this over with." Ginny stood up and started walking back up the hill. If she had to be paddled for laughing, she might as well get it done with. She might not agree with their rules, but they were their rules and she was not the one to change things.

Ian could not believe his ears. This young, impetuous English girl was going to take her punishment without argument. It seemed that the last few days were nothing but arguments when it came to her. She stopped and turned around to look at him. "Are you coming?" she asked indignantly.

"Aye, I'm coming." Ian stood and followed her up the hill. She had no idea what she was in for and he did not relish making her cry, especially in front of the entire clan.

❖ Chapter 12 ❖

Word spread quickly about the punishment to be meted out to the Englishwoman. Clansmen dropped everything they were doing for a chance to witness it. Some commented on how it would be more fun than a festival. Others pulled out stools and blankets to make a picnic of it. Almost everyone was excited to witness the suffering of one of the English, everyone except Maude. She had never appreciated the need for such humiliation.

Ginny watched as two men wheeled out a contraption made of wood. It was simple... just a box with a rope strung across the top. It had a sturdy base, so it wouldn't tip over. It occurred to Ginny that it was meant for her paddling and the rest of the day would really suck. *When am I going to learn to keep my big trap shut!* Ginny thought despairingly as she walked over to the box.

Ian walked next to her and explained that when the time came, she was to bend over the box and hold onto the rope. He held a vicious looking wooden paddle in his hand. The paddle, smooth from careful sanding, was the size of the cricket bat, but a little wider. It had an intricate design on it, probably Scottish in nature, Ginny surmised. It looked well used and was probably what they used on willful children.

Ian spoke to the clan calmly. "It gives me no pleasure to do this, but as ya know, we have rules that must be followed. Lady Chatham has broken a very important rule by disrespecting me and this clan." The crowd began to boo Ginny and she felt the hate like needles being pushed into her skin. She kept her head high and bore it without complaint. Ian felt even worse for what he was about to do.

"QUIET!" Ian roared at the booing clan. "She is willing to take her punishment for her transgression. She is here of her own accord, no one needed to drag her here or hold her down. She will take her punishment and it will be done."

Ian nodded to Ginny, who quickly took her place on the box. She held the rope, although Ginny didn't think he would paddle her so hard to send her flying. Of course, she didn't know for sure.

"You will receive three whacks," Ian announced right before the first one hit.

Ginny had never felt anything like it. She imagined that it was how it would feel being hit by a ram. Ginny was certain that Ian wasn't holding anything back just because she was a woman. All that was heard was a small grunt from Ginny. She'd be damned again if she would cry. These people didn't deserve her tears, only her contempt.

The second whack was worse since it was hitting sore skin and the third was nearly unbearable. When it was over, Ginny stood up slowly. She fought to keep down the wave of nausea that was building up inside her. Ginny knew that crying would be bad, but throwing up would be unforgivable. As she passed Ian, he stopped her with his hand.

"Ya have done well, little one. Ya took it like a warrior," Ian whispered in her ear. Ginny, who had been looking straight ahead up until that point, turned her head and looked right into his eyes. It was clear that she was angry, but trying to contain herself to avoid another whack.

"Thank you, Laird. That means so much to me," Ginny managed to say before pushing his hand away and walking into the keep. Sarcasm had always been something of an art form for Ginny. She wielded it like a sword against the stupid. Right now, she could think of no one more stupid than Laird Ian and the whole McKenna clan.

Maude followed Ginny into the keep. She closed the door and came to her side. "Please let me help ya," was all she said as she took Ginny's arm and led her the large table in the middle of the room. "I know ya don't want to sit, so lean over the table and I will fetch ya some water."

Maude's kindness was almost Ginny's undoing. After all the hate she received since her arrival, this one young girl proved that she was not some kind of monster. Ginny leaned over the table and wondered if the sting would subside soon.

As if reading her mind, Maude said, "It won't sting forever, my lady. It will hurt for the first hour or so, but it will get better before evening supper."

Ginny received the water gratefully. It seemed that poor Maude had received the same punishment at some time herself. "What did you do?" was all Ginny said.

"I can get myself into some mischief on occasion. The last time I accidentally set fire to my family's hut."

Ginny looked at her incredulously. "Really... all I did was laugh. How many did you get for the fire?"

"Five," Maude turned her face away, but Ginny could see that she was laughing. "It was an accident, but no one would listen. That was before Laird Ian. His father was much more brutal." More brutal? *Dear God*, thought Ginny, *he must have been the devil himself.*

Ginny could hear the giant wood door opening and the light from outside pouring in. She knew who it would be without turning around to look. She wondered if she would hear about her snide remark before leaving him outside. The "emperor" couldn't possibly be happy with her insolence.

"Maude, would ya be so kind as to leave us alone for a moment?" Ian's voice, for once, didn't sound surly.

Maude bowed her head and headed toward the kitchen. Before she left, she called back, "Please let me know if I can be of service this evening, my lady. I've some experience and can be helpful in yar comfort." Ginny couldn't help but smile. Despite Ian's presence, she'd made her displeasure known. Maude was a braver girl than she.

In a uncharacteristically soft voice, Ian asked, "How are ya faring?"

Ginny was in no mood to speak to him. However, she did not wish to endure another paddling session. With her teeth gritted, she said, "As fine as to be expected, Laird." It almost killed her to hold back the smart ass response she so wanted to give him. Ginny also had quite a few names she wished she could call him. Many he would have never heard before, and may not even know were insulting. Ginny considered this while Ian continued to stare at her.

Ian went quite easy on her. He did not swing with as much ferocity as he had in the past on other members of his clan and he certainly wasn't as vicious as his father. He wanted her to know of his compassion. "Ya should be thankful that I was so gentle with ya."

What? Ginny thought. *He has to be kidding!*

Despite the pain, she stood up and faced him dead on. Biting back the worst of the comments that came to mind, Ginny smiled and said, "I will forever be grateful for your kindness and the kindness of your clan. I have never felt so welcome in my life. Your restraint with the paddle was most appreciated. I can honestly say, without a doubt, I barely felt it."

At this, Ian smiled. Her audacity was starting to please him greatly. Since the moment they met, she never shrank from him. Oh, he knew there were times she feared him and what he was capable of, but she never backed down. Ian loved watching the play of emotions on her face as she held back the worst of her thoughts. Yes, this woman would please him greatly.

Ginny stared at Ian's face as he smiled. Yes, he was a handsome man, but most of the time it was hard to notice with the constant snarl he wore. Now, with his smile, Ginny felt a strange stirring. Sexually appealing, she began to wonder what it would be like to sleep with him. Ginny was no virgin, although the body she possessed most likely was. She began to smile thinking about what it would do to him if she responded with as much ardor as a 21st century woman.

Her smile was Ian's undoing. His mind shouted for him to stop, but his body moved closer to hers. His large, calloused hands grabbed her face and pointed it up to meet his gaze. "You please me, Lady Genevieve. You belong to me now and forever." With that, Ian bent his head to meet his lips with hers. Gentle at first, he didn't want to scare her.

Ginny couldn't believe he was kissing her and so gently. It was her chance to shock and horrify him. *Now, Laird Ian McKenna, you'll find out what it was like to kiss this woman who's not afraid of men and not ignorant of sex.* She reached her hand behind his head, laced her fingers in his long hair and pulled him even closer. Opening her mouth, her tongue reached out and traced his lips.

Ian pulled back abruptly and just stared at Ginny. He could not believe her boldness. Shock flashed on his face before he couldn't hold back any more. With a grunt of pleasure, Ian pulled Ginny to his mouth and kissed her. His tongue reaching into her mouth to take possession of her. His hands caressing her face and shoulders. Ian knew that he would not likely be able to stop himself.

Just as his hands reached down to caress her breasts, Ginny pulled away abruptly. She quickly ran around to the other side of the table to put some distance between the two of them. Her plan to shock and horrify him went terribly wrong. Ginny knew that he was turned on. She was no prude, but damn if she would sleep with him after he took a paddle to her ass. Wiping her hand across her wet, swollen lips, Ginny had trouble drawing a breath.

Neither said a word for a long time. They just stared at each other from across the table. When Ian could trust his voice again, he spoke gently, "Did I scare ya?"

What!, Ginny thought, *he has got to be kidding?* It occurred to her that that thought was becoming her mantra. Ginny dropped her face to her hands and was shaking. She immediately controlled her laughter, since that was what got her paddled in the first place. She took a deep breath and looked him in the eyes.

"I'm sorry, Laird, but I thought it was I who scared you!" Ginny retorted. She couldn't help but smile at the look of indignation on his face. There was a part of her that just couldn't help herself when it came to baiting him.

"Surely, ya jest," was all Ian could say. This girl, this Englishwoman, had the audacity to think she could inflict fear on him. *Of all the gall*, he thought. Once again, his desire turned to rage. When he saw the look on her face, he realized that he was scaring her again and immediately calmed himself down. *What was it about this woman*, he thought grimly.

Ginny could see that she'd made him angry again. She wasn't up for another confrontation. She just wanted to find some middle ground that they could both live in. Ginny was tired, hungry, dirty and in pain. She knew she should suck it up and placate him before he went on a rampage once again.

"I'm sorry, Laird. I didn't mean to insult you... again. I know whenever I speak, I say the wrong thing and make you angry. Maybe I should find Maude and she can bring me to her house. I don't wish to inconvenience you any longer," Ginny said forlornly. She knew she sounded pathetic, which was so unlike her, but at this point, she felt pretty pathetic.

"Ya must be tired," Ian was trying to be more accommodating.

"I'm exhausted. I'm also starving and thirsty and filthy and my bottom is on fire. I am not having a good day!"

Immediately, Ian strode from the room toward the kitchens. Ginny could only imagine what he had in store for her. She prayed for a little kindness, which all the romantic novels would offer, but she knew that she'd irretrievably changed this story for the worst.

Ian came back with a tray of ale, bread and cheese. He held the tray in one hand and grabbed her arm with the other. He walked briskly up the stone steps to the upper level where he stopped in front of an enormous wood door, with big metal studs and door pull. Ian used his shoulder to push open the door and dragged Ginny inside.

Inside the room, was a giant hearth, two holes for windows with heavy fabric curtains. The stone floor was covered with rugs and on the one side was a giant bed with a canopy and more heavy curtains. Ginny could imagine how cozy it would be when all the curtains were drawn. Before she could take in the whole room, Ian dragged her to the bed and released his grip. He put the tray down next to the bed and turned to Ginny.

"This is my bedchamber. Please partake of it until ya feel better. Have a bite to eat and get some rest. I'll fetch Maude to attend ya."

With that, he left the room. Ginny stared at the doorway and began to cry.

Maude found Ginny, still standing in the same spot, staring at the door. Somehow, Ginny managed to stop her tears before Maude came in, but it was obvious from her red eyes and tear stained cheeks that she'd been crying. "My lady, are ya unwell?"

Ginny laughed. "That would be the understatement of the century."

Maude tilted her head slightly and looked at her funny. "Ya say the strangest things, my lady. Let me assist ya so ya can get some rest. Everything will seem much better tomorrow."

"Why, are they finally sending me away?" Ginny was only half kidding.

Maude helped Ginny undress. Two women from the kitchen began to arrange for a bath. There was a small tub, more like a bucket, that was placed next to the hearth. While Maude built a fire, the two women began to fill the tub with hot water. Leaving two buckets of water behind for rinsing, the women disappeared through the door. Maude then had Ginny kneel in the tub so she could help her wash.

Such a personal activity, Ginny was slightly embarrassed, but not enough to ask Maude to leave. With a sweet smelling soap, Maude washed the spit and mud from Ginny's hair.

After she was rinsed, Maude had Ginny dry herself by the fire and began to clean up after the bath. Finally, clean and dry, except for her hair, Ginny felt a thousand times better.

It was only then that Ginny realized how cold it was. Waking from her shock, Ginny's mind railed against this situation and place she found herself in. She knew that she should be enjoying herself. Obviously, the smell, the unsanitary conditions, the lack of clean anything was wearing thin. But she knew that she was living someone else's life and should be free to do whatever stupid things she wanted, consequence free.

As it was turning out, she was living very much as she had, in a time that had little tolerance for any freedom afforded the female gender. And, she was paying for it. Ginny couldn't help that the clan hated her for being English, but she could help by being more demure and accommodating. It might just save her ass from being paddled again.

"Are ya feeling well, my lady," Maude asked tentatively, staring at Ginny's face. Ginny must have seemed a thousand miles away.

"Huh... oh, yeah, I'm fine. Just thinking about how to make my situation more tolerable," Ginny said hoping to be alone soon to consider her options.

"Why don't ya eat a little and then get some rest. I know you dinna sleep verra well last night," Maude said, with her sweet smile.

"Thanks, Maude. You don't have to hang around here. Go do whatever it is you're supposed to be doing. I'll be fine," Ginny returned the smile.

Maude bowed her head and left the room. This gave Ginny time to feel sorry for herself and try to figure out how to make things better. She needed to formulate a plan, but her mind just kept returning to things she shouldn't do. Ginny considered running away, after all, isn't that what the damsels in the books always did. Then the mega-hunk would have to race to find her in the middle of whatever trouble she'd gotten herself into, save her and then proclaim his undying love and live happily ever after.

Ginny was starting to turn this around in her head. If she could accelerate the timeline, or plot line, she might be able to finish this drama and return to her own body in the future. *I guess it's worth a try,* she thought as she slowly ate the hard black bread and moldy cheese. She tentatively tasted the ale. Ginny liked a good beer, and to her, anything from Mexico constituted a good beer. This ale tasted more like warm light beer on a bad day. But, beggars can't be choosers!

After finishing her meager offering, Ginny laid down on the bed. Part of her did not want to sleep on this "mattress." Too many stories about bed bugs and lice were swimming in her head (and possibly would make a home on her head if she laid down). Looking around the room, she didn't see anything that would be an acceptable alternative. Eventually, she was too tired to care and settled down on her stomach, to allow her bottom to heal.

As she began to relax, Ginny started thinking about the Cat Steven's song *Wild World: Oh Baby, baby, it's a wild world, it's hard to get by just on a smile, Oh baby, baby, it's a wild world and I'll always remember you like a child*. Despite an intense case of heebee jeebies, Ginny was asleep in minutes. Snoring away, as she always did when she slept on her stomach.

Sometime after dark, Ginny began to shiver. Not quite awake, she suddenly felt a warmth move towards her. She moved her body to be closer to it and felt both relieved and comfortable. She settled back into her dreamless slumber.

❖ Chapter 13 ❖

The next morning, Ginny woke up suddenly and couldn't remember where she was again. She sat up in bed too quickly and the pain in her rear reminded her of both where and when she was. Ginny laid back down and groaned. *Why can't this be over? I want running water again!*

She stepped gingerly out of bed, not wanting her bare feet to touch either the filthy rugs used as carpeting or the cold hard floor. She had little success avoiding either. No sooner had she stepped out of bed, did Maude come in.

"I thought I heard ya. Are ya feeling well today?" Maude was all smiles.

Despite her initial fears about the bed, she had to admit, it was very comfortable. Although the room was absolutely frigid, Ginny was nothing but warm and toasty in the bed. "Maude, I feel a thousand times better today. I believe I can get through an entire day without being paddled," Ginny said it, but she didn't actually believe it.

"Let's get ya dressed and find ya some food. Then I will show ya around the village."

"No thanks, Maude. I'm quite through with being spit on," Ginny was not about to let the clan have another crack at her. Their treatment on her first day was enough to convince her that maybe she should just run away. After all, what would Ian do? He must be just as tired of dealing with everything to bother coming after her.

"Oh, I think ya will be surprised, my lady." Maude pulled out some new clothes for Ginny to wear. Hardly fashionable, they were at least clean. Ginny pulled on the chemise. The cloth felt coarse against her skin, like burlap. Maude handed her the long tunic dress next. The sleeves were wide, and the fabric was heavy, but it would keep her warm. Next came some heavy hose and strange slipper like shoes.

Surprising Ginny for a moment, Maude handed her a cloth and some powder. It took Ginny a moment to realize it was for her teeth. Reaching into the knowledge she gained from Lady Chatham, Ginny knew that although hygiene wasn't the top priority, Medieval people weren't as unclean as she always thought. The powder wasn't as good as her toothpaste at home, but it would work.

After her bath the day before, her good night's sleep and the opportunity to clean her teeth this morning, Ginny was ready to face whatever came her way.

After some breakfast, Maude went about the tour. Outside the large stone keep, there were many huts that dotted the landscape. As they passed each hut, Ginny noticed small gardens, growing beans, peas and spinach. The huts themselves looked to be made of mud bricks and some stone with thatched roofs. The windows and doors were covered in linen and provided little protection from the elements.

Further out were plowed fields of wheat, barley and rye. Maude began to chatter on how their clan was famous for their bread and ale. They sold or bartered it to many of the other clans that bordered them. As they passed building after building, Maude would rattle off its name and purpose. Ginny was only half listening, since she was expecting to be attacked at any moment.

Maude noticed her inattention and said, "Ya will not be treated so badly again, my lady. Many of the clan were impressed by how ya took yar punishment yesterday."

Ginny smiled and sighed her relief. It was a beautiful day, for Scotland. The sun was making a rare appearance and it wasn't as cold as it usually was. The grass smelled fresh and the animals were downwind. It was still painful to witness the poverty of these people, but it was just the way it was. In a mere 800 years, things would be better, at least for more people. Even with all the world had in the future, there were still too many people who lived like this.

Grim thoughts for a such a beautiful day, Ginny thought. She was determined to get into the spirit of this place. She had a part to play and hopefully it would lead her back to her time. *To what?*, she thought again, *being alone but being well fed? To a home by myself, with no one to share it with.* Ginny shook her head in disgust. Living in a romance novel was beginning to make her crazy.

Maude continued to chatter on about this and that. She showed Ginny her family's hut. Ginny met Maude's mother, a short, round woman with mousy brown hair flecked with gray. Her father had passed away only a few months earlier. Maude spoke on about how the rest of the clan helps their family out and now she had a job as her servant so she would be able to help more, too.

"Servant? You're not my servant, Maude," Ginny replied to Maude's assumption.

"Laird McKenna asked me to assist you. I was willing to help ya for no reason, since I like talking to ya, but the laird insisted on paying me. He is a generous man."

Ginny could see the pride Maude had in her new found position and didn't want to deflate her enthusiasm, but she had a problem with this young girl being a servant to her. "Listen, Maude. I appreciate your help and God knows I need it, but can we call you something else? How about 'mentor,' since you're teaching me all the things I need to know so I don't get paddled?"

Maude laughed and made a musical sound. "If it makes ya feel better, ya can call me whatever ya want. I am just happy to have you as a friend."

"So am I, Maude. You can now be my mentor. I do warn you though... If I get paddled on your watch, you may be out of a job!"

Maude laughed again and continued the tour. Ginny began to wonder what she was supposed to do now. Feeling useless was not something she enjoyed feeling. She could use her skills to help doctor these people. It was the best she had to offer. Maybe she could start with bathing and how it kept one healthy. *Baby steps, Ginny, can't move mountains*, she smiled.

And so it was, Ginny became the clan's psuedo healer. Psuedo because most of the clan wouldn't come near her because she was English. The older the clan member, the more they refused to be treated. Ginny was learning about all sorts of plants used for healing. Many she'd known about from her grandmother, but many were new and interesting in their uses.

The hardest part was trying to treat those that would be instantly cured with antibiotics or surgery, but were left to suffer slow and sometimes agonizing deaths. Often left to pure guessing, Ginny tried to help with everything from hangnails to cancer. Mostly, she just tried to make the clan member more comfortable.

Ginny was working from morning 'til night. She would see patients inside the main room of the keep, since she had no hut of her own. Maude was her assistant and nurse. No matter what Ginny asked her to do, she grinned and bore it with grace. Maude was not allowed to assist with the men's treatment. It seemed that no one cared about Ginny's sensibilities.

When Ginny wasn't seeing new patients, she and Maude would travel to check up on the sickest in their huts. Ginny had become very good at masking her feelings when entering some of the horrific conditions these people lived in. Dirt floors, sleeping on hay in corners, no clean water, clothing or bodies. It was no wonder they suffered so much. Their diets were bad enough: not enough protein, high in fiber, but low in Vitamins A, C and D. The diet, coupled with the unsanitary conditions often made Ginny wonder how anyone survived past infancy.

Ginny was beginning to feel the effects on her. She seemed tired all the time. When the sun did make an appearance, she stood outside for as long as she could, willing her body to soak in the Vitamin D. There was no explaining nutrition, since they had only so much food to go around. They were poor, but were also very generous and caring. It was awesome to witness.

Every night, Ginny would retire to Ian's bedroom. He had been very generous to loan her his bed. She had no idea where he spent his nights and probably didn't want to know. Every night, she would begin to shiver and suddenly there would be warmth. She'd snuggle against it and sleep soundly. Every morning, she would be cold again. Despite her initial reservations, the bed was comfortable and she had yet to get lice. Pretty good considering.

Days drifted into weeks and nothing new was happening. Ginny barely saw Ian, as he was often working with his warriors to hone their skills. When she had some time and she wasn't trying to make better concoctions with her herbs and plants, Ginny would sit and watch them fight. It was brutal and she knew she would probably be called to set a broken bone, but she was fascinated by the skill and cunning many of the men displayed.

She watched as they practiced with swords and bow and arrows. Most of the time, it was hand to hand combat, wrestling and full on cage fighting. Ginny got the impression that if someone didn't walk away bloody, it wasn't a worthy match.

Ian would often stare at her from a distance. Since the kiss after her paddling, he had avoided her like the plague. Ginny was willing to make the sacrifice of sleeping with him if it would get her home quicker, but she knew that was not how these books worked. She would have to fall in love with him despite his flaws and he would have to do the same. Ginny just didn't want to fall in love. It seemed so cliché.

And so, they barely spoke, they barely stood within a few feet of each other. If they were supposed to fall in love, this wasn't the way to do it. Something had to change. Ginny rolled her eyes to herself as she pondered what she had to do. *How embarrassing,* she thought grimly. *I'm going to have to change something here and probably humiliate myself in the process.*

Ginny didn't know what was worse, having to execute a silly plan to make Ian fall in love with her or the fact that she was completely incapable of coming up with a silly plan. She would sleep on it and consider her options in the morning. Maybe Maude would have some silly suggestions.

❖ Chapter 14 ❖

"My lady, please. Come quickly. Roslyn is having problems with the baby. She is asking for ya. Please," Maude was pulling Ginny's arm to get her moving.

"What are you talking about? Who is Roslyn?" Ginny, who was half asleep, had no idea what Maude was telling her. She tried to wake up, but the dream she was having was too good to abandon. Ginny was lying in the sunshine, warmed by the rays, surrounded by wildflowers. This was her happy place and she didn't want to get up and out into the cold.

"Ginny, wake up. Roslyn needs ya now," it was Ian's voice, standing half naked and looking somewhat agitated. Ginny could barely remember a time when he didn't look half to fully agitated about something, so this was nothing to her.

"Okay, okay," Ginny was still reluctant to give up her warmth, but as her head started to clear, she realized both Maude and Ian were worried about something.

Ginny dressed as quickly as possible, mostly having Maude do the work. *God, when am I going to get used to how freakin' cold it is here,* she thought miserably. Her hands were like ice as she was led to Roslyn's house. Ginny looked around the sleepy village. There were no lights, of course, but the moon was full and bright enough to lead the way. She only stumbled a few times on the way. Every time she tripped, she could feel Ian grab her and set her right and hear him mumble something about her clumsiness.

The small hut was situated along the valley to the west of the keep. Ginny was led inside where every available light source was being used. In a small bed was Roslyn, laying on her side and panting. It didn't take a medical degree to see that this woman was having a baby, and judging by her behavior, she was having it now. What the cold didn't do to wake her up, the situation was making up for it.

The old midwife came to Ginny's side and began rattling off in Gaelic. "Wait, I'm not that good with Gaelic... please slow down," Ginny stared at Maude to translate.

"She says that Roslyn is in trouble. The baby, it's too big. She knows ya're a healer and is asking for help."

Ginny stared incredulously, first at Maude, then at the old woman. When Ginny was in school, she had done her rotation in OB, but never delivered a baby by herself and certainly never did it with complications. Maude looked at Ginny, imploring her to help. Her eyes begged as if it she were the one lying there.

"Okay, let me take a look at her. Can someone go back and get my bag with my herbs?" Before Ginny could finish the sentence, Ian was out the door.

Ginny walked over to the small bed and felt the woman's forehead. Fever had already set in. "How long has she been laboring?"

The midwife spoke softly to Maude, who replied, "Almost two days."

Ginny didn't want to alarm poor Roslyn, but that was obviously not good. She concentrated on softening her face before turning to the laboring mother. "How many kids do you have?"

"This be my first, my lady."

Ginny heart broke at the sound of the exhausted woman. She bent low down, so only Roslyn would hear her. "I may only be able save one of you. If I have a choice, who do you want it to be?" Ginny was nearly certain of the poor girl's answer, but had to ask regardless.

"Save me baby, please."

Ginny turned swiftly to the midwife and Maude. She began shouting orders of what she needed. The three women prepared the hut. With all the activity, Ginny was not able to be nervous about what she was about to attempt. She knew that she couldn't do a Caesarian under these conditions, not that any conditions would ideal for her to do one in. Ginny was going to have to pull the baby out the regular way and knew that Roslyn may very well die from the experience.

Ian returned with her herbs. Ginny walked over to him and spoke quickly, "Where's her husband?"

"He's right over there," Ian stated pointing at a man pacing back and forth with two other men watching him. "Do ya need him?"

"Ian, I don't think Roslyn will survive this. He should come and be with her for a bit to say his goodbye," although sounding matter-of-fact, Ginny felt like crying. She couldn't afford tears at this point, though, so she kept it together.

"I'll tell him," was all he said and strode off to speak to the husband.

The night air was a relief to the heat inside the hut. Taking one last breath, Ginny re-entered the hut and began to prepare Roslyn. Not a minute later, Roslyn's husband, a man named Angus, had entered the hut and was by Roslyn's side. Ginny wanted to give them their privacy, but still had a lot to prepare, so she made herself busy and ignored them as much as possible.

Angus bent over his wife and put his hand to her cheek. In the soft light of the candles, Ginny could see Roslyn's fear, but she tried to be brave for her husband. There was so much to say and no time to say it, so the couple just stared at each other as if understanding without words. A small smile came across Roslyn's face, like she'd been given some peace from the pain. Angus kissed her forehead and stood up slowly.

"What do ya need me to do, my lady? I am at yar service," Angus spoke quietly, but with authority.

"I may need you to hold your wife while I retrieve the baby. Did Ian prepare you?" Ginny didn't want to say too much in front of Roslyn, but needed to know that Angus was aware of the possible outcome.

"Ian told me," was all Angus said before resuming his position at the head of the bed.

Opening her bag, Ginny looked through what she had available. The first thing she wanted to do was block as much pain as possible. She pulled some herbs and mixed them with hot water making a tea. She handed the cup to Angus and told him to feed it to his wife as quickly as possible.

The midwife began yammering again, so Ginny turned back to see the blood coming from Roslyn. "Crap," Ginny began moving with speed. She had some needle and thread and the sharpest knife she could get. Everything was sterilized as much as possible.

"Angus, Ian, hold her arms. Roslyn, you need to do exactly what I say. Maude, and you," Ginny never did get the name of the midwife, "hold her legs. Bend them and open them wide. Now, Roslyn, with everything you have, push."

Roslyn's face contorted from the effort. Ginny could feel the head and knew it was a big one. Rubbing the skin to try to get it to open further, Ginny kept ordering Roslyn to push. The contractions were one on top of the next, which didn't help Roslyn much since there were no breaks. The air inside the hut, incredibly, got even hotter.

Ginny forehead was covered in sweat as was everyone else, especially Roslyn.

The head moved slowly down the birth canal and finally seemed to be making its way out when it stopped. Several pushes and contractions did nothing to move it along. This was the part Ginny dreaded. She grabbed the sharp knife and made as small a cut as possible. Roslyn barely felt the cut with all the other pain. Ginny tried to get her fingers around the head to move it out. Roslyn was screaming now, an unholy sound. Finally, Ginny heard a small pop and the head was out

"Almost there Roslyn, just one more big push." Ginny looked Roslyn in the eye to try to will her just a little more strength for the task. "Ready... Push!"

Roslyn beared down and with what little strength she had left, she pushed. Ginny maneuvered the shoulders out and with a sudden swoosh, the baby was out. The midwife was there to assist with cutting the cord. "Have her breastfeed as soon as possible. It will help with the bleeding."

The midwife grunted and went about cleaning up the baby. After the placenta was delivered, Ginny examined it carefully to make sure all of it came out. The last thing anyone wanted was another complication. Ginny repaired the cut she'd made with the needle and thread. While Roslyn fed the baby for the first time, the midwife massaged the belly to get the uterus to shrink. Ginny cleaned up Roslyn as much as possible to prevent infection.

The baby, a beautiful boy, was a giant. He had soft brown curls and big brown eyes. He was the most beautiful thing Ginny had ever seen. She sighed softly and realized that she was about to cry. *I need to get out of here,* she thought. Ginny went outside and looked around. At the bottom of the hill was a small grove of trees.

Dawn was breaking to the east and the clan was already up and about. Ginny did not want to lose it in front of the village, so she ran as fast as she could to the trees. Once safely inside the grove, she kept running. She pushed her way past a tight knit grouping of trees and came to a small break. Ginny stopped and looked around quickly. No one was there.

First the tears came, streaming down her cheeks. Then came the anger. Ginny started picking up stray sticks and rocks and throwing them at the surrounding trees, all the while screaming every dirty word she knew. Her hands shook violently as she picked up objects to take her anger out on. She spotted a big rock and turned to hurl it, only missing Ian's head by inches. She stopped, noticing he didn't even flinch.

Ginny dropped to her knees and began to weep. It took Ian only seconds to reach her side and wrap his large arms around her. He was speaking softly, trying to sooth her. He wanted desperately to take her pain away.

Finally, when there was nothing left, Ginny calmed down and began to breath deeply. Although she was grateful for his comfort, she was also embarrassed for her display. "I'm sorry. I don't think I have ever been so terrified in my life. I was never one to enjoy feeling helpless."

"No one enjoys it, lass. Ya did verra well. Ya saved her and the babe."

"I guess that remains to be seen," Ginny looked at Ian's face. "Do you think it's fair that the man gets to have all the fun when it comes to making babies, and the woman gets to do all the suffering?"

"I dinna know if Roslyn had any fun in the making of her son. I know my wife will enjoy making me sons. As for suffering, I'm sure that Angus was suffering right along with her."

Ginny made a sound like it wasn't the same thing. Ian continued to stare into her eyes. He looked impressed and that made Ginny smile. "Yar the bravest lass I have ever met, Ginny." Before she could respond, Ian leaned down and kissed her softly on the lips. After so much terror, Ginny just wanted to feel good. She began to kiss him back in earnest.

Ian knew he should stop this before it went too far, but Ginny tasted so good. She used her tongue, unlike many inexperienced girls. *Maybe she's not as inexperienced as she claims*, he thought while continuing to assault her lips and mouth with his own. His hands wound up along her neck into her hair, which was coming out of its braid. As if they had a mind of their own, his hand slowly moved further down to caress the outline of her breasts.

When Ginny didn't flinch from his liberties, Ian kept going. He laid her on the ground next to him and stretched his long body beside her. With his one hand still caressing her head, the other began to massage her breasts, her back and bottom. Meanwhile, he kept kissing her lips, face and neck. When Ian would pull away from her lips,

Ginny would sigh so sweetly that Ian knew he had to stop this. He could feel himself lifting her skirts to get to the skin beneath.

Ginny was thoroughly enjoying herself. Ian was a great kisser and smelled so good right now, like wood smoke and outdoors. He was particularly tender, which made her hunger for more. *If we just do it, maybe I can go home*, Ginny thought, but realized that the idea of leaving him made her a little sad.

Ian began to nibble at the space behind Ginny's ear. This had always been one of those "sensitive" spots on Ginny and had the power to completely undue her. When he began to use his tongue, Ginny went wild and threw her one leg over Ian's, while rubbing his arms and chest. She managed to get her hand under his shirt and was rubbing the soft hair over his chest. She felt his hard stomach and was continuing to move her hand down when Ian all of sudden jumped up and turned away from her.

"What?!" Ginny was angry. *If he thinks to leave me hanging, I will castrate him right here*, she thought as she listened to her ragged breath. Suddenly it occurred to her that she should not be behaving this way. She was a virgin, after all, and should not be seducing him. *He probably thinks I'm a whore.*

Ginny sat with her head in her hands and her elbows on her knees. She willed herself to calm down so she could come up with some stupid excuse for her behavior. It was getting very difficult to play this part and the pretense was wearing thin. Never one for playing games with the opposite sex, Ginny found that she wasn't very good at it anyway.

With a humpf, Ian turned to face her. He was disgusted with his behavior, knowing that he was very close to stripping her naked and taking full advantage. Ian watched her for a moment, while Ginny was still composing herself. *Dammit*, he thought to himself, *I can't be falling in love with this lass.* To Ian, there was nothing worse.

He knelt down beside her and took her chin in his hand. With a soft smile that made his face so much more handsome, he said, "Now, that should no' have happened. Ya make me forget myself, sweet Ginny."

Searching his eyes for the correct reply, Ginny just sighed. No, it shouldn't have happened, but it had felt right. There was a stirring in Ginny that she'd not felt before. There were men that she'd wanted, and a few that she'd had, but this felt different. Is that my purpose, to fall in love? Will that appease whatever god put me here. Lesson learned?

"Ya'll be wanting to get some sleep now, eh? It has been a long night," Ian stood up and held out a hand to help Ginny. It was all suddenly too much, the night, the cold, and the moment with Ian. Ginny felt like she weighed a thousand pounds. She held out her hand and Ian picked her up as if she weighed nothing. Walking hand in hand, they set off back to the keep, where God willing, Ginny could get some warmth and sleep.

Ginny slept hard for most of the day. When she finally woke, she hurried to Roslyn's house to check on her and the baby. She'd left so abruptly that morning, trying to hide her weakness from the clan, that she hadn't even made sure everyone was alright. The clan had to know, they had to have heard her throwing rocks and sticks and making such an awful racket. While walking to the hut, Ginny chose not to think about it. Instead, she began to softly sing one of her favorite Crosby, Stills and Nash songs, *Teach Your Children: Don't you ever ask them why, if they told you, you would cry, so just look at them and sigh, and know they love you.*

As she approached the hut, she could hear the baby boy screaming bloody murder. That was a good sign, healthy lungs. She smiled as she announced herself.

Angus came to the doorway and invited her in. He was holding his screaming son with the proud look of a first time father. "He's my little warrior, dinna ya think, my lady."

"He's quite a big, healthy boy. Congratulations to your family," Ginny flushed with pride, knowing that she was able to help. She turned her head and saw Roslyn asleep. Her color was good, so the bleeding had stopped. Relief washed over Ginny. Maybe this could have a happy ending.

"She has been so tired. A touch of fever, still, but she says she feels better. I can wake her if ya want to visit," Angus looked concerned to wake his tired wife.

Ginny immediately declined, "No, please, let her sleep. You'll both be needing what sleep you can get. I left so abruptly this morning that I wanted to make sure everyone was alright. Also, make a tea with this," Ginny handed Angus a small pouch, "Have her drink it. Hopefully it will help her recover faster."

"God bless ya, my lady. Ya gave her the strength she needed and now I have my son," Angus was practically beaming with pride.

Ginny smiled and said she would return the next day. She walked down to the lake and sat at the edge. The water was so clear, it reflected the mountains perfectly. It was as if two mountains existed, exact opposites, both beautiful. The breeze was chilly, but for once, Ginny wasn't cold. She was content to sit and admire the beauty of her surroundings.

Enjoying the private moment, Ginny began singing again. Part of her wanted to keep singing songs to remind her of her real life. Part of her just liked listening to this strange voice sing future songs. So, in the quiet by the lake, she sang the most mellow song she could think of, The Carpenters *Close to You: Why do birds, suddenly appear? Everytime, you are near, Just like me, they long to be, close to you.*

She felt him before she heard him. Ian sat beside her and stared out at the landscape beside her. He remained still and quiet for a while, so Ginny didn't feel the need to speak. The companionable silence was pleasant and neither wanted to disturb it.

Finally, he glanced at her sideways and said, "Are ya faring well?"

"Aye," was all she said, with a small smile on her face. She was starting to pick up the lingo and maybe she was beginning to feel a little at home. She still missed her own home, friends and running water, but this place wasn't so bad. At least she had a handsome hunk desiring her.

Ian smiled as well. He turned his face towards her profile and was suddenly struck dumb. She was so beautiful to him and he wanted her in his bed, but at this moment, he saw something in her he hadn't seen before. She seemed older and wiser than her years. He felt he could see into her soul and he realized that she didn't belong here. His frown was fierce.

Ginny turned and stared at his frown for a moment, wondering what she'd done now. As she stared into his eyes, she saw something fierce, something primal. "What is it?" she asked, for once knowing it wasn't her fault, his bad mood.

"Ya belong to me, do ya hear? I canna let ya go," Ian's stare was intense and for a moment, Ginny was frightened. She was breathing heavy and her body began to tingle. The fear left and the desire came, nearly overwhelming her. Her eyelids drooped and Ginny began to stare at his mouth, willing it to kiss her.

When nothing happened, Ginny looked up and saw him staring at her mouth. "Are you going to kiss me? Or do I have to sit here all day?" Her boldness made him smirk. She was not like any other woman he'd ever known and every encounter brought that into sharp relief. His erection was strong and immediate. Before she could say anything else, he stood, grabbed her and began walking to the nearest grove of trees. Dragging her by her arm, quicker than she could handle, he had her in the protection of the trees in less than a minute.

He turned her, pushed her back up to a tree and covered her mouth with his. Ginny immediately opened her mouth and began to tease him with her tongue. Ian knew he was beyond reason. He started to kiss her neck and ear. Ginny released a small moan and lifted her leg to rub against his thigh. *Dear God*, was his last thought as he practically threw her to the ground and laid on top of her. He was desperate and acting like a teenager, his lust ruling his thoughts.

His hand began to reach under her skirt and feel its way up her leg. He kept waiting for her to stop him, to make any protest at all, but she continued to writhe under him and use her hands to explore his chest.

I must stop this, he kept thinking, his personal mantra that did nothing to stop his advances. He found what he was searching for, the center of her femininity. He stared down at her face as he invaded her slowly. Her eyes were glazed over with passion, but he saw nothing of fear or protestation.

He began to play gently with her nub, circling over and over again, until he saw her reaction. Ginny closed her eyes and her breathing became more heavy. It had been a long time since she'd been touched so passionately and the body she possessed had probably never felt anything like this before. The simple act of playing with her clitoris was driving her mad. She could feel him kissing her nipples through her clothing, as he continued to bring her to orgasm. When it happened, it happened quickly, but powerfully. Ginny arched against his fingers, spasming over and over again.

Ginny was shocked by her body's reaction to something so simple. She'd never been able to find release so easily, mostly faking it to end the encounter. Most of the men she'd been with cared little for her satisfaction, or were just unable to give it to her. But this man, this incredible man, had just given her the most earth shattering orgasm she'd ever experienced. And with so little effort. When she opened her eyes, she had to pry the lashes apart, as if she closed them so hard during the experience that they melded together.

Ginny wanted to give as good as she got. She looked into his eyes, a proud smugness was painted there. She smiled at him as she reached under his kilt. The smugness was replaced with shock. Ginny grabbed hold of his shaft and began to caress it. He moved from on top of her and laid next her. His eyes began to smolder with his unspent passion.

Ian laid back and allowed her to continue her caress. He watched her lift his kilt and use both her hands, guiding her fingers up and down, squeezing hard. Ian was completely unprepared when she lowered her head and began to suck lightly on the tip. The shock was nearly his undoing, and he almost spilled his seed at that moment. Ginny was taking him in, continuing her assault with her warm, wet mouth while using her hand to rub up and down at the same time. He couldn't take his eyes off her, watching as she pleasured him with her hands and mouth.

Ginny had never really enjoyed blow jobs, but somehow she knew this would be different. Her mouth wasn't too small, so her jaw wouldn't lock up from trying to take him in. He wouldn't smell of bodily functions or sweat, only of his outdoorsy male scent. She was enjoying the fact that she could give him what he'd given her.

When the time came, he could hold out no longer, he pulled her up to his mouth and began to kiss her thoroughly again. Ginny continued use her hand, increasing the speed with his urgency, until he finally came. Ian threw his head back, closed his eyes and moaned with satisfaction. In his lifetime, with the women he'd had, it had never been like this. The instant passion, the complete release. They both laid together, still, but panting, until their heartbeats returned to normal.

Neither of them knew what to say. Ginny realized that she had, once again, done the wrong thing. She wondered what repercussions would come of this. Although the wrong thing, she could not feel guilty about it. It was incredible, satisfying and a long time coming. She sat up and looked down at him. She smiled tentatively, trying to judge his mood.

Ian stared at her while she smiled at him. She wasn't upset about his advances and she had definitely knew how to pleasure a man. *Perhaps she's not the innocent that she pretended to be.* This thought brought back the feeling like she didn't belong here, that she was older than her years. Slowly, he smiled back at her, trying to ease any nervousness she had over what had transpired, because he fully expected it to happen again.

He sat up, cupped her face with his calloused hand and said, "Now, that probably should no' have happened, aye?"

Ginny laughed. Still smiling, she said, "No, but I don't regret it. Do you?"

"Nay. I canna bring myself to regret it either."

He stood up and began to adjust his clothing when he heard Broderick calling his name. He watched the disappointment on Ginny's face when she realized that their time together was at an end. "It seems you have work to do."

"Aye." He reached down, helped her stand up and picked the leaves off her back. "I will see ya at supper," he said as an order before quickly kissing her then turning around and leaving the trees. Ginny leaned back against a tree and watched him walk off. What was she going to do now, knowing he was capable of that? She smiled to herself and walked off to clean herself up.

❖ Chapter 15 ❖

At supper, Ginny was seated next to Ian at the large table in the great hall. She had often dined with him and his entourage, but usually was seated at the end of the table, away from their discussions about their clan and other clans. She was almost beginning to feel like one of the family. Broderick, as usual, was scowling at her. Ginny had come to realize that nothing annoyed Broderick more than when she was nice to him. So, she would often pour on her charm.

"Broderick, you look very nice this evening. Have you done something different with your hair?" she asked knowing it would bug him.

Broderick responded with something unintelligible and went back to shoveling food into his mouth. She smiled sweetly at him and asked one annoying question after another. Finally, having enough, Broderick excused himself and promptly left the hall.

Well, that was fun, she thought merrily when she noticed that Ian did not find it amusing. She stopped smiling and went back to eating. Eating had been a problem since her arrival. She'd always been picky, not enjoying anything fancy or unusual. Most of the meals, the meat was unidentifiable. It made it almost possible to eat it, not knowing what it was. Other times, she would pick slowly until she could reasonably get up and forgo the rest of the meal.

What she wouldn't give for a cheeseburger and anything whose main ingredient was chocolate. Ginny would often eat any raw vegetable she could get her hands on. Spinach was especially important for the vitamin C. The rich sauces they used, probably to cover up the meat having gone bad, left her stomach protesting most the next day. Having diarrhea on a chamberpot was not only difficult, but disturbing to clean up later.

After the meal, Ian asked Ginny to sit with him by the hearth. There were two upholstered arm chairs facing the the fire. Ginny took the nearest chair, turning to stare at the fire. It felt so good, she finally felt warm.

"I need to speak to ya," Ian looked like he was in an awful mood. Ginny figured it had to do with their antics that afternoon. He obviously did regret it.

"Very well," was all she could manage to say. She was terrified that he was going to chastise her for being so wanton. When the hell did she start caring about what he thought anyway.

"Ya shouldna provoke Broderick so much. The man canna take much more."

Huh, what? Really? "Yes, you're right. I will try to leave him alone. I really wanted to be friends, but my being English makes that impossible, doesn't it?" The relief on her face was obvious, but fortunately, Ian wasn't looking at her at the moment. He continued to stare into the fire.

"No, he doesna like the English and he has good reasons for it." Ian slowly turned his face to look at her. His eyes spoke of something else, something hidden. "Sweet Ginny, I have something to tell ya..."

He never finished his thought. The door to the keep slammed open and in came a small boy. He ran directly to Ian and said, "Laird, yar brother needs ya. It is Aileana."

"What happened, boy?" Ian stood up and was walking away when Ginny stopped him.

"Should I come... maybe I can help," she looked at Ian.

"Aye, come."

They walked out of the keep into the courtyard. Ginny knew the way, as she had been visiting with Aileana often. She and Maude were her only real friends here, so Ginny coveted the time she got with them.

As they approached the hut, they could hear Aileana screaming. Things were crashing around the hut. Ian began to run to the hut and stopped before going inside to say, "Stay here."

Ginny stood with the boy, rubbing her arms against the cold of the night. The sun was down and the air was chilled. She was covered with goosebumps, but some of those may have been caused by the unholy screaming she heard.

Alec appeared at the doorway and called Ginny in. Before she could set foot in the hut, Alec warned her. "She isnae being reasonable. I dinna know what is wrong. She willna talk to me." His eyes were frantic and desperate.

Ginny placed a hand on his shoulder. "Maybe you and Ian should go. Leave her to me." Alec was shaking his head.

"Nay, Ginny, it wouldna be wise. She is out of her mind."

Ginny put on her most serene face and said, "Trust me."

Alec calmed down slightly and put his head in his hands. When he looked at her again, he nodded and turned to his brother, who was avoiding the attack as much as possible, "Ian, let us go outside. The women need to be alone."

Ian turned and glared at Alec, then Ginny. "Get out now, Ian. I need to talk to Aileana. You've no place here right now." Two could play at the "leave no room for discussion" game. Ian took a deep breath and followed his brother out.

Ginny turned to Aileana, who had exhausted her ammo and was curled up into a ball on the floor. Ginny didn't dare touch her, but wanted her to know she was there. She sat down in a chair at the small table, keeping her voice even she said, "Do you want to talk to me?"

A sob escaped the fragile figure on the floor. Her shoulders shaking, deep sobs began to rack the small body. Not able to resist any longer, Ginny knelt down and wrapped her arms around Aileana. She didn't resist Ginny's touch, only continued to sob. After what seemed like hours, Aileana's face turned toward Ginny and asked, "What am I to do?"

"Do about what?"

With a sigh of resignation, she said, "The baby."

It took a moment for Ginny to realize what she'd said. *Baby? Was Aileana with child?* A child conceived by rape and torture. By men hardly worth being associated with human beings. Now she understood... the screaming, the violence. Although every one of those men had been killed, at the hands of her own family, they were still torturing her beyond the grave.

"You're sure. The baby was conceived during your... your... captivity?"

"The pain wouldna be so bad if I was sure. But, Alec and I... were... intimate, before I left to visit my family. Truth be told, Ginny, I dinna know whose baby I carry and I dinna know how to tell my husband," anguish filled her face and she began to cry once again.

Ginny put her arm around her again and waited for her to compose herself. No DNA tests were available, so Aileana would never have piece of mind. Alec would always wonder too, even if he was too much a gentleman to ever reveal that to his wife. Ginny had no consoling words, nothing to give her for comfort.

"Can ya tell him for me?" Aileana asked. "I dinna think I can. I canna watch the look on his face. He doesna know that I see the pity, and the shame, when he doesna think I am looking. I canna take much more."

What could Ginny say? She wanted to help this tortured woman, but didn't relish the job of telling her husband the news. She stared into Aileana's eyes and nodded. Of course she would do it. Of course she would take whatever pain from her she could. Even as little as it was and as impotent that she felt.

"Do you want me to wait. Stay with you a while longer," she sounded cowardly, but didn't care.

"Nay, it needs to be done. I owe ya so much, Ginny. I dinna deserve a friend like ya."

"Ha! You're one of the few people here who never treated me like a pariah. You've paid me back a thousand fold just by accepting me." Ginny smiled and got up to leave. "He'll be in here as soon as I tell him. Prepare yourself."

"Aye," was all she said as she slowly got up and sat down on the bed. The last thing Ginny saw before leaving the hut was her head drop to her hands.

Ginny forgot how cold it was outside and immediately began to rub her arms. Ian and Alec strode over to her, determined to find out what she'd learned. Alec's face grew forlorn when he saw Ginny expression.

"Do ya know what is wrong," Alec asked, trying to sound hopeful and failing miserably.

"Yes, I know. Can we take a walk?"

Ian and Alec exchanged a glance, but nodded and slowly began to walk away from the hut. Ginny spent the time trying to phrase what she was going to say. No one ever likes giving bad news, but especially in Ginny's line of work, it was inevitable.

"Alec, I'm going to tell you what's wrong and you have to promise to stay here until I'm completely finished. Agreed?" Ginny didn't want Alec running off as soon as the words were out of her mouth.

"Aye."

Ginny took a deep breath and said, "As if she hasn't been through enough... Aileana is pregnant."

Unfortunately, they hadn't moved far enough away that Aileana would not have heard the tortured cry of Alec. He was angry and the look in his eye spoke of murder. Ginny backed away and Ian came to stand in between them. Alec fell to his knees and buried his face in his hands. How much more could this one family take.

Ginny was determined to get through to him. She moved to his side and knelt beside him. "Listen to me, Alec. She doesn't know who the father is. She told me that you two were together before she left. The baby might be yours. There is no way of knowing." Alec began to cry harder and started to pound his fists into the ground.

He slowly looked up to her face. His anger was palpable and suddenly, Ginny was scared. He was going to lash out and she had stupidly put herself in the target zone. She spoke as calmly as she could, trying to keep the tremble from her voice, "She needs you. She needs you not to be so angry because she knows how you feel. She needs you to go into that hut, put your arms around her and let her know that no matter what happens, you still love her. That nothing could ever change that... even your own guilt."

Anguish flashed across Alec's face and he looked around for something to get his anger out on. Ian stepped forward, reached down to help his brother up and said, "Hit me."

Alec closed his eyes for a moment, then, without warning, punched Ian in the face. Ian went down on his butt, but got up immediately and said, "Again."

Alec wasted no time punching Ian's chest and head. Ginny was appalled, but kept quiet. Ian took each hit and stood for another. He was his brother's punching bag, and hopefully, Alec would be sane enough to speak to Aileana when it was over.

When his anger was spent, he turned to Ginny and said, "Thank ya, lass. Thank God yar here. I canna ever repay ya for yar kindness." He turned to the hut and began to walk back. After a few steps, he turned and said, "Ginny, yar my family now. Yar my sister and I will always protect ya with my own life. Know that." He turned and walked toward his hut.

Ginny was humbled. She didn't feel she deserved such feeling, but she was appreciative of it nonetheless. She wished she could hug him, to let him know how much it meant to her, but now was not the time. Ginny turned to look at Ian, who looked a little swollen and wore a fierce scowl on his face.

Looking down at her, he said, "Yar not my sister, that is certain. But I would protect ya as well." His eyes darkened and the lust was apparent. Ginny smiled and stood there hoping for a kiss. She was not disappointed.

Ian lowered his head and met her lips gently. Molding his lips to hers, he hesitated to deepen the kiss. There were things he needed to tell her before this relationship went any farther, but he hadn't found the courage yet to speak to her. He had tried before they were summoned to his brother's home. Ginny, of course, had different ideas and opened her mouth to use her tongue. A man only has so much willpower. With a growl, he took over her mouth with his tongue and let her know who was in charge.

Ginny reached her arms behind his neck and Ian winced. She pulled away, realizing that he did just take a beating from his brother. With a laugh, she said, "Come. Let's get you back to the keep so I can clean you up. You look like hell."

"Hell, ya say. Hmmm, ya canna mind so much if yar willing to kiss me like that."

"I didn't say I minded, did I?" He laughed as he walked her back.

No sooner had Ginny cleaned up his face, did Ian tell her to go to bed. She was getting used to his ordering her around and, at times, found it somewhat endearing.

She changed and climbed into bed. It was always the coldest when she first got in. When she began to warm up, she dozed off. The dream was so vivid, she thought for sure she was awake. She felt Ian climb into bed with her and put his arms around her. The warmth was exquisite. She cuddled close to his hairy chest, smelling his outdoorsy, male scent.

Her hands began to explore his body, finally settling on his erect penis. God, he was huge. She wanted him so badly, but heard him say no. She was confused. Why would her dream Ian refuse her. Damn, she couldn't even get laid in dreams. In frustration, she turned her back to him. He pulled her back against his chest and whispered endearments in her ear. This wasn't so bad. At least she was warm. Ginny didn't remember anything after that.

❖ Chapter 16 ❖

The next morning, Maude came in as cheerful as usual. She began to chatter on about people in the clan that Ginny didn't even know. She stoked the fire to life and added more wood as another woman, a maid named Rhona, brought in the large washtub. Several women began to bring in buckets of steaming water and pouring them into the tub. Ginny finally realized she was going to get another bath. Maybe not as good as her jetted tub at home, but still, a chance to get every part of her clean.

Maude insisted on helping her. As Ginny stepped into the tub and knelt down, Maude rinsed her and washed her hair with a sweet smelling soap. Ginny was just enjoying sitting in the small tub full of water. Maude was massaging her scalp, just like in the nicer salons. *Now if only I could do this everyday, I could definitely live here*, she thought merrily.

Once she was clean, rinsed and dried off, Maude combed and braided her long hair. As if possessing someone else's body wasn't strange enough, there were things you just didn't get used to. One was having hair so long it reached your butt. Ginny's normal hairstyle was as short as possible without looking boyish. The weight of this new hair was ridiculous. One more thing that women suffered with in the good ole days.

Once dressed, Maude and Ginny went in search of breakfast. They entered the great hall and there was Ian and Alec, speaking in low voices and obviously arguing over something. Maude offered to fetch her some porridge and scampered off. It is difficult to be so independent and have someone waiting on you, but Ginny didn't begrudge Maude wanting to hightail it out of the room. The atmosphere was grim.

Ginny walked up to the two men and said, "Good morning, gentlemen. Alec, how is Aileana doing today?"

"Better. We have decided to raise the baby together. It doesna matter who the real father is. I will be the father."

Ginny beamed. She was really proud of him. Although Alec blamed only himself for what happened to Aileana, she could imagine

106

how hard it would be to raise a child if you're not sure of the true parentage. "I'm glad to hear it. I'll be happy to help in any way." After a pause, she added, "I want to thank you for your kind words to me yesterday. It's humbling to have you as my champion."

"He is not your champion, Ginny. I am!" Ian looked angry. But, what else was new.

"Very well," Ginny moved to the table and began to eat the porridge Maude had brought her. She also had a shiny new apple. Maude knew Ginny loved her fresh fruit and vegetables and would often bring some from her own garden. Before Ginny could thank her, she disappeared again.

Ian and Alec continued their discussion. Ginny didn't want to eavesdrop, but it was impossible not to listen.

"We havenae found out who was behind the taking of my wife. Sealing this alliance will only aid us if it comes to war," Alec said, once glancing at Ginny.

"Aye. I will do what is best for the clan," Ian responded.

"I am sorry, brother. Ya do a great service."

Ginny wondered what awful duty Ian had to undertake for his clan. Just then, Broderick walked into the keep. It was a good thing, since Ginny hadn't tortured him yet today. Just as he walked up, she was about to ask him about his tunic, when he spoke, in a loud voice, "Ian, I am ready to leave to bring back yar bride. I willna be gone more than a few days." Ginny was staring at Broderick and he was staring right back.

Bride? Bride for Ian? That was the duty he had to undertake for his clan. Seal the alliance? *Great, just great!* she thought grimly. That was what he hid from her yesterday. Probably what he'd been trying to tell her for days. Ginny's head dipped down to look at her porridge.

Ian was madder than hell. He had every intention of telling Ginny of the situation, but Broderick decided to take the insensitive approach as usual. "Leave us!" Ian practically shouted at the two men.

Alec and Broderick walked to the door and went no further. They still had much to discuss with Ian and were just waiting for him to explain himself to the girl and be done with it. Broderick didn't care what he said, she deserved no explanation as far as he was concerned. Alec felt truly sorry for her, since he was certain she had fallen in love with Ian. Both men watched from the doorway.

"I am truly sorry, Ginny. I dinna know how to tell ya."

Ginny was quite surprised when the tears started to form in her eyes. *Please don't cry, please don't cry,* she kept telling herself. She took a shaky breath and without looking at him, said, "How long have you known you were marrying someone else?"

"The betrothal was arranged a few months ago."

Ginny fairly whispered, "A few months ago." She took in another shaky deep breath and stood up. The tears were now gone, replaced by anger. He had used her, plain and simple. She was a fun toy, but now that business needed to get done, she was cast aside. Nice!

She turned to him, stared him in the eye and spoke with an eerily calm voice, "So, the kissing, the... other stuff... what the hell was that?"

"Now, Ginny, ya must know that I dinna want to marry this other woman," he didn't even finish when the torrent opened and Ginny let loose.

"Well," she screamed, "that's just great! You don't want to marry her. How nice will that be when she comes here and meets me and finds out she was a means to an end. God dammit, Ian. Thank God we didn't sleep together!"

At that last statement, Ginny heard gasps from the kitchen. *I guess they're all listening to this juicy bit,* she thought as she tried to contain herself. Maude came running into the room and put a protective arm around Ginny. Maude had seen what Ginny's temper accomplished and was trying to save her from another paddling.

Ian just shook his head, turned and left with the other men. Ginny couldn't believe he wasn't going to say anything else. Didn't he care that he had shown her Nirvana and now left her with nothing. Ginny closed her eyes and tried to get her heart to slow down.

"Ginny, what did ya mean ya havenae slept with Ian?" Maude asked tentatively.

Now she had to have a sex talk with her fifteen year old friend. "Maude, I hope you don't think less of me, but Ian has kissed me a few times," Ginny had to fairly choke those words out, "and it never came to... came to... coupling, so to speak. Do you know what I mean?"

"So, when ya and Ian shared a bed each night, ya never..." Maude had more trouble finding the words than she did.

"Shared a bed? Maude, what are you talking about?"

"Ian sleeps in his own bed every night. I found him there when

Rosalyn had the baby. How dinna ya know that?"

Like a bolt out of the blue, Ginny finally realized why she suddenly got warm at night. She closed her eyes and began to silently berate herself for being so dumb. She never asked him where he was sleeping after giving her his bed. Well, now she knew where, with her, the whole time.

Something else occurred to Ginny, "Maude, who knows about us sharing a bed?"

"Everyone, by now. Broderick was verra angry and had a loud fight with the laird over it. I never heard Broderick yell at the laird before."

Ginny closed her eyes and prayed for patience. The prayer went unanswered.

She strode to the door and slammed it open. There, standing a few feet into the courtyard, were Ian, Alec and Broderick. Judging by the look on their faces, hers must have been telling of the coming storm. Ian just stared at her and lifted an eyebrow. The condescension was obvious.

"HOW DARE YOU!" Ginny screamed at the top of her voice.

Calming down slightly, she said, "You've been sleeping in my bed every night. And everyone in this village thinks we're lovers. What's wrong with you?"

In a calm voice, Ian replied, "It is my bed, Ginny. Ya would do well to remember that."

"Fuck you, Ian McKenna," Ginny said while pointing her finger into his chest. "You have the nerve to treat me like some kind of plaything. You can go to hell!" Ginny walked down the steps and through the courtyard. Just then, the stable boy came with a saddled horse. Without considering that she'd only ridden a horse a couple of times, she lifted her skirt, put her foot in the stirrup and pulled herself up. Then, before the stable boy knew what was happening, she kicked the horses flanks and off it rode, out the gate.

"My horse!" Broderick fairly screamed as she rode off.

Ginny had no idea where she was going. She headed south, at least she thought it was south. She held on for dear life and hoped the damn horse knew where to go. After a few minutes, Ginny pulled back on the reins and got the horse to slow down. The horse was walking now, so Ginny took some time to adjust her skirt so it wasn't so indecent. She could no longer see the huts of the village, could no longer see the keep. Ahead she saw a field with a small stream running through it. Fortunately, she was able to stop the horse and get off it without killing herself.

She walked over to the stream and scooped up water into her hands. She rubbed the water onto her face, trying to cool down her temper. Ginny couldn't remember a time when she was this mad. Maybe that time she caught her boyfriend Victor sucking face with her co-worker at the hospital Christmas party. No, not even then.

Ginny sat remembering their few sexual encounters together. They had been brief, but they had also been passionate. Could Ian have been faking it? No, he wanted what he wanted and as laird, he got what he wanted.

Ginny was muttering to herself. Why the hell did he continue to insist that she was his when the whole time he knew he was marrying someone else? She knew he wanted her, but why would he use her like that? Ginny guessed it had something to do with an over abundance of testosterone. He simply didn't consider her feelings.

"Well, well, what do we have here?"

Ginny turned to face the voice. Three young men, barely no longer boys, were standing there facing her. Judging by the sneers they gave her, there intentions were less than honorable. They were a gruesome bunch. The tallest, who was well over 6 feet, had bright orange hair and a bad complexion to match. The second, was only slightly shorter, and had a lazy eye. The third, who wasn't much taller than Ginny, was missing an extraordinary number of his teeth. The effect made his sneer even more laughable.

"Yar the Englishwoman, aye?" the orange haired boy said.

"Yes, I'm Ginny," was all she said, staying on her guard.

"Isnae she the laird's mistress? That's what my da told me," that came from lazy eye.

"Aye, his mistress. Do ya think she might want to demonstrate her wares?" Orange hair was having a good time.

"Never had a whore before," came out of Shorty's mouth and it made them all laugh.

Ginny had had enough. "Really, what a shock! Although, considering you haven't had any woman, I can see the appeal of having one you had to pay for." Oops, wrong answer.

"She dinna just disrespect me, did she?" Shorty took offense to her response.

"Aye, she did. What kind of whore doesnae like to relieve a man's suffering," Orange hair looked perplexed.

"I'm not a whore, gentlemen. The stories of my sleeping with McKenna have been greatly exaggerated," Ginny did not like where this was going. Three against one was never good odds, but then as a female, with limited strength, it made the odds even worse.

"If I say yar a whore, then yar a whore, aye?" Shorty was getting bold and Ginny was getting pissed.

Her morning had started off so promising. She remembered thinking the day would be so much better because she had gotten a bath. It went downhill from there. Finding out about Ian's marriage to a woman only for the sake of an alliance, finding out that the entire village thinks she's a whore, and Ian's obvious lack of repentance over the situation. If anger gives you strength, then call her the Hulk. "Careful, gentlemen, you wouldn't like me when I'm angry."

All three started laughing. The loud guffaws made something in Ginny snap. She moved forward to Shorty and clocked him upside his head. The other two stopped laughing and came at Ginny. She was able to kick Orange hair square in the nuts, but lazy eye grabbed her from behind and lifted her off the ground. She couldn't move her arms and her legs were thrown out in front of her, so she couldn't kick his shins.

Shorty came over, looking particularly pissed. Ginny's heart was beating so fast, she could both hear and feel it pounding in her ears. It was probably why she didn't hear the horse approaching. Shorty stayed out of the way of Ginny's flailing legs, but managed to back hand her. Then suddenly, Ginny was on the ground.

All three boys were looking toward a frightening sight. There stood Ian, breathing heavy and scowling viciously. The boys ran in different directions, but Ian caught Shorty and proceeded to pound him into the ground. His yell stopped the other two in their tracks.

"Ya dinna want to make me run after ya. Get over here, Malcolm, Hamish," Ian's voice indicated that this was one order that wouldn't be disobeyed. As soon as they were in front of Ian, he took their heads and smashed them together. The sound was a sickening thud and both boys crumbled to the ground.

He stepped over the boys and walked toward Ginny. His face was still frightening and Ginny wanted nothing to do with him. She got up and began to back away. She felt the tears streaming down her face. Wanting nothing more than to be anywhere else, she quickened her steps and promptly fell over a rock. This gave Ian more than enough time to catch up. Without a word, he scooped her up and walked back to his horse.

How he was able to climb onto a horse while cradling her, she could not fathom. But there she was, once again in his arms, riding on his huge horse. Before heading back to the keep, he grabbed the reins of Broderick's horse. They were back in the courtyard within a few minutes, since she'd only managed to get over one hill during her flight.

Broderick snarled at her, muttered something about stealing a man's horse, then quickly climbed up and left, presumably to pick up Ian's bride. Ian dismounted and brought Ginny into the great hall, where he gingerly put her down on one of the chairs by the hearth. Ginny just stared into space, not willing to make eye contact, not willing to listen to anything he had to say.

"How are ya?" Ian asked, trying to keep his voice low. He was kneeling in front of her, caressing her hands.

Ginny continued her stare. She knew that men hated it when women went silent. It was her only weapon, so she employed it. She turned her head, not realizing that it would show off her newly forming bruise from Shorty's back hand.

"Och, Ginny. Yar hurt." Ian strode over to the kitchen and was giving orders. In less than a minute, he was applying a cold compress to her face. He was being gentle and Ginny felt herself wavering. But, in the end, she held firm. She didn't want to be used again.

"Will ya no' talk to me?" Ian sounded a little desperate and she really liked that.

Ginny decided that the only thing better than silence was guilt. "Do you know why those boys were attacking me?" She stared at him with her eyes still wet with tears.

Ian looked down. Ginny didn't think he realized the extent of his guilt, so she continued to elaborate.

"They were calling me a whore. Your mistress. They wanted me to show them what I was capable of. I suppose you can't blame them. It is the impression everyone has of me."

Ian's head shot up and stared. "Och, Ginny, they can and will be blamed for their actions. And no one thinks yar a whore."

"Why not? I'm unmarried and have been apparently sharing a

bed with you since Day One. The one boy said he heard I was your mistress from his father."

"I dinna mean for this to happen." Ian's voice dropped to a whisper, so only Ginny could hear him. "I have wanted ya from the moment I saw ya fighting in that keep. When ya thought ya were saving me from attack. Havenae ya known that?"

"It doesn't matter, Ian. After our few stolen moments, you've had to know that I wanted you too. But that's not how it works here. You know we have to be married to go that far. It's the one thing I have to offer to a marriage. If you take it, no matter how much we both want it, then I have nothing." Ginny knew she didn't care, but for some reason, she didn't think she'd be in this body forever. And if she couldn't leave that much for Lady Chatham, Ginny would have cheated the life she'd only been borrowing.

"I dinna take you last night. Even after ya grabbed me," Ian fairly snarled at her. Obviously, this woman had no idea how much restraint he'd employed. He, after all, was used to getting what he wanted and Ginny was on the top of that list.

"What? Jesus Christ, I thought I was dreaming. That certainly explains a lot," Ginny retorted. Well, that would be why she couldn't get laid in her dreams, because she hadn't been dreaming. She did wonder something, though. "You stopped me. Did you know I was half asleep and would regret it. Is that why you stopped it?"

"Nay, Ginny. I stopped ya because I want to marry ya. I want ya to give me sons. I dinna want this other woman. I havenae even seen her. I marry her only for the alliance."

Ginny felt herself weaken. A large part of her wanted Ian to carry her upstairs and make love to her. She knew it would be spectacular and she needed a little spectacular after the day she was having. But that was what she wanted, not necessarily what Lady Chatham would want. On the other hand, it might be all she got. Of course, if this was a romance story, something had to change in her favor. Could she wait just a little while longer, to see what was yet to come? Ginny knew she had to.

"When will your bride be arriving?"

"It will take Broderick a few days to get there and back again."

"Very well. We have a few days together before you become forever unavailable to me. What would like to do?"

Ian looked confused. Did she think he would send her away

once he was married? "Ya still belong to me, Ginny. I wouldnae send you away after the marriage."

"First, stop saying that. It reminds me of things I can't have. Second, I will not sleep in this keep after you're married. I need to find alternative housing. It's not like I can leave, Ian."

"Nay, ya willna ever leave."

"And what, exactly, will you do if I decide to marry someone else? Or do you plan to just keep me here, unmarried, for the rest of my life?"

Ian looked like she struck him. He hadn't really thought what he would do if she married someone else. He was fairly certain he would never let her marry anyone else. It wasn't fair, but he didn't care.

"We dinna need to talk about that now. What did ya want to do today?"

Ginny bowed her head thoughtfully. When she looked up into his eyes, it occurred to her that it would be nice to spend some time with him. "There is a grove of trees, just down the hill from where your men train that I wanted to look at. I was wondering what kind of plants were growing there. I remember a moss that's great in healing."

Ian smiled. "I will take ya there."

"Just let me get some things..." Ginny said as she stood and left him in the hall. She called over her shoulder, "I'll meet you in the courtyard in fifteen minutes." With that, Ginny walked up the stairs to where she kept her herbals.

❖ Chapter 17 ❖

He was there, on top of his horse, waiting. Ginny decided to make him wait, as she used the disgusting chamberpot, got some water, grabbed her apple and then finally made her way out to the courtyard. He lifted her up to his lap and rode off to the grove she had spoken about. Four of Ian's men followed on horseback, fully armed with swords.

When they slowed down, Ginny started munching on her apple. Ian stared at her and asked, "Are ya no' going to share yar sweet apple?"

"No, I'm not going to share. You got to eat your breakfast this morning. I did not."

Ian began to laugh. It was a booming laugh that could only make you smile in response. Ginny had to decide how mad she still was at him. She had to maintain some anger, or he would easily convince her to fool around again. Above all else, Ginny could not allow that to happen.

They dismounted in front of the grove. On the other side of the trees was a steep hill, on top of which, Ian's men trained. "Why are you not training your men today, Ian?" Ginny asked.

"Alec will handle it. Besides, I am spending some time with ya." Ian's voice could be soothing and sexy when he wanted it to be. Ginny wasn't falling for it.

She finished her apple and threw the core into the trees. After wiping her sticky fingers on her tunic, she began to inspect the different varieties of flora. She knew a lot of plants by sight, few by name, often referring to them by their characteristics: yellow leaves, small red buds, etc... She wasn't having much success when she came out to see Ian talking to one of his men.

As she walked out of the trees toward him, she heard a strange whistle. Not a second later, an arrow hit the tree next to her head. Now, Ginny isn't stupid, but she just stood there staring at the arrow trying to figure out what was going on. Suddenly, she was on the ground, underneath Ian, within the tree line.

"What's going on?" she asked, as she finally started piecing it together.

Ian growled at one of his men, "How many?"

"I canna tell. At least fifteen on the ridge line. The plaid, if I am no' mistaking, is MacBain," the man turned to Ian with a look like that was some seriously bad news.

"Damn! Five against fifteen. If it were any other clan, I wouldnae be worried. But not McBains," Ian took only a second to consider his options.

He turned his fierce stare to Ginny and said, "Ya need to run up the hill, Ginny. Ya need to get Alec and more men down here as quickly as possible. Can ya do that?"

"Of course." Ginny stood up and began to make her way through the trees. As she forcing her way through, she yelled back to Ian, "Stay safe. All of you. Or I will be pissed."

She heard their laughter as she made it to the other side of the trees and began running up the hill. The hill wasn't that high, but it was steep. She had always been a quick runner, but never lasted very long. About a quarter of the way up the hill, the stitch in her side started and her lungs began to burn. Ginny pushed past the pain and kept going. *Damn Scotland for being so hilly*, she thought, but continued to push herself up the hill. She didn't know how long Ian and his men could hold out.

The rocky slope was killing her feet. The only shoes she had to wear were not very sturdy. More like ballet slippers with a hard sole. Ginny would have killed for a pair of sneakers at that point, or her reliable hiking boots.

She saw the top and started spouting, *I think I can, I think I can*, over and over in her head. When she finally reached the top of the hill, she could barely breathe, so she started waving her arms to catch Alec's attention. Another warrior saw her and ran over, just as Alec spotted her and rode the horse he was still on top of over to see what was going on.

"What is it, lass?" the warrior asked.

"Ian... attack... MacBains..." she started pointing toward the grove of trees at the bottom of the hill, like some kind of pantomime. The warrior called out to Alec, then let out a piercing war cry. Men were running down the hill as fast as they could, carrying their swords high and yelling to let Ian know they were coming. Ginny dropped to the ground and was soon surrounded by four of the clan's newest warriors.

When Ginny caught her breath again, she said to the nearest man, "Go, take care of your laird. I'll be fine."

"Nay, we know our duty. We canna let ya be taken or hurt."

Ginny stood back up, but the cramp in her side bent her over. One of the men came over and helped her back to the ground. Ginny looked up to thank him and realized it was the boy she'd stitched up after the first battle when she first met the clan McKenna. She smiled at him as he offered her his waterskin.

"Thank you. Ronald, right?" she asked while taking a big drink from the skin.

"Aye. I never thanked ya for yar help healing me that day. I am verra sorry about acting so badly," he looked quite remorseful. Ginny thought Ian could take a lesson.

"It's alright. I know it was probably a little embarrassing for you. I think we can now be even," she said, holding up the skin and taking one more drink before handing it back to him.

"Nay, I still owe ya," Ronald said with a smile. As Ginny tried to get up again, he helped her and her side didn't burn as badly as before.

They all stared at the grove and beyond, not really seeing anything because of the trees. Finally, Alec came riding up the hill. He had a smile on his face, so she assumed it went well.

"Damn MacBains. So brave facing five McKennas... not so brave facing far more," he was laughing with her guards. "Come Ginny, yar needed. Some men are hurt." He held his hand out to her and was promptly lifted onto his lap.

"Is Ian alright?" Ginny could hear some panic in her voice. Alec heard it as well.

"Nay, he was injured," Alec stated with a grim expression. He wanted to see how Ginny reacted to the news. She reacted as he assumed she would.

"What happened? Was he hit by an arrow, sword, what???" Ginny was frantic. "Can't you ride any faster?"

"Ginny, he will be fine. He will have ya to tend to him," Alec said evasively. He knew a little about love. He loved his wife with a passion he didn't know was possible. As the wind whipped past them, riding down the hill, Alec knew for certain that Ginny was in love with

117

Ian. He also knew that she wasn't likely to live her life in happiness with Ian married to someone else.

He pulled the horse around the trees and Ginny caught her first sight of the battle. There were a few bodies on the ground. Some looked beyond repair. Ginny was relieved to see that they wore different plaids than the McKennas. When Ginny spotted Ian, she barely let Alec stop the horse before she jumped down and ran to him. His back was turned to her and he was giving orders to his men. She didn't want to disturb him, but needed to touch him.

Reaching out, she gently touched his arm. Ian turned suddenly, causing Ginny to jump in surprise. He laughed when he saw her shock.

"Alec said you were injured," Ginny said trying to cover up her impatience.

"Aye," he said. Then lowered his head and whispered, "but I'd rather show you when we are alone." His eyebrow went up and a boyish grin formed on his face. Ginny could do nothing but smile.

"I'm guessing you'll survive. Are there others who need my immediate attention?"

"Aye, come with me." As they walked away, Ian continued to give orders to his men in Gaelic, so Ginny only caught part of the conversation. Ian had scouts that he would use to hunt down any other MacBains on McKenna land. They would prepare for war and they would call in their allies.

When Ian stopped, Ginny stared at a man who was pretty beaten up. His face was covered in blood, along with a huge gash that ran the length of the man's chest, from right shoulder to his left hip. He laid on the ground, shaking slightly.

Ginny didn't think she could save him, but was willing to do something to make him comfortable, when Ian commanded, "Keep him alive, Ginny. He wants to die, but I need information from him. He likely knows the MacBain's plans, since he is his younger brother." The last part Ian stared directly at the prisoner. Ginny could see the shock in his expression at being found out.

"Curse ya, McKenna. I wouldnae tell you anything. Ya might as well keep yar English whore away from me."

Before Ian could speak, Ginny said calmly, "Sir, you are not the first person to call me a whore today. My guess is that you don't want to end up like the others. I mean you no harm. Please let me help you."

Ginny had dealt with difficult patients and could be very sweet and charming if it had to come to that. In this case, she definitely had to be sweet and charming.

The man calmed down and stared her in the eye. "Verra well, lass. Do what ya will."

Ginny smiled and turned to ask the nearest warrior to grab her bag, "I think it must have fallen near the tree line," she said, pointing in the general direction. Ian gave orders to two other soldiers to stay close and make sure the MacBain prisoner didn't try anything troublesome toward Ginny.

Upon closer inspection, the wound to the man's chest was only superficial. It could be easily sewn up, but that wouldn't help him against infection. When the warrior returned with her bag, she asked if he could get her hot water. The warrior just stared at her incredulously.

They were still arguing when Ian returned. Ginny stood and spoke softly to him. "I need hot water to treat him or he will come down with fever and die. What do you want me to do?"

Ian looked thoughtful for a moment and said, "We will bring him back to the keep. Ya canna help him much out here."

" Fine," she replied and watched them as they threw him on a horse and rode to the keep. *That will be one unpleasant ride for him*, she thought as she sat on Ian's lap, holding on for dear life as he rode faster.

Once back at the keep, Ginny employed Maude to assist her in getting everything she needed. Although Ginny could have used Maude's help, the soldiers told her to leave once everything was set up. Couldn't have such a young, impressionable girl in the presence of the evil enemy, after all. The men finally arrived with the prisoner and plopped him on a table.

With a pot boiling in the hearth, she deposited her knife, needle and thread. She took more hot water to wash her hands and to meticulously clean the wound. Although the man never said a word, his face would contort with pain during her deeper inspections.

"What's your name, sir?" Ginny wanted to distract him before the real fun began.

"Why do ya care, English? Ya know he only means to kill me soon anyway."

"Why would Ian ask me to save you then?" she asked, perplexed by his logic.

"So he can ask me questions. Torture them out of me if necessary. Ya canna be that naïve," he said contemptuously.

"Are you the one who shot the arrow that nearly took off my head?" she asked tartly.

The man laughed in response. "Aaah, yar a brave one. If it weren't for the accent, I would think ya a Highlander. No wonder the McKenna keeps ya around. Alas, nay, twasn't my arrow. Mine wouldnae have missed."

It was Ginny's turn to laugh. "I asked your name, sir."

"Campbell MacBain," was his only response.

"Well, Campbell MacBain, let me give you a bit of advice. Perhaps, Ian plans to torture information from you, but right now, you should be worrying about me. I can do this nicely, or I can do this... not so nicely. Do you get my meaning?"

"Aye, I think I do."

"Good. Now that we understand each other, I can continue," Ginny continued cleaning the wound. She then moved onto his face, which was more blood than deep wound. Once she washed away the blood, she could see how handsome he was. His wavy brown hair framed his strong jaw. He had light blue eyes, the color of the sky. His nose, although perfect for his face, was slightly askew, probably having been broken a few times. Ginny enjoyed the view for a moment.

"It seems that my biggest job is closing the wound on your chest. Do you faint at the sight of needles?" she said with a smile on her face.

Campbell laughed. "Och, English, what ya must think of me."

"My name is Ginny and so far I'm quite impressed with your restraint. Let me just get what I need." She turned to the fire and retrieved the needle and thread from the water using some wooden tongs. She set herself up and carefully washed her hands. Once the needle was threaded, she began to sew up the wound, making the stitches as small as possible.

Campbell's chest was muscular, with a smattering of hair the same color as on his head. She was leaning over him, working from top to bottom, having to lean across him so as not to disturb her light. As she worked on his right shoulder, she could hear him breathing. At one point, she was certain he was smelling her hair. The two McKenna soldiers were still standing there, in case the prisoner tried anything, but didn't say anything while she worked.

It took some time, considering the size of the wound. It felt overheated in the keep, but Ginny was certain it had more to do with the fact that their enemy's brother was here, rather than the heat from the hearth. At times, it got so quiet, when Ginny dropped something, it echoed throughout the room. The soldiers soon became bored and were talking in low whispers to each other, so Campbell began to speak to Ginny.

"Yar a bonny lass, Ginny. Has anyone offered for ya yet?" he eyes sparkled with mischief when he asked.

"No, I'm not spoken for." Ginny voice sounded a little forlorn. Campbell immediately called her on it.

"Were ya hoping that the McKenna would offer for ya?"

Ginny looked up from her work and stared into his beautiful eyes. She could feel an attraction there, despite the whole blood enemies thing. Ginny didn't want to reveal too much, but she felt herself opening up to those eyes. *Better be careful*, she thought to herself. *Danger, Will Robinson, Danger.*

"No. Why would the head of a Highland clan offer to an Englishwoman?"

"Well, normally, he wouldnae. However, if she were a particularly bonny lass, with a healing touch and a compassionate nature, he may be swayed," his eyes fairly shone in the dim light of the keep. She noticed that he had a great smile. His teeth, very straight and white, seemed abnormal for this time period. Once again, the absurdity of romance novels, where the heroes were always clean, good looking and healthy.

Right answer, considering, Ginny thought wistfully. A girl could really get lost in those eyes. Ginny wasn't a fool, she could tell she was probably being played, but she could enjoy the ride. He would find out that she wasn't ever going to betray Ian, but let him think she was all mushy about him.

"A good looking man like you must have a sweetheart at home," she said, leaving it almost like a question.

Campbell smiled again and tilted his head to the side. He knew his smile was one of his best features. Many a lass swooned at the sight of his smile. "Nay, no sweetheart."

"No sweethearts, huh? Well, then maybe a few broken hearts," Ginny was flirting with unexpected skill, lowering her eyelids and staring at him while she continued to work. She was often at a loss when speaking to strange men, but she was quite good at engaging Campbell. She thought it had something to do with it all being make believe.

"Och, Ginny. Ya make me forget yar the enemy," he smiled at her once again. This girl could be helpful to him. If he could convince her to help him escape, he would take her with him and make her his mistress. He'd already heard that she was McKenna's mistress. He could make her a lot happier with him.

"I'm not your enemy, Campbell. I don't see what you have against the McKennas though," Ginny said trying to assuage any guilt over flirting with him.

"Ya dinna know them like I do, Ginny. Ya should beware. The lot of them have no honor," he replied.

"What do you mean? What have they done to you?" Keep him talking, she thought and maybe something useful will come out.

"It is a long story. A long time ago, the Laird McKenna stole a MacBain for his bride. When my clan fought to get her back, she was killed in the battle. It caused the bad blood."

Ginny didn't mean to be so blunt, but said, "Was it your men who killed the McKenna soldiers, stole Aileana and sold her to those animals?"

Campbell's eyes turned away for a moment, then returned to her eyes. "Nay, Ginny. I wouldnae ever let that happen." He was lying about something. Ginny could not have known better if he was hooked up to a polygraph. She silently finished sewing up his wound.

When done, she slathered the stitches with a salve to help prevent infection and dressed it as best as she could. She had him sit up, while she wrapped long strips of cloth around his chest. He hadn't attempted to speak to her again either. The silence became uncomfortable, especially after the easy rapport they had earlier.

Just as she was washing her hands, Ian stormed into the keep. Walking right up to the prisoner, Ian eyed him suspiciously. He grabbed a chair and ordered Campbell to sit in it. Ginny went about cleaning up her things, while Ian paced around the chair where the prisoner sat. Suddenly, Ian lashed out and back handed Campbell so hard he was thrown to the floor.

Ginny gasped and ran over to Campbell. "I just spent all that time putting in stitches. You don't need to pull them out so quickly."

"Ginny, leave now. Ya havenae a place here." Ian left no room for argument, but naturally, that didn't stop Ginny.

"Ian, may I speak to you? Please." she asked as nicely as she could after helping Campbell back into the chair.

"Nay."

Ginny turned to him so Campbell couldn't see her eyes. Silently, Ginny was trying to convey that speaking to her was in his best interest. But of course, most men couldn't take a hint even if it were gift wrapped. "Please, Laird." Then she mouthed she had information. Ian squinted his eyes, sighed loudly, grabbed her arm and dragged her across the room.

"What?" Ian hissed at her when they were out of earshot.

"I just spent the last hour with the man. Did it occur to you that maybe I'd gleaned some information from him that might be helpful to you?" she hissed back. Ginny always considered herself a patient person, but this man could drain the patience from a saint.

"Verra well, what do ya know, Ginny?" It took all her willpower not to walk away from him and leave him hanging. The condescension in his voice was aggravating her to no end.

"Well, first of all, he thinks I'm your mistress. The man is from another clan and thinks I'm your mistress. And he made overtures that he would happily take over that position if I were amendable."

"And what was yar response to that?" Ian could barely keep the anger from his voice. He would now feel no remorse when he killed the bastard.

Ignoring his question, she continued, "He spoke about the bad blood between your clans. Some relative stealing a bride, her getting killed, yada, yada, yada..."

"How does this help me, Ginny," exasperation filled his tone.

"I asked him about Aileana. He knows something, but I don't think he, or his clan, is involved. But he definitely knows who is and is probably willing to die to protect them. So I suggest you consider the MacBain's allies."

Ian thought about what she said. He went through the MacBain allies in his head, trying to determine if any of them seemed likely. Then he thought again about the bastard wanting Ginny for himself. He looked at her, with a gleam in his eye, and said, "Ya never looked at my wound, Ginny. Ya spent all that time with the enemy, but ya didnae take care of me."

The soft burr in his voice was intoxicating. Hadn't she decided to never let him touch her again? Ginny was having a hard time remembering why that was. His cerulean blue eyes were looking at her so intensely, his head bent low as if he was going to kiss her. Then it occurred to Ginny why. He wanted Campbell to see and realize he had no power over her. Ian held all the power.

"If you wish me to treat your wound, perhaps we should go upstairs where it is more private," Ginny had no intention of letting him have her, not after all that had transpired, but she was in the mood for a little payback. She felt for sure he would take the bait.

He chuckled low. His arrogance was intolerable. It's true she wanted him and he knew that she could have him anytime she wanted.

"Nay, lass. Perhaps later... I have something to take care of right now," Ian finished his sentence with a growl.

"Don't pull out those stitches, Ian." Ginny still wanted some payback. "I'll have to take another hour restitching him, bent over him, providing him a clear view of me." Her eyebrow shot up in mock understanding.

Ian growled. "Ya willna be near him again. Ya best go and find Maude. She will have ya to supper tonight. I will be busy in here." Ian turned and watched Campbell, who had been staring at the pair the entire time.

Ginny did find Maude and had supper with her family. She returned to the keep, very late since Maude's mother kept her there with funny stories about Ian as a child. There were a dozen soldiers milling around in the great hall. Ginny looked around, but didn't see Ian among them so she continued up to her room. The chamber was dark, since no one had bothered to light a fire or candles. *Great*, she muttered to herself. It was bad enough being so useless, but being reminded of it for something so simple was nearly intolerable.

As Ginny crossed the threshold, she was suddenly grabbed from behind and pulled up against a tall, muscular body. There was a large hand over her mouth and another large arm across her chest. She relaxed a bit, thinking it was probably Ian until she heard the voice.

"Good evening, Ginny," the voice rasped quietly. Ginny still recognized it immediately. It was the prisoner, Campbell MacBain.

"If I take my hand away from yar mouth, will ya promise me not to scream?" he asked in the whispered tone.

Ginny slowly nodded her head up and down. She felt the hand move from her mouth and move lower to the top of her tunic.

"Thank ya, Ginny. I will release ya now, please dinna do anything rash." Campbell released her and Ginny slowly turned around to face him. In the dimness of the room, she could barely make him out.

"Didn't anyone ever tell you that if you want to escape, going up stairs isn't the best move?" she asked, sounding impatient and sarcastic.

He chuckled over her tone. "Well, ya might be right. I do have a problem now if I dinna wish to get recaptured."

"How did you escape in the first place?" she asked curiously, not particularly afraid.

"Those McKennas thought I was asleep, so they weren't paying much attention when I came from behind."

"What? You didn't hurt them, did you?" Ginny was appalled. Not surprised, just appalled. These people didn't seem to think anything of killing and maiming.

"Nay, they will recover. I dinna envy their headache though. When I went to leave, some more men came in and I ran upstairs to hide. It was just lucky ya came along."

Ginny sighed in disgust. "Well, what's your plan for getting out now? You know I won't help you and you know I won't just sit here and wait for you to..." Ginny stopped. She could be a complete idiot at times, but this had to top the list. Was she just telling him that he would have to eliminate her before leaving. Thankfully, in the dark, he couldn't see the look on her face.

He chuckled again. Obviously her blunder did not go unnoticed. "Well, now, Ginny, it seems we have a problem, aye? I canna verra well leave ya here, now, can I?"

"You could tie me up, gag me. It would be a while before someone stops by to check on me. If you wish to drag me along with you, I promise not to make it easy on you." Once again, Ginny thought that she had to be the dumbest person on the planet. That all her years in school had done nothing to provide her with the common sense to shut the hell up.

Before she could talk him into another plan of action, she felt something heavy hit her head. And then, she felt nothing.

❖ Chapter 18 ❖

The first thing she felt was cold. Nothing unusual about that, Ginny was always cold, but this was different. She felt exposed and wet. She opened her eyes slowly. Although cloudy and raining, the light was blinding compared to her unconsciousness. It took her a moment to remember what happened and when she remembered Campbell, the anger woke her up fully.

She sat up and noticed that she was in a large field. Looking around, Ginny couldn't see anyone or anything. No huts, no keep, just nature. The field was sloped downward, with groves of trees dotting the landscape. *Where the hell am I?* she thought, still trying to shake the last cobwebs from her mind.

It was then that she realized that her arms were tied behind her back and her legs were tied together at her ankles. *That bastard*, she thought, realizing that Campbell left her to rot in the middle of nowhere, while he undoubtedly ran home. A slew of curse words flew from Ginny's mouth, worse than a sailor. "Whatever happened to chivalry?" she screamed at the top of voice. "Whatever!"

Ginny knew that if she was going to get anywhere, she was going to have to at least get the binding off her ankles. Walking with your hands tied together was possible, but she had no plans to hop around trying to find help. The ankle sheath, which had once housed a knife, was unfortunately sitting in Ian's room back at his keep. It seemed she would have to think of a different way to free herself.

Ginny got to her knees and reached down to see if she could untie the ropes on her ankles with her tied hands. Ginny knew in her own body, this would be impossible, since she was as flexible as steel. Of course, she wasn't in her body and Lady Chatham was smaller and more flexible. Ginny was able to lean back enough to reach the ropes. After a few frustrating tries, she managed to loosen the rope enough to kick them off.

She laid on her side for a few moments, catching her breath. As she rolled over to get up, Ginny felt a rock at her back. Rolling to look at it, it had several large, sharp edges that would do quite nicely. Even nicer, the rock was large enough to be firmly stuck in the ground.

Ginny carefully rolled over so the ropes at her wrists rubbed against the rock. Using what energy she had left, after not eating anything in quite some time and with a nagging headache that could possibly be a concussion, Ginny rubbed the binding against the rock.

After a few minutes of trying to move her body against the rock, the binding gave way. Finally, she was free. But free to do what, exactly? She had no idea where she was and no idea which direction to head in. The overcast sky was a perfect backdrop to her mood: gloomy. Thirsty, hungry and in the worst mood she's had since arriving, Ginny began to walk down the slope to the first big grove of trees. The going was slow, especially with the pounding in her head.

"After all I did for that ungrateful son of a bitch," she mumbled to herself. "First, I sewed his chest, cleaned him up, probably kept him from dying of some nasty infection." As Ginny kept mumbling, she didn't immediately notice the sound of horses coming. When she did finally hear them, she was just outside the trees, so she quickly ran inside and hid behind a tree, looking out to see who was coming.

Please be Ian, please be Ian, she kept whispering to herself. Of course, that would have been the easy way and she knew that romance novels never did things the easy way. First, she saw the wrong plaid, but of course she could recognize it anyway. MacBain. *Dammit*, she thought, continuing to hide.

She watched the men up the hillside stop where she ditched the ropes. Squeezing her eyes together, trying to recognize Campbell among the men, she noticed them arguing over the cut ropes. *Ha, stick that in your pipe and smoke it, gentlemen.* Aaaah, the first smile of the day. Nothing like sticking it to the man!

Ginny was casually watching them look around. She still didn't move as they retrieved their horses and began to follow something down the hill. As a matter of fact, she didn't even consider they were looking for her until they started to gallop down the hills toward her increasingly smaller grove of trees. *Crap*, she thought, too late to actually effectively hide or run away. *I used to be considered smart, until I came here*, she shook her head in disgust.

Giving in to the inevitable, and knowing that she'll only make them madder if she made them work for it, Ginny left the cover of the trees and walked into the open. The air seemed even heavier, the clouds darker, as the men came to halt in front of her. She searched each face until she saw the one she recognized.

"My lady," Campbell said with an exaggerated bow. Well as much as one can do on top of a horse.

" Campbell," was her only reply, still staring at his face. *It really is a pity*, she thought, *he is a fine looking man. Too bad he's a scumbag.*

"Verra good getting out of the binding. I thought we would be long back before ya even woke up."

"Sorry to disappoint you, Campbell. By the way, very nice knocking me unconscious and leaving me alone in a field. I really appreciated that," he'd have to have been deaf and incredibly stupid to miss the sarcasm of her statement.

Well, stupid at least. "I am sorry for that. With my injury, it was difficult to carry ya and ride at the same time. I did leave ya on MacBain land, though. Ya were never in danger." She took it back, quite the gentleman.

Releasing a heavy sigh, she scanned her audience as she said, "Well, what now?"

Campbell raised an eyebrow as he considered how to respond. Suddenly, he let out a laugh and beamed his gorgeous smile at her and said, "Ya will come home with me. I canna give ya back to the McKenna and I see only one way to keep him from stealing ya back. Ya will marry me, Ginny."

Ginny bowed her head and closed her eyes. Her head was still pounding and she would have given her soul for a Tylenol. She reached up and began to rub her face with her hands. *Fine*, she thought, *whatever. This guy, Ian, whoever. Does it matter?* She wasn't where she was supposed to be, she wasn't when she was supposed to be anyway.

"Do I have a choice?" she asked, just to be contrary.

All the men laughed. Ginny just smiled and shook her head. Of course there was no choice. She looked up at Campbell once again and thought at least it's not Broderick.

" Fine. Who has water?" she asked. Before she could move forward, someone threw a skin at her and she promptly drank the whole thing down. As she walked toward Campbell, she threw the skin back to the man who had thrown it. She held out her hand to Campbell, waiting for him to lift her up to her new existence. It was then she heard the sound of horse hooves. *What now*, she thought grimly.

All the men turned and started talking at once. Before she knew what was happening, Ginny was on Campbell's lap and the men where galloping toward the group of horsemen. It only took a moment for Ginny to recognize the McKenna colors. And there was no mistaking Ian, riding in front, looking quite put out.

Both groups stopped within thirty feet of each other, Campbell taking point for the MacBains and Ian for the McKennas. It was silent, no one moved or spoke. The only sounds were the horses snorting. Ginny looked to the sky and realized it would start to rain at any moment, which would turn this battle into a cold, muddy mess.

"Yar on MacBain land, McKenna. I can kill ya for just that," Campbell said, sounding intimidating, with his low snarl.

"Aye. Yar welcome to try," Ian could sound just as intimidating.

Ginny realized that this was probably the last place she wanted to be right now. So, without too much thinking, she elbowed Campbell in his chest, right where she knew it would hurt the most. He dropped her, and she promptly ran to the middle of the clearing between the clans. Both clans tensed and Ginny realized that she had a little power now.

"Ginny, come to me now," Ian's voice was low, but menacing. Ginny stood her ground for the moment. She wasn't sure she wanted to go back to the McKenna clan to watch him marry someone else. Of course, it was at least a "known," where the MacBains were completely "unknown."

She decided to hedge her bets and try to make Ian jealous. Stupid, yes, but her only weapon at the moment. "Campbell has offered me marriage, Ian. With you marrying someone else, maybe I should take him up on his offer."

Ginny chanced a glance at Campbell, who was smiling like he'd won Publisher's Clearing House. Then she looked at Ian, who was not smiling, and also looked a little sad. He let out a heavy sigh and said, "I wouldnae stop ya, if that is what ya want. But ya should know that the MacBains are heathens and would treat ya badly."

Campbell spoke up immediately, "Dinna listen to him, Ginny. He is only jealous ya would choose me over him. I will treat ya well. Ya willnae want leave my bed." The MacBains laughed and snickered. Ginny rolled her eyes at the arrogance. Her only consolation was that people didn't live very long in this age and her potential husband, with all his arrogance, would probably die soon in some battle.

Ginny looked Ian in the eyes. Despite everything, she still wanted him. Maybe it was the time they spent together or maybe she saw something else in him that no one else got to see. Ginny liked bantering with him and felt herself tingle at the thought of his touch. And dammit, hadn't she put up with enough to justify having the best sex of her life? Hadn't she lived without showering, pasteurized food, all the shows racking up on her DVR so she could fall in love with an unlikely individual, get married and have non-stop fantastic sex where she would orgasm by just being naked near him?

Before she could think anymore, Ginny walked over beside Ian. He grabbed her and hauled her up onto his lap. Ginny turned and saw the frown on Campbell's face. "Ya made the wrong choice, Ginny. He willnae marry ya. He wants his alliance too much for that."

Not wanting Ian's arrogance to get out of hand, Ginny turned to Campbell and said, "Sorry, Campbell. I just can't see myself marrying a man who would knock a woman unconscious, then leave her tied up in the middle of nowhere. You're a swell looking guy, but a girl has to have her standards." Hopefully, Ian wouldn't think she chose him because she wanted very badly to sleep with him. She doubted her deception worked at all.

"Get off my land, McKenna. Ya have what ya came for, now go."

"I dinna get everything I came for, but we will go. Be warned, MacBain. If I catch ya near my land, I willnae leave anything to be healed. Aye?"

Campbell laughed. "Aye."

The McKennas turned their horses around and began galloping off. Ginny remained silent. Ian figured she was forlorn about his impending marriage. He hadn't been brave enough to tell her that they were heading to intercept Broderick and the Laird MacDonald's daughter. The marriage needed to take place sooner, rather than later. All signs pointed to war and Ian wanted as many allies as possible. Ian only wished he knew exactly which clan he should declare war against.

❖ Chapter 19 ❖

When Broderick arrived at the MacDonald keep, he was tired, hungry and thirsty. He and his men rode hard, late into the night, getting up early the next day. It was essential that this alliance be made, especially without the knowledge of who the true enemy was.

There was also something in it for Broderick. He loved Ian like a brother, fought beside him in many battles, risked his life for his clan, but he could not accept the Englishwoman as part of his clan. Somehow, she managed to get Ian to care about her, bewitching him. It was more than he could handle.

When this task came up, he gladly took it. Both to guarantee it was done and to get away from her and her non-stop chatter. She spoke strangely, using words he'd never heard before. Although he didn't relish hurting Ian, making the Englishwoman suffer added to the joy of this task.

A few MacDonald men met the McKennas outside the courtyard walls. Although not an official alliance, the MacDonald's had always been friendly to the McKennas. And so the men began to talk, exchange information and gossip, find out about relatives. They walked together to the keep, into the great room where the MacDonald laird was waiting with his daughter.

Broderick was stunned. She was, by far, the most beautiful woman he'd ever seen. She had red hair, not the dull brown kind, but true red hair. It was long and hung in a braid down her back. Her skin was pale, but covered in delightful freckles. They covered her nose and cheeks and made her look younger than her seventeen years. The girl had a thin face, long nose and a pair of mesmerizing green eyes. She was tiny, probably only came to Broderick's chest, but she carried herself regally.

Broderick instantly felt horrible. How could he feel lust towards his laird's future wife. He bowed his head to the MacDonald laird. "It is my pleasure to escort your beautiful daughter back to the McKenna." Broderick was a man of few words, but did he really just call her beautiful to her own father?

When he looked up and saw her eyes on him, he felt himself

getting hard. He immediately turned to the laird and put on his best grimace. The laird did not seem to notice his slip, since he was yammering on about the alliance and information he recently acquired.

"Please, have your men sit and partake of a meal. I need to speak to ya about yar enemies," MacDonald said, waving a hand to the table set up behind him. It was covered in food, meat pies, bread, cheese and ale.

" Thank ya, Laird. That is kind of ya," Broderick followed the older man to one end of the table and sat down to eat. Once seated and served, he noticed that the laird's daughter had also joined them. *How strange*, Broderick thought. Since when would a laird allow a woman, even his daughter, to join in a conversation about war.

The laird was too busy eating to start the conversation, so Broderick turned to his daughter and asked, "What is yar name, child?"

Her chin immediately came up and she took on a haughty air. "I am no' a child. I am old enough to marry yar laird, am I no'?"

She was a true Highland lass, with backbone. Ian didn't realize how lucky he was to receive such a gift. It made Broderick jealous and he knit his brows together over the confusion of his feelings. He took another bite of bread and continued to stare at her.

"My name is Elspeth," she finally revealed.

"Tis a beautiful name," Broderick replied. What was with his sudden use of the word beautiful. He was beginning to think there was something wrong with him. Broderick was no virgin. He'd had many women over the years, many young wenches who begged for a strong bed partner. But this was different. He felt this woman could be a true partner in life with him, not just in bed.

Casting his eyes downward, he silently shamed himself. This was his laird's bride. He shouldn't have such thoughts about her. He glanced at her again and noticed that she had particularly large breasts for her skinny frame. This led to him getting hard again. Thankfully, she wouldn't be able to tell with him seated at the table.

Suddenly, the MacDonald turned to him and stated plainly, "I have come to find out which clan committed the treachery."

"What?" Broderick was furious that he waited this long to tell him.

"One of my men has family in the Sinclair clan. When he went

133

to visit his sister, she told him the story. She had heard it from one of the warriors."

Broderick looked puzzled. "The Sinclairs? We are no' friendly, but the McKennas have done nothing so bad to cause this."

"Aye. I have heard rumors that the leader is hell bent on revenge. Tis war they want."

"Tis war they will get," Broderick said through gnashed teeth. "I need to get Elspeth back as soon as possible. With your permission, we will leave before dawn."

"Aye. That would be best. I will have five of my men ride with ya. I canna have anything happen to my daughter."

Broderick, perfectly serious and without reservation, said, "I will defend her with my life." As he said it, he stared at the young enchantress. With her head bent, she stared at him through her long lashes and smiled.

After a few hours of riding, Ginny finally became curious. "I didn't realize Campbell rode so far from your keep with me. He complained to me that it hurt too much, which is why he left me in that field."

"Ya werenae that far from my keep, Ginny. We are riding somewhere else." Ginny furrowed her brow at him. Was that all the explanation she was going to get. Where the hell were they going and why would they be bringing her along?

"Okay, so where the hell are we going then?" she asked insolently.

Ian smiled. It was her most endearing trait, her inability to accept his leadership without question. It was probably not a trait he should allow, but Ian found it refreshing at times. She could be so insolent, so hard headed. It made him ache just thinking about it.

"We are going to meet up with Broderick. To bring ya back to the keep would take too much time. I need this alliance now," Ian didn't want to reveal that truth to Ginny, but he wasn't going to lie to her either.

" Oh," was all she said. *Great, I get to attend the wedding as well,* she thought. Ginny closed her eyes and tried to rest. The jarring of the horse and the constant feel of his hard chest against her kept her awake. She tried to envision what their sex would be like. Ian, of course, would be quite skilled and know exactly how to bring her to orgasm over and over again. Although she was a virgin, the pain would be temporary and quickly forgotten. It made Ginny's nipples hard just thinking about it.

They finally stopped for the night. With her head still pounding, partly from her attack and partly from thinking about her potential lovemaking, Ginny begged to get some sleep immediately. Ian took her to the stream running nearby, so she could wash up. The water was freezing, but it felt so good against her skin.

With just Ian there to witness, Ginny took off her tunic, leaving just her chemise like undergarment. She smiled to herself when she heard his gasp. Taking the small handkerchief she carried out, she began to wash as much of her exposed body she could. It was cold, but Ginny knew that Ian would warm her up if she asked.

She worked on washing her neck and shoulders. Then she reached into her garment to wash her armpits, which were disgusting and hairy. Ginny could admit that not having to shave had its advantages, but after so many years, it just grossed her out being so hairy. When her armpits were clean, she sat down and worked on her legs and feet.

Chancing a glance back at Ian, she saw that he stood as still as a statue, staring at every move she made. It wasn't so dark that Ginny couldn't tell that he was hard as a rock, pitching a tent with his kilt. She wasn't even sure that he was breathing.

Ginny wanted to wash her most intimate area, but also didn't want to chance sending this laird off the deep end. She turned away from him fully, and reached under her garment to washed as quickly as possible. When done, Ginny put her tunic back on. It seemed kind of ridiculous, washing at all knowing she would put on the same dirty outfit, but it had felt so good to be clean, even for only a moment.

When done, Ginny turned and stared at Ian. "Thank you, for bringing me here so I could wash up. It was quite... refreshing." Ginny spoke the last word as a whisper.

Ian was a man of great discipline. He had great endurance and patience when the situation called for it. This woman would undoubtedly be his ruin. She had just spent this time teasing him. Did she think he would be able to keep his hands off her? A man can only take so much before he breaks, and Ian had reached that breaking point.

Before she could speak one word of refusal, Ian grabbed her. His lips kept her from voicing any objections. He opened her mouth with his tongue and began making love to her with it. His tongue took possession of her mouth and his hands held her face. He vaguely felt her hands on his arms. Ian knew she was responding to him. She was kissing him back, using her tongue to duel with his.

Ian moved his hands down her delicate neck, to her small shoulders. Now that she was kissing him back, he could use his hands to explore her body. First, he moved them down her back, pulling her closer to his body, against his hard arousal. Then he cupped her bottom and pulled her off the ground slightly to allow him to kiss her deeper. Just as his hands came back up to feel her hard nipples, even under her layers of clothing, one of his men called out to him.

"Laird. Are ya alright?"

Ian stopped kissing Ginny long enough to scream something derogatory to his soldier. Unfortunately, it was enough to break the spell for her. Ginny pulled away and quickly returned to the camp. Instead of following behind her, Ian stood by the stream and washed himself down. The cold water helped to reduce his throbbing erection, but did nothing to lighten his mood. What was he doing? He couldn't have her, not in the way she wanted. He needed to stop this before he married the MacDonald girl.

Ian completed his washing and returned to camp. He saw that his men had made a small pallet for Ginny to sleep on to keep her from getting damp. With her back to the fire, she pretended to be asleep. He would leave her be for now, but he had every intention of keeping her warm tonight. Just as he had every night since she came to his keep.

Dammit, dammit, dammit, Ginny kept repeating in her head as she lay as still as stone by the fire. She had hoped to fall asleep before Ian returned, but she was so hot and bothered at the moment, sleep would allude her for hours. What was wrong with her? She had told herself that she wouldn't sleep with him. So why, exactly, had she teased him by taking half her clothes off? Why had she kissed him back when he grabbed her? Why weren't they having sex right now!

It was so dark beyond the firelight. They camped near a grove of trees, and Ginny could barely make them out in the darkness. The light of the stars twinkled against their black backdrop. With so little surface light, you could see millions of stars in the sky. Large clusters of stars that looked like dust across a black floor. Ginny had only seen it like this one other time, when she was at Lowell Observatory in Flagstaff. As spectacular as that was, it didn't hold a candle to this glorious sight.

I just have to wait a little longer, she thought. *I just have to be patient. This story will come around and I will get to have sex with Ian. Or someone just as spectacular. Only a little longer now.*

She smiled to herself in the dark, even though she was uncomfortable, sore, hungry and tired. But, she was somewhat clean. *Why couldn't we just stay at the Hilton?* No matter which way she turned, she couldn't get comfortable. No pillow, a thin blanket that would never keep her warm and a long day on a horse were all conspiring to keep her from slumber. Ginny felt the tears starting. Now, on top of everything else, she was feeling sorry for herself. Great!

As if on cue, Ian walked over to her prone figure. He slowly lowered himself to lie down along side of her. He used his arm to cushion his head and his other arm to drag her up against his chest. He bundled up the top part of his kilt to make a small pillow for her head. As he continued his ministrations, he felt the tears on her cheeks. His heart broke at her pain. Finally, he realized his dilemma. He was in love with her. He wanted her above all others and didn't know if he could marry the MacDonald girl after all.

Ginny decided to enjoy this potentially last night with him. No matter what happened tomorrow, she could pretend they had a relationship tonight. He was so gentle and caring. Right now, this was the best she could hope for. She turned slowly and faced him. Placing her cold hands on his warm chest, she slowly settled to sleep. Her last thoughts were of Ian, what he meant to her and how she was going to prevent him from marrying that other girl.

❖ Chapter 20 ❖

Before dawn, Broderick and his group set out for McKenna land. It was slow going in the dark, but worth the extra few miles they could put behind them. Although on her own horse, Elspeth made sure she was always next to Broderick. Whenever he looked at her during supper the night before, she could feel strange tingling sensations going through her body.

He was so big. His shoulders were probably as wide as she was tall. His hands looked like they could crush stone and his legs were like tree trunks. Even his head seemed oversized, covered in jet black hair and scruffy cheeks. His eyes were gray, like looming storm clouds over the countryside. Elspeth was certain she had never seen a more magnificent man in all her life.

"Are ya married, then, Broderick," she asked as they rode. She kept her voice quiet, so only he could hear her.

"Nay," was his only response. He wanted to talk to her, learn more about her, but he was concerned about their vulnerability. He hadn't been kidding when he said he would protect her with his own life. He just wanted to make sure it wasn't necessary.

Elspeth took no offense to his short answers. She rather liked talking anyway. "Did ya know I am the only child of the MacDonald laird? My ma, God bless her soul, died during childbirth. My da was so in love with her that he never remarried, even though it cost him an heir. My cousin, Arran, he is being groomed to take my da's place." Elspeth fell quiet for a moment, looking to the rising sun thoughtfully.

Broderick, concerned by her sudden silence, looked over at her. Her face was just as beautiful, but sad. Normally, he would just ignore it and continue with silence. But, for her, he needed to make her feel better. "Are ya unwell?"

Elspeth looked up at him, her eyes brimming with unshed tears. "I will miss my da."

Broderick didn't know what to say to that. It was always tough on women when marrying. They had to leave the only homes they'd ever known and sometimes live with virtual strangers. There was only one thing he could do for her. "Anytime ya want to visit, I will take ya.

Ya only need to get permission from the laird."

"Really! Thank ya, Broderick. Yar the sweetest man I have ever met, except for my da."

Broderick looked uncomfortable with the attention. His feelings were getting stronger for her and soon she would be married to his laird. He needed to distance himself or risk breaking his own heart. It seemed such a crazy notion, since he was not known to have such feelings.

He meant to say something curt and ride up ahead so she couldn't speak to him anymore. Instead he said, "My pleasure," and continued to ride next to her. Elspeth picked up where she left off, speaking about her clan and her friends and her family. Every word she spoke was like an angel speaking to him, every look a gift.

Broderick couldn't be sure, but he knew that he was in serious trouble of falling head over heels in love with this girl.

Ian rose early to continue the journey to the MacDonald land. The more Ginny thought about it, the more she realized that her being miserable was unacceptable. She was a grown woman, from a very different century, millennium even, and she was getting herself caught up in a romance novel. It wasn't anything short of ridiculous and even somewhat embarrassing. For all the hemming and hawing she did about reading the damn books in the first place, now she was actually pouting over her mega-hunk's impending marriage. Crazy was the perfect word for her situation.

The day was turning glorious. The sun was rising and there were no clouds to indicate rain. The azure blue sky was flawless and was offset quite nicely by the rolling green hills. The further they went, the more rocky the terrain. The air was fresh after the recent rains, and filled with the scents of nature: grass, dew, and wildflowers. She smiled just at the sight of such glory.

They had ridden in silence since they started off and Ginny felt it was time to put an end to it. She turned her head to look up at him. His face, beautiful and serious, was staring at the horizon. He didn't seem like he was in the mood for conversation, like a prisoner being led to the hangman's noose. It occurred to Ginny how apropos that analogy was.

Ginny decided to be subtle, "How are you feeling?"

Ian hrumphed and continued their journey in silence. "Really, Ian... How are you?"

He looked down at her face, read the expression and smiled a small, tentative smile. "I will do what is best for my clan, Ginny. No more, no less."

"Yes, that is important. Especially with war looming over you. It's a shame it doesn't coincide with what you want, huh?" She made the statement lightly, even smiled a little as well, but he heard the bitterness it contained.

"Aye, tis a shame." Ian lowered his head and began to nuzzle in Ginny's hair. She smelled good to him, like roses and campfires. He had decided that he would do one thing for himself. If he couldn't wed the woman he wanted, he would have her anyway. If they did not meet up with Broderick today, tonight, he would take her. She would offer no resistance, not once she was convinced of the pleasure he would give her.

He didn't even know what the MacDonald girl looked like. It didn't matter. Ginny would be his lover and she would give him sons. His wife would learn to live with this and he didn't really care anyway. He would marry the MacDonald girl for the alliance, but Ginny would be the love of his life. It was the only way he could survive.

His silence was deafening to Ginny. She had decided earlier that what Lady Chatham would want should matter to her. That her feelings were important. Now, Ginny thought that idea was stupid. This was make believe, a fairy tale as such. Ian never existed in history, she didn't travel back in time, so what difference did it make. She was simply re-writing a story, written by some woman in the 21st century, in the hopes of making some money at her craft.

Ginny was tired of holding back. She was tired of letting this happen on its own. Now she was going to take over and take what she wanted. Like from the beginning, she figured there were no consequences when she picked up the knife sheathed to her ankle and threw it that big, ugly guy. This was her body now!

With that in mind, Ginny had every intention of seducing Ian tonight. No consequences, no regrets. Tonight would be the night, provided the guy didn't marry someone else instead.

❖ Chapter 21 ❖

They rode through the day, stopping for an extended time so Elspeth could refresh herself. The men stood around, eating the rations given to them by the MacDonald laird. Broderick kept a close watch on where Elspeth disappeared into the trees. When she didn't return, he went looking for her. Entering the woods, first he called out her name. When she didn't respond, he became frantic, running around trying to find her.

He found her, alone and unharmed, staring into space, deep in her own thoughts. He breathed a sigh of relief. "Elspeth. What is wrong?"

She turned so quickly, she nearly fell over. Broderick was right there to keep her upright. The first thing she noticed was his strong arms around her. Just as she was beginning to enjoy the feeling, he moved away.

"I am sorry to intrude on yar privacy. I was worried when ya dinna return."

"I am sorry. I got caught up in my own thoughts. I dinna mean to make ya worry." She smiled at him with a dazzling smile that took his breath away.

Grumbling under his breath, he turned to leave her. "I will wait for ya in the..." he never finished his sentence. One of the men called out the alarm.

Grabbing her arm, Broderick dragged Elspeth back to the clearing. One of the McKennas, a warrior named Cameron, turned to Broderick and pointed to the north. There was a large group of men on horseback. Broderick knew they were too close to outrun them. "We need to make our stand here."

"Aye," Cameron agreed. "What should we do with the lady?"

Broderick thought about this for only a second and turned to her. "Ya will go into the trees and find somewhere to hide. Ya must no' come out unless ya hear my voice. Aye?" His look intense, she was almost frightened of him... almost.

"Aye," she agreed and ran into the woods.

The strangers began riding their horses toward their group.

Broderick took point, not bothering to get back on his horse. He needed to be able to get to Elspeth if it became necessary. Broderick met the group with his legs apart and his hand on his sword. He recognized the plaids they wore: Sinclair.

The leader of the Sinclairs dismounted and stood before Broderick. The men were almost evenly matched in size. The Sinclair leader smiled at Broderick, perhaps trying to look friendly, but Broderick wasn't falling for it. Nothing was said for some time, while both groups sized each other up.

"Yar on Sinclair land. I dinna remember ya asking permission," the Sinclair soldier stated, still smiling.

"This is no' yar land. We are riding along the border of MacGregor land," Broderick kept his voice even, somewhat bored. He didn't want to provoke a fight, not when he needed to keep Elspeth safe.

"Perhaps. What are ya doing here? Pretty far from home, McKenna."

"I am bringing something back from the MacDonalds. Not that it is any of yar concern." Broderick could feel it before it happened. The sudden tension, the looks in their eyes. They were planning to fight and there was nothing he could say to stop it.

Elspeth had run, but she didn't hide. She was watching the exchange, trying to ascertain if they were there for her. She wouldn't let Broderick die for her. If the Sinclairs wanted her, she would come out and give herself up.

Suddenly, the Sinclairs pulled their swords and charged. Broderick was ready, pulling his sword at the same time and running toward the leader. The other McKennas and MacDonalds joined the melee. The once pleasant day was now filled with the sounds of clashing swords, battle crys and screams of agony.

Elspeth watched in awe as Broderick fought. His giant, muscular body seemed to be made to swing a sword. He was almost elegant, like a ballet dancer, moving each way to avoid a killing blow. Her heart raced, her mind spun and she shook slightly watching the grizzly scene.

When it was over, the remaining Sinclairs rode off, most likely in search of others in their clan to bolster their numbers. Two Sinclairs lay dead and one MacDonald lay wounded seriously enough to cause concern. Despite all this, Broderick's only concern was for the young girl hiding in the woods.

He ran toward the trees calling her name. Before he even entered the forest, Elspeth walked out, revealing that she hadn't listened to him and stayed close by to watch. Broderick didn't know if he should be angry, disgusted or happy. Angry because she hadn't listened. Disgusted that she was forced to watch such a display, watching him as he killed another man. Or happy because she was safe for the moment.

Before he could think twice, he hugged her tight and whispered that everything would be alright. The look on her face confused him. She seemed pleased, if not almost excited. Broderick didn't have time to figure it out. He called out to the men, ordering two of the MacDonalds to accompany their injured man back to their keep. The rest would continue their ride back to McKenna land. God willing, they would make it without incident.

Broderick insisted that Elspeth ride with him. He reasoned that it was for her protection, but in reality, he knew it would be one of the last times he got to hold her. He wanted to feel her soft skin and smell the scent of her hair. She was so beautiful and perfect, he had a hard time thinking about letting her go.

As they rode on, Broderick felt his skin prickle and the hair on the back of his neck rise. Something was coming and it wasn't good. Before he could consider the possibilities, he heard the battle cry. Without a second thought, Broderick and the rest of his men began to ride their horses hard, trying to find a defensible position where his handful of men could ward off the greater numbers.

It was late afternoon and the sun was already on its decline toward night. The group of McKenna soldiers, Ian and Ginny had made steady progress toward their destination. Ian was relentless, only allowing a single break for Ginny to relieve herself in the bushes. The tedious journey was having its effect on her and she wasn't all together sure she would be able to put her plan in action after riding on a big horse all day.

Ian had explained, in very few words, that he wanted to be on the outer edge of MacDonald land before they stopped for the night. It would be safer, she assumed, but would it save her ass from being bruised and abused? She thought not.

Daydreaming about getting off the horse, Ginny was shocked when the soldiers and Ian came to an abrupt halt. Looking around to see what had caused the change, Ginny could see a group of men, all on horseback, riding dangerously fast toward them. Ginny squinted to see who they were, only to notice a larger group of men riding dangerously fast behind them. *What the devil?* she thought only seconds before Ian screamed and raced forward at breakneck speed.

Ginny didn't think, she only held on for dear life. All the men in their group had followed suit and were racing toward the first group. When they had gotten closer, Ginny could finally see that the first group comprised McKenna's, with Broderick's unmistakable mass in the front. Holding onto him, much like Ginny, was another woman. Presumably, the MacDonald girl.

All at once, Ginny was on the ground, while Ian and his men continued forward. The second group, wearing kilts that Ginny had not yet seen, were barreling down after the united McKennas. Standing alone, in the middle of the field, Ginny felt exposed, but strangely calm. She watched as Broderick broke off and rode with his passenger toward Ginny.

"Elspeth, stay here with Ginny. I swear on my honor that no man will get past me to ya," Broderick stated as he set the MacDonald girl down with care.

"Aye, thank ya, Broderick," she replied, looking mesmerized by the large, gruesome man.

With that, Broderick rode off to join the melee, which now consisted of two groups, no longer on horses, with swords drawn and angry shouts rendered. It was an awesome sight, with the numbers nearly even, slightly favoring the other clan. Large men, mostly hairy and dirty, ready to slash each other beyond repair. It made Ginny somewhat sick.

"My name is Elspeth MacDonald," she spoke in a quiet, unassuming tone. It almost made Ginny laugh at the lightness of it, like she were introducing herself over tea.

"I'm Ginny," was all she could get out before the ringing of swords broke over the sounds of cursing and shouts. Still, Elspeth was bound to know more than she did. "Who are they?" she asked pointing to the unknown clan.

"The Sinclairs. They dinna want this alliance between the MacDonalds and the McKennas. This is the second such encounter we have endured. Broderick was able to protect me from the first onslaught."

Well, well, well, it would seem that young Elspeth has a thing for Frankenstein, she thought to herself as a smile formed on her face. Before the young girl could spot it, Ginny quickly went back to looking grim. It's not like she didn't know who would win this battle.

"Were they the ones who stole Aileana?" Ginny asked, before realizing that Elspeth probably wouldn't even know what she was talking about.

"Aye. My father received information exposing them. He would have aligned our clan to the McKennas after the treachery, but that was when Broderick came to collect me." With her head down, she whispered, "I am to marry the Laird McKenna."

"Yeah, I know. You don't seem too pleased about it."

"Why should I be? I am sure the Laird is a fine man, but I dinna know him. Will he be kind, like Broderick has been? Will he generous and sweet, like Broderick? Or will I be miserable for the rest of my life without love?"

Ginny eyes widened as she listened to the drivel. *Dear God, really?* she thought to herself. Maybe she hadn't learned her lesson, since she was still in it for the sex. Ginny could admit a large attraction to Ian. She could also admit that she did care for him, quite deeply. Love, though? Would she jump in front of an arrow to save his life? Maybe not. She didn't even know if she was capable of such emotion.

"So what are you going to do about it? Stand here and whine or put down your foot and demand what you want," Ginny resisted the urge to roll her eyes. Damn she could play the part when she wanted to. This situation, of course, would get her what she wanted as well. Ian, in bed, forever. It suddenly occurred to Ginny that it might just mean that: forever. She had no idea if she would ever leave here, or would her brain continue to concoct this story as long as she lay comatose somewhere else.

The sound of swords clashing brought her out of her reverie. Two of the Sinclairs lay on the ground, covered in blood and not moving. The rest were back on their horses and riding off, into the sunset so to speak. The rest of the McKennas came running over with their horses to the two women standing there. Ian was at her side in

145

moments, speaking volumes if Elspeth were paying any attention. She wasn't, of course, because her attention was solely on Broderick, who was by her side in a moment as well.

One of the other McKennas spit on the ground and said, "They be back and in greater numbers. We shouldnae stay here too long." Ginny smiled. It sounded like a line from Star Wars, when Obi Wan warned about the Sand People. Ginny had to admit that sometimes, she was a big nerd.

"Aye," Ian agreed. "We need to find a priest."

Ginny spoke up. "A priest? Did someone die," she looked over at the two Sinclairs on the ground. When no one answered, she turned at saw that they were all looking at her like she was an idiot.

"What?" Ginny asked her large audience.

Ian took her by the arm and walked her away. When they were out of earshot of the group, he turned her to face him and said gently, "It is for my marriage, Ginny. I dinna care about the Sinclairs. They can rot in hell. If I dinna marry Elspeth, I canna expect the alliance with her father."

Oh, right, she thought to herself, now knowing why they all thought she was an idiot. Turning her eyes to the ground, she spoke softly, "I'm sorry. I guess I forgot about that." She looked up into his eyes and saw something she didn't expect to see. She saw regret. Had he thought about them being together once before the marriage? Ginny imagined he was feeling exactly the same way she was. Strangely enough, it made her feel better.

Putting on her game face, knowing that she had put a bug in Elspeth's ear, she said, "Well, let's go find a priest, shall we?" Ginny linked her arm with Ian and led him back to the group.

The change in Ginny's voice disconcerted Ian. All of a sudden, she seemed quite fine with the idea of him marrying someone else. They walked back to the other men and she waited for him to give his order. Why was she so... happy? The entire trip had felt grim and now she seemed almost excited to continue.

"Ewan, where do ya think we might find a priest?" Ian asked one of his soldiers. Ewan was famous for knowing where to find anything.

"There is a small village to the north with an abbey attached to the land. One of the monks can marry ya."

Ian mounted his horse and reached down to grab Ginny to

haul her up. Ginny stepped away quickly and suggested, "Ian, maybe now would be a good time to get to know your fiancée. I'll just ride with someone else." As Ginny walked over by Broderick, it took only one look from him to know that he was not willing to be her partner. So, she walked back to Ewan, who was smiling in her direction.

"Ewan, would you mind carrying me?" she asked, almost chipper, knowing full well that Ian was probably madder than a hornet right now.

"Aye, my lady. It would be my pleasure."

"You're so kind," she said, chancing a look back at Ian, who was indeed, rather pissed off. Ian fixed his gaze on Ewan. The look, which left no room for misunderstanding, spoke of murder for any inappropriate action made on Ewan's part. Ian then fixed his gaze on Ginny. He was angry and maybe even hurt. This would have been their last chance together. Ginny expected otherwise, so she simply smiled and winked.

Ewan took hold of Ginny and placed her gently on his lap. Not as big as Ian, Ewan still had powerful thighs that made a nice cushion for Ginny. He looked strange, having jet black hair and sharp brown eyes. His olive complexion looked more worthy of an Italian man, than Scots. He did not suffer from insufficient conversation, and spoke almost non-stop to the abbey. Knowing nothing would come of it, Ginny flirted with him and kept up her end of the conversation.

Ginny watched Ian and Elspeth as they rode to the north. Ian was stiff as a board, which was nothing compared to Elspeth, who looked as if she would snap at any moment. Not much in the way of conversation transpired between them. Ian was making it very clear that he was no more amendable to this marriage than she was. Thankfully, they wouldn't be marrying each other, Ginny was certain of that.

Ginny began to sing snipets of America's *Sister Golden Hair: Well I tried to make it Sunday, but I got so damned depressed, that I set my sights on Monday and I got myself undressed. I ain't ready for the altar, but I do agree there's times, when a woman sure can be a friend of mine.*

The further they rode, the colder it got. Ginny had almost forgotten about the cold. She turned her head to look at Ewan and said, "Ewan, I'm sorry. I'm very cold. Do you mind if I lean up against you to warm up?"

Ewan looked at Ian and smiled wanly. "Of course, my lady. I

would be happy to assist ya." Then he whispered, "I dinna want to anger the laird though."

Ginny saw his predicament. If he kept Ginny warm with his own body, Ian would probably pound him into the ground. On the other hand, Ewan certainly didn't want to say no to her. "Maybe I could just discreetly put my hands on you to keep them warm. That would help."

"Aye, my lady. Discreetly," he whispered, which almost made Ginny laugh out loud.

Ginny put one hand on Ewan's chest, outside his shirt, so it looked like she was only steadying herself. The warmth tingled through her fingers and up her arm. Her mother would always tell her, "Cold hands, warm heart," but Ginny would have preferred to have warm hands anyway. When she got older, she would tell her mother that she'd rather be a cold hearted bitch if it meant having warm hands and feet.

❖ Chapter 22 ❖

Just north was a two hour horseback ride. By the time they reached the abbey, Ginny's ass was as numb as her hands and feet. As soon as her feet hit the ground, Ginny was walking around trying to regain some feeling. She kept tripping, with the pins and needles in her feet making her uncomfortable. Ian always seemed to be right there to keep her from falling though.

Broderick walked up to the abbey gate and rang the bell. The bell, large and rusty looking, clanged loudly in the peace of the early evening. While waiting for the summons to be fulfilled, Ian took Ginny aside and whispered, "I must marry her, Ginny. Ya do understand that."

"Ian, have you asked Elspeth what she wants?"

"It doesnae matter what she wants. Her father and I agreed to join our clans. She must marry a McKenna."

"Fine. But does that McKenna have to be you?" She saw him begin to object and she quickly added, "She's in love with Broderick. She all but told me flat out when you were butchering Sinclairs. Wouldn't her father be alright with her marrying him instead?"

"Why dinna ya tell me this earlier?"

Ginny looked as if she was thinking about what he said. She even put her hand on her chin and looked back thoughtfully at him. "I don't know. I guess torturing you for a couple of hours was in payback for you not telling me you were betrothed when we were fooling around with each other." With that, she gave him a dazzling smile.

"Och, Ginny. Ya made me watch ya with Ewan for hours so ya could get some revenge?"

"Aye, I did. You really must learn not to mess with me, Ian. I can be really mean when I want to be!" Her smile was devious, but dazzling. Things were definitely started to look up.

He put his head in his hands and starting shaking. Ginny wondered how much trouble she would be in for this, until she saw the smile on his face. He shook his head and walked quickly away. She watched Ian approach Broderick and Elspeth, who had naturally stood by him while waiting for the monks to arrive at the gate.

Ian spoke to both of them. Ginny saw Elspeth's face light up and Broderick, as usual, remained implacable. Elspeth began to shake her head up and down vigorously. Ginny watched Broderick as he agreed slowly to the arrangement. Ian slapped his first in command on the back and walked back to Ginny.

"Well, it is done. Broderick will marry Elspeth. And ya will marry me."

Ginny was so happy to hear about Broderick and Elspeth that she didn't fully comprehend his other statement. "We're getting married... today?"

"Aye, Ginny." Ian lowered his voice to a whisper and said, "And ya will be mine tonight."

A flutter started in Ginny's stomach. This was it, finally. Ginny was going to get what she'd been waiting for since day one of coming here. Would it be done after that? Would she get to go home? Her face dropped at the thought. As much as she wanted to go home, she really did like Ian. It was too late to consider it, since a monk finally appeared at the gate.

Broderick spoke quickly to the monk, who then opened the gate and allowed only the couples and two witnesses inside. Ian quickly gave orders to the others to be on the lookout. One of the MacDonalds, a man named Liam, had been sent to the MacDonald laird to tell them the marriage would take place and war would be declared on the Sinclairs. Liam was to meet them here, hopefully with some MacDonald soldiers at his side.

Another man was sent to the McKenna keep. He would rally Alec and the other McKenna soldiers here as well. It seemed that after the festive marriage of the McKenna Laird and his first in command, there was to be a battle. Probably in the field outside a small village, where an abbey stood watch over the land.

❖ Chapter 23 ❖

Before Ginny knew what was happening, she was herded into a chapel inside the old keep of the abbey. She and Elspeth were taken aside, far enough away from Ian and Broderick that they wouldn't be able to hear, and asked some very pointed questions by a monk named Douglas.

"Do ya both come here of ya own free will? I willnae marry ya otherwise," he said. Ginny looked at his old face. Brother Douglas probably wasn't that old, but the years had not been kind. The monk was shorter than Ginny and rounder as well. He had an easy smile and kind voice, so both girls were instantly put at ease.

Elspeth was the first to answer and quite eagerly at that, "Oh yes, Brother. I am more than willing to marry Broderick." She was smiling from ear to ear. She had thanked Ginny a thousand times for her help as they entered the abbey.

Brother Douglas turned to Ginny. "And ya, child. Are ya certain ya wish to marry Laird McKenna?"

Both Ginny and the monk turned to look at Ian at the same time. Ian, who had been staring at them already, lifted an eyebrow at her in challenge. He obviously knew what the monk was trying to ascertain and knew that Ginny would probably be difficult about it. Ginny smiled a dazzling smile and turned back to the monk. "Yes, I think I would like to marry the Laird McKenna today."

Impatience got the better of him and Ian yelled from across the room, "Brother, we havenae all day."

Brother Douglas' easy smile disappeared. "I willnae be rushed, young man. I will take what time I need to make sure the two of ya didnae steal these girls from their homes." Ginny watched Ian roll his eyes at the announcement.

Ginny smiled at the monk. She'd rarely seen anyone willing to stand up to Ian, other than herself. It was refreshing to see that the monk was not so easily intimidated. Ian could probably snap him in half, but Brother Douglas had a duty to do and wouldn't be put off from it.

"Now, as I was saying, were either of ya taken against yar will? It is a sad practice in the Highlands. But a tradition at that. So, were ya?"

Elspeth, again in her enthusiasm, said, "No. I was to marry the laird, but I fell in love with Broderick. I wasnae forced in any way."

At her announcement, the monk looked curious. "Lady Chatham, did ya know that Elspeth was intended for the Laird?"

"Aye," was the only reply she gave, still smiling in Ian's direction.

"Ya havenae an issue with marrying him instead?"

"Nay," again, still smiling.

"Verra well, then. I will marry ya both right now."

The ceremony, if you could call it that, was very brief and informal. Questions of whether you take so and so, and do you promise to honor, cherish and obey. Truthfully, Ginny wasn't too jazzed about the obey part, didn't feel it was necessary since she had no intention of obeying anyone. Alas, if she was going to get her wedding night, she would have to lie a little.

At the end of the ceremony, Brother Douglas took a piece of both men's kilt and wrapped it around their joined hands. Ginny smiled again at the symbolism and was in a kind of awe over what she'd done. She'd just married a man. Never did that before. Of course, she wouldn't have married someone just to have sex either. She would have just had sex with him.

After the final blessing, the group walked back to the great room of the keep. Brother Douglas offered everyone some wine in celebration. Not wanting to be rude, everyone accepted a glass and toasted the newly married couples. Even the two McKenna soldiers, enlisted as witnesses enjoyed a glass. Finally, the monk offered the married couples lodging for the night.

"We have some special chambers for overnight guests. They are simple, but warm and comfortable. Would ya care to stay?" he asked the men. Ginny thought it was a no brainer, of course they would stay, but apparently it wasn't that simple for the men.

"We should prepare the troops, Laird," Broderick stated.

"Aye, but we need to consummate the marriage to ensure the alliance," Ian retorted.

"I think Elspeth and I would be far more comfortable in these lodgings than out in the field in front of the abbey," Ginny was getting slightly perturbed by the casual banter, interfering with her best sex ever.

Ian called to the two soldiers and gave them quick instructions. Then he turned to the monk and said, "Thank ya, Brother Douglas. We will accept yar hospitality."

"Verra well. I will show ya the way."

The monk walked them down a dark corridor that was damp and musty. Ginny decided that you shouldn't build a stone house in a humid place. How she hadn't caught a nasty cold yet was beyond her. Although it probably had something to do with Ian keeping her warm every night.

Each man carried one candle to light the way. Brother Douglas opened a door toward the end of the corridor. He motioned to Broderick and Elspeth. Elspeth practically ran into the room, without the use of the candle that Broderick held. Broderick raised an eyebrow in response and promptly followed his new wife into the room.

Ginny had a slew of rude things to say, but held her tongue. Wouldn't do her any good to irritate her new husband. They continued to the next and last door in the corridor. The monk opened the door and bid them goodnight. He left in quite a hurry, probably not wanting to think about what was going to happen next, let alone listen to it. Ian eyed her intently. "After ya, wife," he said with a smile on his beautiful face.

Ginny entered the small cell and looked around. There was a bowl and pitcher of water on a small table in the corner. On the floor, was a straw mattress, covered with what appeared to be clean linens and a heavy blanket. In the corner by the door, was a small brazier, which Ian began to build a fire using the wood provided.

The water in the pitcher was cold, but Ginny knew better than to ask for hot water. She poured some water into the bowl, found a small towel under the table and began to wash her face. The only sound was the clanging of Ian building the fire. She went about taking off her tunic and placing it on the bed. Standing near the wash basin in only her chemise, Ian stared hungrily. Finally, he would get what he'd wanted for so long.

Ginny continued to clean as much as she could reach. She truly wished she could have taken a bath first. Suddenly, Ian was right behind her. Ginny could feel his breath on the back of her neck. His voice, raspy and rough, said, "Can I help ya with that, wife?"

Ginny swallowed hard. Her own voice was just as thick with passion, "Yes, of course. Please do."

Ian reached down for the bottom of her chemise and lifted it over her head. He discarded it next to her tunic. Although not shy, Ginny could feel herself blush from standing before Ian naked. He then knelt down to remove Ginny's shoes and hose. When completed, Ginny stood before him completely naked, but surprisingly not cold. The fire that Ian had built had warmed up the small room. Ian began his ministrations, taking the washcloth and washing her body. He started up top, on her shoulders and arms. Then delicately working his way down, paying close attention to her breasts and stomach.

He finished rather abruptly with her legs, having bypassed her hips and bottom. Ginny wondered if he was afraid of scaring her, so he neglected those areas for the time being. When completed, he stood before her and smiled. Ginny smiled back, to let him know that she was quite looking forward to their time together.

Ginny took the washcloth and put it down in the basin. Then she turned to him and began to undress him. Ian couldn't believe how bold she was. She started by taking off his boots, then undoing his kilt. When she unlatched the belt, the fabric fell away and Ian was left standing in his long shirt. Motioning him to bend over, she promptly removed that as well. Ian immediately grabbed her, but Ginny pushed him away. She picked up the washcloth and began to wash him from head to toe as well.

Unlike Ian, Ginny paid special attention to Ian's groin, making sure to thoroughly wash his erect penis. It was enormous and Ginny wondered if he would tear her apart. Once complete, she put down the washcloth and turned to him. "I'm done. What would you like to do now?" she said with her eyebrow raised and a smile on her face.

Ian picked Ginny up as if she weighed nothing. He turned and gently placed her on the mattress, then covered her body with his. Ian began to kiss her face, eyes, nose and finally her mouth. With no encouragement, Ginny opened her mouth to him and Ian used his tongue to dominate her mouth and body. His one hand was caught in her hair while the other hand began to gently caress her breasts. When he took one nipple between his fingers and squeezed, Ginny let out an involuntary moan of pleasure.

Ian leaned down and began to suck gently on her nipple. Ginny wound her hands through his long, auburn hair and let him have his way with her. His tongue was like magic, bringing each nipple to stand erect at his touch. Even in bed, Ian expected total submission, from all his subjects. He began to kiss the valley between her breasts as his hand went to explore her soft mound. Parting her slowly, he found her clit and began to play gently with it, first circling it, then softly pulling at it.

Ginny could feel the orgasm building in her middle. She knew that Ian had to do very little to give her tremendous satisfaction. His finger began to circle the outer edge of her opening, stroking gently, but purposefully. When finally he entered her with his finger, Ginny came off the bed and moaned loudly. Ian laughed softly. "Aaah, Ginny, yar so wet for me. I can feel yar warmth." His own painful erection was pressing against her, looking for its own satisfaction.

His finger entered and withdrew, mimicking what his cock would do soon. Ginny felt the building storm, knew her orgasm was reaching its zenith. All at once, Ginny was rocked with pleasure, forcing her hips to grind against Ian's hand as she involuntarily shouted his name. The waves of pleasure continued for what seemed like hours.

Enjoying the lingering effects of her orgasm, Ginny continued to rock against his hand. Ian smiled briefly at her, just to let her know that he was pleased with himself, and continued to kiss her breasts and stomach. Suddenly, his hand was gone, and Ginny realized he was kissing the inside of her thighs. *Oh God*, Ginny thought as he began to kiss her inner folds, lapping at her nub.

Ginny so rarely orgasmed that when she felt it coming on again, she was utterly shocked. It was one of the best parts of being female, multiple orgasms. Ginny grabbed the blanket beneath her, twisting it in her fists. The fire was building inside of her, the heaviness, the pleasure. Closing her eyes, she felt the waves of pleasure wash over her again. Ian lifted his head and in his low, raspy voice, exclaimed, "Och, Ginny, ya taste like the best wine. It makes me heady for more."

Ginny opened her eyes to see that Ian was between her legs, his erection pressed against her stomach. His face was only inches from hers, his stare intent. He waited until she was able to fully focus on his eyes and said, "I told ya, Ginny, that ya would be mine forever. Ya belong to me, wife. Do ya understand?"

What, huh? Ginny thought she nodded her agreement, but

couldn't be sure. She was still panting heavily from her orgasm, her limbs heavy. Suddenly, he entered her. Ian did it swiftly, breaking her maidenhead in one quick motion. Fully embedded inside her, Ian breathed slowly, trying to gain some control. He knew he hurt her and needed to allow her to get used to the intrusion.

Pain, like nothing else, can startle you back into consciousness. Ginny felt the tearing pain when Ian entered her. *This was precisely why no woman should have to give up her virginity more than once*, she thought grimly. Still, it was hard to dismiss the pleasure, so it was worth a few moments of pain. Having read all those novels, Ginny knew the pain would disappear quickly, replaced by another earth shattering orgasm. Unlike her real "first time," when her boyfriend John didn't know what he was doing and only followed his own instinct to pleasure himself.

Soon, the pain was gone and Ginny felt herself moving underneath him. "Nay, Ginny," Ian sounded like he was in pain, "Dinna move yet. Ya need time to get used to me." Ian's eyes were squeezed shut and there was a fine sheen of sweat on his forehead.

Ginny took his face in her hands and turned him toward her. When he opened his eyes, she gave him a look that said that not only was she okay, she was ready for more. Ian kissed her hard and began to move his hips. Slowly, he would withdraw and thrust into her again. Kissing her neck, Ian could hear the pleasure moans coming from deep in Ginny's throat. It fueled his need and he began to thrust more heartily.

Ginny couldn't believe it, but she was about to climax again. She opened her eyes and stared at her husband with an imploring look to hold out for just a moment longer. The warmth was spreading, building in her middle and with a sudden spasm, it released to her body, making her limbs weak and warm. Ian shuttered with his own release, expelling his seed deep inside her.

Ian laid motionless on top of her. Ginny could feel him breathing, but otherwise, he was dead weight. After a moment, Ginny tapped his shoulder and said, "Ian, I can't breathe."

He chuckled softly as he finally moved off her and lay next to her on the small mattress. He grabbed Ginny, pulled her up next to him, cradling her in his arms. Ian then reached down and grabbed the blanket and covered her up, knowing his wife's propensity toward being cold. Ginny snuggled up against him and purred like a kitten.

She was finally satisfied, warm and laying in her own Greek god's arms. She couldn't think of anything better than that. Which was the last thought she had before falling asleep.

The dream was both vivid and horrifying. Two sides battled against each other to the bloody death. Protecting his clan and seeking revenge, Ian was in front, fighting his way through the throngs of men to get to one in particular. Horrible screams, from both those fighting and those injured, filled the air and the ground turned dark with blood.

Ginny woke with a start, covered in sweat. She lay shivering as Ian took her back into his arms, panting slightly. "What is it, love?" Ian sounded concerned. The single candle was still lit, casting huge shadows on the stone walls.

"Bad dream. Why did the Sinclairs take Aileana?" she asked finally, having wondered since their battle before the wedding.

"I dinna know for certain. The McKennas and the Sinclairs have never been on good terms, but we havenae done anything to cause this. We enjoy raiding them, but they give as good as they get. It makes no sense."

"What will Alec do when he finds out?"

"He will want blood. And I will help him get it."

"Could you be killed?" Ginny shuddered at the thought. She still didn't think she was in love with Ian, but she did care about his well being, and wanted to be able to have more nights like this.

"Och, Ginny, dinna worry about that. I can take care of myself." Ian sounded almost perturbed by her question. No wife should lack confidence in her husband, especially after only a few hours of marriage.

"I'm sorry. I know you're quite a gruesome fighter," Ginny said to placate him. "As your wife, I'm allowed to worry about you, though."

"Aye. Ya need to make sure my hunger is satisfied," he said as he began to nibble on her ear.

"Did you want something to eat," Ginny smiled, playing with him once again.

"Nay, not food. How are ya feeling?" Although the question was asked in general, Ginny knew what he specifically meant.

"I'm a little sore," she said, feeling his increasing erection against her. "But I can still take care of you."

"What do ya mean by that?" he asked, sounding genuinely curious.

Ginny got up and walked to the basin. She threw old water into the chamberpot and refilled it, walking back to Ian. She hurried her steps, since the floor was cold beneath her bare feet. She took the washcloth and began to wash the blood from their lovemaking off his erection. She gently washed him, up and down, while he sat with his hands behind his head, enjoying the attention.

She cleaned him thoroughly and began to play with his sack. She ran her hand up and down his penis causing a huge grin on her new husband's face. Continuing to gently massage his testicles, she lowered her mouth to take him in. Ian gasped, with pleasure rather than shock since this was not the first time Ginny had used her mouth on him.

Ginny continued her gentle assault, using her hands and mouth. She used her tongue to trace a line around the head and licked softly into the cleft at the top. Ginny could taste him, salty and male, which only bolstered her resolve. She bobbed her head slowly, taking as much as she could into her mouth, then used her tongue to tease him even more.

Ian suddenly grabbed her and threw her to the side of him. Kissing her deeply, she felt him come on her leg. When replete, he looked down on her face, deep into her eyes and said, "Dear God, Ginny. Ya make me forget all my discipline." He gently brushed her hair with his fingers, showing Ginny that he did indeed have a softer, more gentle side. She smiled up at him, quite satisfied at what she had accomplished.

Ian reached over to the bowl and grabbed the same washcloth she used on him. First he cleaned up after his orgasm, then went about gently cleaning up the proof of her virginity. Ian smiled while he worked, knowing that he was her only lover and God help him, hopefully the only lover she would ever know. When complete, he moved the bowl back to the table, stirred the embers of the fire and added more wood and came to lie back down next to her.

Ginny immediately moved into his arms, resting her head on

his chest. Listening to his heartbeat, she played with his nipples and chest hair. After a few minutes, his hand stilled hers. "I could easily be ready again, Ginny, but I canna do that to ya." She chuckled softly and fell back to sleep.

❖ Chapter 24 ❖

Loud banging, then silence. Ginny continued to sleep. Then, she felt someone shaking her. Slowly, she was coming awake. First, she felt annoyed. Then, seeing Ian and Alec above her, she felt really annoyed. Pulling the blanket higher up her, she stared at the two men. "What?" she asked, wondering why Ian would allow his brother to see her naked in bed.

"Ginny, ya must get up. We have to leave." Wow, such a useful explanation. Ginny remained where she was. "What are ya waiting for?"

"For your brother to leave so I can get dressed," she said calmly, but her eyes betrayed her real feelings. "Unless you'd like him to see me naked." Ginny began to stand up as Ian physically forced his brother from the room. The door closed and all Ginny could hear was Alec's laughter.

The room was so dim, with only one candle to light the darkness. There were no windows in the small cell, so she had no way to tell what time of day it was. They were married in the early evening, but Ginny had no idea how long she was asleep. It couldn't have been long, since she was still very tired.

After dressing in her already filthy clothes and using the chamberpot, Ginny left the room. The corridor was empty, with only a few torches to light the way down the hallway. The door to Broderick and Elspeth's chamber was open, obviously empty. Ginny wondered how their evening went. No doubt she'll hear all about it from the frantically and appallingly in love Elspeth.

Down the dark hall, there were voices in the distance. The last torch didn't reach into the entryway of the Abbey, so Ginny wasn't sure which way to go. As she entered the dark space, she saw light to her left, coming from under a door. Walking slowly, so as not to trip, she reached the door and opened it to the great room of the keep. There was Ian, and a few of the McKennas, another large, older man, and a few of his clan standing by the hearth. Ian spotted her and called her over.

"Ginny, this is Laird MacDonald. MacDonald, this is my wife."

"Aaahh, ya the lass who stole the Laird from my daughter," MacDonald said looking quite put out.

"The decision not to marry Ian was hers, not mine," Ginny stated, keeping her voice even, but not giving an inch.

The MacDonald laird laughed a hearty, warm laugh. "Aye, she did." Turning to Ian, he said, "Ya werenae joking about her boldness. Tis a rare find, especially for an Englishwoman."

"Aye," Ian agreed. "Ginny, go and get some food. We will be leaving soon."

Ginny was never known to miss a meal and she had missed several over the last few days. This reminder nearly doubled her over with hunger. Walking to the table, she began to eat the bread and cheese left out. Helping herself to a tankard of ale, she sat and began her repast. The men were discussing strategy and some such. Obviously all the players were present, it was only a matter of time before the battle began.

The men began to walk out of the room, leaving just Ginny and Ian. He sat beside her and stared at her profile. Not interested in hearing about what the next few days would be like, Ginny continued to eat, but without much gusto. Finally, not being able to take the silence any longer, Ginny turned and stared back. Her frown was a testament to her feelings.

"The Sinclairs are gathering with their allies, the MacBains. We have the advantage, since we are now aligned with the MacDonalds. I have also called on our allies to the North, the MacGregors."

"Do you even know why you are fighting?"

"Och, Ginny. They killed my men and they all but killed Alec's wife," his frustration was evident, but Ginny wanted to make her point.

"I know that, Ian, but why? Why would they put an innocent woman through that. What do they perceive you did to deserve that kind of revenge? Are you the least bit interested? Maybe it could prevent bloodshed."

With that Ian jumped to his feet and began pacing back and forth. Ginny knew she was in trouble, she had come to know the signs. He was fairly shaking, obviously trying to regain some control. When he did finally speak, his voice was low, but very menacing. "Ya willnae question me, wife," he spit out the last word sounding regretful of marrying her. "They dinna deserve yar compassion. They only deserve yar contempt."

Putting her head down, speaking barely above a whisper, she said, "I don't believe everyone should be punished for the bad decisions of their leaders. I've seen it too many times, where the innocent, following blindly or forced to follow, end up paying for the sins of those in charge." Looking into his eyes, she continued, "You don't think it was everyone's decision to take Aileana. Yet they will die for it, at your hands. Is that fair?"

Like a father instructing a child, he said, "No, it isnae fair. Few things are, though."

"Maybe you could change that, Ian. Maybe you can be different."

"Ya stand with me or no'. Ya must make yar decision, now. If yar no' with me, ya may stay here. I willnae bother ya ever again."

Ginny felt her lip quivering and her eyes tear up. Ian saw her face and turned away. He could not be swayed. His new wife had to know that his decisions were akin to law and she was not above the law. The die had been cast when the Sinclairs engaged in such treachery. A clan is just a large family. The sins of the father always fell upon the son.

The tears were flowing down her face now. Ginny could feel herself giving in and following him blindly, but she would not be able to live with herself if she did. They say if you don't learn from history, you're doomed to repeat it. Well, in this case, Ginny had the knowledge of her time. The senseless killing done by terrorist cowards. Strapping bombs to naive men and women, telling them they would receive their reward in the next life. Telling them to walk into groups of innocent people, whose only crime was being born in a hated country. In the end, nothing changes, only the hate is escalated. The retaliation repeated, back and forth, with the leadership making decisions that end up killing the innocent. Useless and stupid, but ultimately inevitable. Or was it?

Taking a shaky breath, Ginny knew that her decision would end this relationship. But principals were not something so easily destroyed or at least they shouldn't be. "I can't stand by you Ian. I know you think I'm just a dumb girl with a big mouth. Truth is, I know a lot more than you do." She could see his disbelief and continued anyway. "You believe different things and maybe I thought I could change your mind, make you see things a different way, but I know I can't. This is who you are and I can't change that. And you, of course, can't change me either."

"What would ya have me do, Ginny?"

"I would have you speak to all the lairds and find out what happened to bring this about. I would have you be diplomatic, rather than automatically fighting. If it comes down to something petty, I would have you fight the Sinclair laird alone, without killing his entire clan. Or let Alec fight him, since he was the one who lost the most."

" Impossible. Ya know that." Ian seemed to waver for just a moment, then he turned abruptly and started walking toward the door. Ginny stood still, watching him leave, feeling the sinking, empty feeling inside. The tears were flowing freely and her breathing was coming in short pants. *Who am I to change things*, kept cycling through her head. But the truth was, she could only account for herself and she knew what he was doing was wrong. Humanity had a way of screwing everything up, but individual humans could be brave and just. So, in the end, she stood her ground.

"Good luck to you Ian," she called out as he left the room.

He turned suddenly, captured her eyes and said, "I love ya, Ginny. I dinna know when it happened, but I do. I wish ya only happiness." And with that, he left.

Ginny dropped to her chair as if some unseen force sucker punched her in the gut. Grabbing her middle, she began to cry. *What's wrong with me?* she asked herself. *This is make believe. Why does it feel like this?*

Not even hearing his approach, she felt his arm slip around her shoulders. Brother Douglas was trying to soothe her, like a father would soothe his daughter. "It will be fine, my dear. Ya must trust in God's divine vision. He will look after him."

Ginny stopped crying for a moment and looked at the monk. "It doesn't matter. He won't come back for me. I wanted to take a diplomatic approach and as you know, Highlanders don't take the diplomatic approach."

The monk smiled. In his smile were many years of trying to win the same argument. "They can be a stubborn lot. Ya must trust that when it is over, he will take ya home."

She thought about what the monk said. Take me home. Indeed. But which home would she go to. She had such a hard time believing this was make believe, but her logical side couldn't grasp this being real. In the end, she was at a loss... a loss of how to get home, how to make this right, how to not feel like a piece of her had been ripped away.

Suddenly, Ginny knew. She stood up so abruptly, the monk almost fell over. "I need a horse. Do you have a horse I can borrow?" she asked the stunned man.

"Nay, we have only one horse and one of the brothers has used it to administer to the sick."

Ginny's mind was working furiously. "Where are the McKennas?"

"Right outside our gates."

Great! she thought. She would steal one of their horses. If this was make believe, she would be fine. If this was real, she would be dead and could go home. It didn't matter, because something had to change. She did not want to spend the rest of her life cloistered with a bunch of monks.

"Thank you, Brother. You've been most helpful." With that, she ran out of the room, heading to the door to the courtyard.

Ginny peered through the gate of the abbey. The large open field was crowded on both sides by the two different groups. It looked like this field existed just for the battling clans. Low grass, no trees nearby, just wide open expanse, with only the occasional boulder to mar the landscape. On one side, the Sinclairs and the MacBains. On the other, right outside the gates of the abbey, the McKennas, the MacDonalds and the MacGregors.

The early morning sun was just peering over the horizon. Ginny had hoped for some darkness, so it would be easier to steal a horse. Glancing around, she finally spotted the horses in the back, near the outside wall of the abbey. Only a couple of boys stood there, guarding the horses. Formulating her plan, she slipped unnoticed outside the gate and headed to the horses.

As she expected, all the men were facing their enemy and not paying any attention to her skulking along the wall. The guard boys were standing together, speaking in low tones. Ginny caught only a snatch of their discussion. It revolved around how many Sinclairs Ian and Alec would kill. Each had a bet on who would get more, but they were having some trouble deciding how to count.

Ginny crept into the middle of the horses and searched for Ian's. Nothing would get that man's attention like having his wife of less than twenty-four hours steal his horse. However, in the end, Ginny decided that if she was to die today, there was only one man who she would rather piss off more. Stealing Broderick's horse, again, would be like the ultimate middle finger to the man who was never nice to her, always full of contempt and had, of course, back handed her when she first arrived to the McKenna keep.

After locating the horse, Ginny quietly mounted and prayed that she would be able to hold on long enough to get past the McKennas and out toward the Sinclairs. Not being particularly religious, but having had heavy Catholic training, Ginny performed the sign of the cross and kicked the enormous animal forward. She was well past the soldiers before anyone realized what was happening.

Holding on, and feeling somewhat confident, Ginny galloped across the field. She could hear Broderick's bellow from halfway across the field and it made her smile. *Screw you, jackass,* she thought merrily as she continued to hold on. She began to sing Bob Dylan's *Steelers Wheel: Clowns to the left of me, jokers to the right, here I am, stuck in the middle with you.*

Now was the time to put the rest of her plan into action. Quickly contrived and not very clever, she moved her horse directly in front of the Sinclair men. They all stood still, openly gawking at her, when she screamed, "I want to speak to the Sinclair laird."

No one moved, they just continued to stare. Ginny wondered if they didn't speak English. So, in what could only be the most insulting of pronunciations, she said, "C'aite a bheil ceannard?" This finally elicited a response from the men. They began laughing uproariously. Some even fell over with laughter. *Great, this is working great,* Ginny thought watching the men enjoy themselves thoroughly.

Finally, a young man came forward and looked at her. Speaking English, thank God, he said loud enough for everyone to hear, "I am the Laird Sinclair."

The laughter died down and the men watched her carefully. Ginny knew she only had one shot at this and wasn't even sure what she was going to do. The whole plan depended on her thinking on her feet and acting quickly. Turning her head slightly to the side, as if sizing him up, she said, "A little young to be laird, aren't you?"

Raising an eyebrow, the young man scrutinized her back. He was tall, over six feet, with broad shoulders and huge muscles in his upper arms. His hair was an indistinguishable brown and his eyes were gray. His face was handsome, but hardly beautiful and he had a huge scar that ran across the bottom of his chin.

Ginny was thinking he should grow a beard to hide the scar, but then wondered if he was too young to manage one. The silence went on for under a minute, but it felt much longer with all the tension everyone was feeling. Finally, he spoke, "The former laird, my father, died recently. I have taken his place."

"Perhaps you can tell me why you plan to battle the McKennas today," she asked the question so only the laird and a few others could hear.

The Sinclair laird moved a few steps closer and in response, Ginny directed the horse a few steps back. She did not want to be within striking distance of the laird. Seeing how she responded, the laird stopped.

"Did the McKenna send you here to ask?" he asked with an amused look on his face.

"Do you really think he would do that?"

"Nay. I think yar no' a good mistress. He may even kill ya for yar desertion."

"I didn't desert him and I'm not his mistress," Ginny marveled how quickly information moved around the Highlands despite a lack of technology. "My conscience dictates that I try to stop this bloodbath. Your blood, by the way."

That brought a new round of laughter to those who could hear her. "What makes ya think we will lose?"

"Passion. They are so angry at you for what you did to one of them, they are beside themselves with revenge. They are focused and determined. What do you have?"

The laird's eyes narrowed. "What happened to his brother's wife was in retaliation."

Before he could continue, Ginny asked, "Retaliation for what?"

"My father told us of what happened all those years ago. The raping of Sinclair women who found themselves anywhere near a McKenna."

"What? When did that happen? I know that Ian has no idea why you're so angry with his clan. How long ago was that?"

The laird looked confused. He was hiding something, although she wasn't sure what. Ginny noticed that many of the men who had heard the conversation also looked uncomfortable. It suddenly occurred to Ginny what was going on. They were caught up in a revenge plan of someone else's making. They weren't even sure what they were fighting for and now that the person who wanted the revenge so badly, for whatever reason, was dead, they were simply carrying on where he had left off.

"You don't know, do you?" she asked incredulously. "Did it even happen? Can anyone in your clan corroborate his claims?"

"It doesnae matter. My father's dying wish was for every McKenna to pay for those sins."

"You would risk your clan's lives for something you're not even sure happened? Do these men have wives and children to care for? You would make them suffer for revenge that may not even be warranted?" Ginny was beyond stupefied. She was struck dumb, not able to speak another word. There wasn't anything left to say.

The laird walked closer to Ginny, but this time she didn't make any retreat. He looked peaceable enough. She waited until he stood next to her and looked down at his face. There was great pain in his eyes. He spoke quietly, obviously not wanting his clan to hear, "Tis too late now, lass. When my father took the McKenna woman and sold her to those lowlanders, I knew that no McKenna would rest until he'd had his fill of blood. I canna blame them either. My father had us all convinced of his claims, but toward the end of his life, it became clear he was no' himself."

"You would destroy your clan and the MacBains because you don't want to admit that your father was..." Ginny didn't know how to finish that sentence. "Maybe he suffered from a sickness that made him crazy. Ian never said anything bad about the Sinclairs before he found out about this treachery. He might understand that this fight wasn't yours, but your father's."

"Could ya convince him..." he began as Ginny shook her head.

"No, you need to convince him. After this, he won't ever listen to me again."

The young laird looked her in the eye, then yelled over his shoulder for someone to bring him his horse. "Why would a mistress go to so much trouble?"

"I told you I wasn't his mistress. I'm his wife."

The laird's head snapped up to meet her eyes. His anger, fueled by how he would feel if his wife behaved the same way, was evident. But in a moment it was gone. He knew she had risked a great deal to prevent the battle. He owed her his gratitude. "If I cannae convince him, and ya need somewhere to live when the battle is over, I would be honored to take ya home with us."

Ginny smiled. "I'll let you know. Get your horse and meet in the middle of the field. You may want to bring the MacBain laird as well."

"Aye. Thank you Mistress McKenna."

Turning her horse back toward the McKenna side, she said over her shoulder, "Don't thank me yet." With that, she kicked her horse into a gallop and held on once again as she faced a far more imposing foe.

❖ Chapter 25 ❖

Ian saw her riding back and couldn't believe it. Why hadn't the Sinclairs kept her? She would be a bargaining chip in their favor. They probably didn't know he'd married her and maybe they didn't think Ian would be too concerned about a mistress. Whatever the reason, she was riding back to him, with a grim look on her face.

Ian felt Broderick stiffen next to him. "Ya willnae touch her, Broderick."

When the giant man said nothing in response, Ian turned toward him. "Ya willnae touch her, aye?"

Begrudgingly, Broderick nodded his head to indicate he would not touch her. If anyone got to touch her, it would be Ian. And certainly not in the way he did last night, in their wedding chamber. He felt closer to strangling her. Sensing his anger, Ginny stopped the horse at least twenty feet away.

"Come here, now, wife!"

Ginny's eyes widened in fear, but she knew that if she was going to make this work, she needed his cooperation. Taking a huge leap of faith that he would hear her out before beating her unconscious, she dismounted from Broderick's horse. She then took the reins and walked the horse over to Ian. Before she could say a word, Broderick ripped the reins from her hands and took back his horse, again.

Ian just stared at her, as did the rest of the clan. They crowded around, hoping to hear her explanation, as well as her punishment. It was like those first few days all over again. All the progress she'd made with the clan had been destroyed. It was something she would be willing to live with as long as they didn't battle.

Before she could open her mouth to explain, Alec walked forward and glared at her. "How could ya, Ginny. Ya saw what they did to my Aileana. Ya know what they are capable of, but ya betrayed us anyway. How could ya do that to my wife?" Alec's face was filled with pain.

Ian hadn't taken his eyes off her the whole time. His face was like stone, but she could sense his anger seething under the surface.

Ginny figured he was too mad to say anything. He needed to control his anger before he could speak. Suddenly Ian looked over Ginny toward middle of the field. There, on horseback, was the Sinclair and MacBain lairds, no weapons, waiting for Ian to join them. Ginny let out a sigh of relief.

Lifting her head haughtily, she stared at one man then the other. "I did what I thought was right. You may not agree and you may hate me forever, but please hear me out."

Before she could continue, Broderick screamed at her, "Yar a traitor and if I hadnae given my word, I would have killed ya myself already."

Ginny felt the tears in her eyes. Taking a deep breath, trying to steady her voice, she said, "Ian, you told me you couldn't understand why the Sinclairs would do what they did. I decided to find out why. Their laird recently died and his son took over. He's willing to speak to you and try to explain. He wants to prevent the bloodshed."

Alec snorted. "Of course he does. It would be his blood he is sparing."

Ian continued to say nothing so Ginny kept talking. "He wants a chance to explain. I thought before you risk your clan and two others, you might want to hear what he has to say." Ginny stared into Ian's eyes. Was there some softening there? She could only hope.

Broderick, barely containing his bitter contempt, questioned, "Why should we listen to them, Ian? They have no honor. And this whore has even less."

Before she could think twice about it, Ginny yelled at Broderick, "You stupid idiot. You would risk your life, leave your wife alone, and not even know why. You want someone to kill that badly, fine! I give you permission to kill me, but only after Ian has spoken to the Sinclair laird."

Stupid arrogant jackass, she thought. Ginny was shaking with anger. What more could she do? She didn't have this much trouble with the damn enemy. "Obviously, the choice is yours. Do what you wish." Looking over her shoulder at the two lairds waiting in the middle of the field, she said softly, "They're willing to talk. What have you got to lose?"

With that, Ginny walked back to the abbey. Just like the first day, the McKennas were staring daggers at her, some spit at her feet, but no one laid a hand on her. The MacDonalds and the MacGregors

170

were staring silently as well. *I am the world's most pathetic romance novel heroine,* she thought grimly. But what were these other feelings? She walked through the gate and back into the abbey.

Ian was dumbfounded. He didn't move for a full minute, considering what Ginny had said. Broderick was the first to speak. "Ya canna be thinking of going over there. Mayhap the whore has been in league with the Sinclairs all this time. It may be a trap."

Ian finally spoke. His voice, barely above a whisper, was full of contempt, "Broderick, ya willnae ever call my wife a whore again." Ian turned abruptly and called for his horse. "Alec, ya will join me to speak to the lairds."

The MacDonald laird and his MacGregor counterpart came over to see what had happened. Ian explained what his wife had done and told them they could join him. All four men mounted their horses and rode to the center of the field. Ian and the others did not see any reason to remove their weapons and this was not lost on Sinclair and MacBain.

"My wife says ya want to talk to me. Well, now is yar only chance," Ian sounded bored.

The Sinclair laird, a man named Bram, took the opportunity to plead his case. He explained that his father had convinced them of some long forgotten McKenna treachery. Bram gave the details his father had told the clan and how he had whipped them into a frenzy of revenge.

Bram and the clan were told they only meant to steal Aileana, and return her for a hefty ransom. It was his father who sold her to the lowlanders. Bram admitted that he knew of it right after the fact, but did not inform the McKenna of where she was, saving them time in finding her.

At this information, Alec cheek twitched, as if he were biting back his anger. Bram knew that this would probably mean his own death, even told them that, but he would not let his clan suffer for his stupidity or his father's madness. At that, Bram turned to the MacBain laird and said, "I release ya and yar clan. I willnae have ya fight on our behalf."

The MacBain laird turned on his horse and rode off, summoning his clan to follow. The Sinclairs, seeing their own allies leaving, looked scared. Then, surprising everyone, Bram got off his horse and told Ian that he would happily give his life for the lives of his clan.

Ian remained silent during Bram's explanation. Taking a deep breath, and thinking he had one big apology to give Ginny, he looked down at the Sinclair. "I believe you have been honest with me. I canna decide yar fate. I leave that to my brother, since it was his wife who suffered. I willnae let my clan, or my allies, fight ya." Then, turning to the MacDonald and the MacGregor, he said, "I release ya as well. Go home and take care. I thank ya for yar service." And without another word, the two lairds left and took their men with them. At the sight, the McKennas didn't look scared, they look surprised.

Alec dismounted and came to stand in front of Bram. Anger, regret, pure unadulterated hate all stirred up his bloodlust. This man had allowed his beautiful wife to suffer weeks of pain and humiliation, just to hide the fact that his father had gone mad. He lashed out so quickly that even Ian was shocked. Bram went flying and landed on his back.

The Sinclair clan ran forward, prepared to defend their laird. This caused the McKennas to run across the field to defend their laird. Before either side could reach the other, the Sinclair ran towards his clan with his hands up to stop them. Bram realized that it might be too late.

Ginny retreated to the same room she had shared with Ian. Without lighting a candle, she entered the dark room and laid down on the straw mattress. She pulled the blanket up to her chin, rolled into the fetal position and laid there, not thinking. As it often does, the mind begins to ask questions, subjects that tend to be too painful to otherwise consider. *Does he still love me? Is he fighting them, right now, killing innocent people over the madness of one man? Will he really leave me here? Did I fall in love with him?*

Ginny began to think about her life so far, the men she'd dated and dismissed. She didn't regret dumping them or being dumped by them, rather that she hadn't found one man who could turn her knees weak and make her giddy in expectation. That is, until now. The cruel hard truth was that after so many years of the dating game, she finally found someone she thought she could spend the rest of her life with, in a body not her own and a time so unfamiliar.

Now what? Should she go out there, confront Ian and let him know that she had no intention of letting him leave her? Did she have those kind of choices? Over the past months, Ginny was forced to confront that there were certain limitations for women in this time period. Some things she could overcome, but some were insurmountable. It wasn't like she was asking to perform brain surgery on the space shuttle, she only wanted to be able to travel to her new home without getting lost or accosted. There was so much to learn, but isn't that what a lifetime with someone was for?

Ginny felt herself slipping away. Lacking in food and sleep, her body had had enough. Not to mention the emotional roller coaster she'd been on for days. She would know soon enough what Ian had decided to do. God knew that she was not brave enough to face it yet. So, she let herself slip away into the void of sleep. Her troubles could wait until later.

❖ Chapter 26 ❖

The Sinclairs were in a frenzy, but were cut short when they saw that the McKennas had stopped their approach. Ian simply held up his hand and the soldiers stopped and waited for orders. Bram turned to see what had changed and was amazed at the discipline of the McKennas. Seizing his opportunity, Bram screamed to his men, "Nay, ya willnae fight them. I take responsibility for my father's actions. Ya willnae pay for his sins, only I can do that."

A Sinclair soldier, presumably the first in command, yelled back, "What if they kill ya? Who will lead our clan?"

Bram looked forlorn, but spoke assuredly, like a true leader. "Ya will take my place, Ewan. The clan will survive. Ya will keep the Sinclairs strong." The laird began to turn around, to go back and take his punishment for his indifference. Suddenly, he ran to his commander and spoke in his ear.

Ian watched the laird with great interest, especially when he turned and pointed to the abbey. It looked as if Bram were trying to elicit an agreement from the commander. The commander looked confused, then tentatively agreed to whatever the the laird was asking. When satisfied, Bram turned and walked back to Alec, to receive whatever punishment Alec deemed necessary.

After hearing the exchange, Alec's anger dissipated. He stared at the Sinclair laird, knowing he couldn't just beat on him while he refused to defend himself. Where was the honor in that? Hearing him take full responsibility had also taken the wind from Alec's sails. But part of him still nagged... what about Aileana? What about justice for what she had endured for weeks, because of this man?

"Ya will fight me. Ya willnae just stand there and take it. If I dinna think ya trying, I will kill ya outright. Aye?" Alec needed to do something for Aileana, but couldn't kill a defenseless man.

"Aye," Bram replied, understanding.

Alec took off his sword. He had no intention of making this an unfair fight. Both men began to circle around each other, eyeing one another closely to see if the other would make the first move. Ian had the horses removed and stood a fair distance from the fighting men.

He would not interfere, only watch his brother's back in case one of the Sinclairs decided to get involved.

The first punch came from Alec, but Bram was prepared and dodged it easily. A smile came across Alec's face. It had been a test, to see if the other man would truly defend himself or continue to allow himself to be beaten. The dance continued, with neither man making a move, simply assessing each other's strengths and weaknesses.

Finally, Bram ran toward Alec, catching him in the middle and knocking him to the ground. Alec rolled him over and was on his feet in seconds. Bram was still getting up when Alec kicked him off his feet again. Rolling quickly to the side, Bram gained his feet. No sooner did he stand again, Alec was there with a vicious punch to the jaw. Before he could connect the fist to Bram's face, Bram was able to turn slightly, catching the worst of the back of his neck.

Since Alec wasn't able to make full contact, it gave Bram time to turn on his heel and bring his elbow into Alec's chest. With the wind knocked out of him, Alec went down for a moment, but was up again quickly, a little more leery of the other man's abilities.

And so it went, each man getting in his punches, each man hitting the ground. Alec's right eye was swollen and Bram's left cheek was bleeding. Both men suffered several bruises, cuts and possible broken ribs. When finally, Alec rammed Bram into the ground, neither man got up for several minutes.

Ian walked over to the men, as did the Sinclair commander. Alec finally got up, limping slightly and looking much worse for the wear. Without getting off the ground, Bram looked up, not quite able to focus and asked, "Are we done?"

"Aye, we are done. I dinna expect to ever see ya again. Aye?"

"Aye," was all Bram said, eliciting the help of his commander with getting off the ground.

As the commander began to half walk, half carry the laird away, Ian spoke. "What promise did ya ask of your commander before the fight?"

Bram turned slowly, wincing at the pain. He wasn't sure he wanted to tell the McKenna, since it meant he might get beaten on some more. However, it seemed that Bram needed information as well, to determine if he needed to keep his promise to the McKenna's wife.

"I told yar wife she could come and live with the Sinclairs if ya wouldnae take her back." Bram kept his eyes on Ian, noting the stiffening of his shoulders and hard line of his jaw. "Should I collect her now, or will it no' be necessary?"

Ian's eyes turned to angry slits as he answered the Sinclair's question in his most menacing voice, "It will no' be necessary. And ya shouldnae ever speak to my wife again. Aye?"

"Aye. I am glad ya came to yar senses. She is a brave lass, and quite bonny at that. Ya would be a fool to let her go," Bram said. The commander continued on, helping the laird onto his horse. The Sinclairs slowly left the field, returning to their lives.

Alec stood on his own until the Sinclair laird was out of sight. Then he leaned heavily on his brother, trying not to vomit. Without a word, Ian helped Alec mount his horse. Then he mounted his own horse and rode with Alec back to the abbey. He wanted Ginny to look over his brother before he rode back to McKenna land.

He gave orders to his men, keeping five with him for the journey back, and sending the rest home. Broderick, who was clearly still angry with Ginny, was told to go home and bring his new bride with him.

"What will ya do with her?" he asked, knowing full well that his Laird was likely to look past this huge transgression.

Pulling his commander aside, he said, "I will take her home."

Lowering his head, Broderick only nodded and turned to leave.

"What would ya have me do, Broderick. Banish her?"

"Aye. My wife stood by me. She understood what needed to be done. What will yar wife do next time? Will she betray ya again?" Broderick's face was red with rage. If given the chance, he knew he would do Ginny harm. What she did, in his estimation, was unforgivable, and she deserved nothing less.

"She did what she did to save us. She risked her own life to keep us from battle. She found out the reason behind the revenge and made the only person responsible pay, instead of asking those who were innocent, or their families, to pay. She is no' like us, Broderick..." at that, Broderick snorted his agreement, but Ian continued. "Nay, she is no' like us. She is better. She understands more, she has seen more, and she wants to do good."

"I dinna think I can live with her."

Ian was incredulous. Lose his commander and best friend?

Impossible. He had to find a way to make it work, because Ginny would be coming home with him.

"Get yar wife home and make her safe. I will be home tomorrow and we will talk then. Dinna do anything rash, dear friend. Please."

Broderick heard the desperation in his Laird's voice. "I will see ya soon, then."

"Aye." And with that, Ian turned toward the abbey with his brother in tow.

❖ Chapter 27 ❖

Ian opened the wrought iron gate and half carried his brother into the great hall of the abbey. Brother Douglas was there, along with a few other monks, who had prepared to assist the injured. When the monk saw only Alec, he looked confused. "Only one?" he asked.

"Aye, there wasnae a battle, Brother. Where is my wife?"

"Yar wife? I havenae seen her since she asked for a horse."

Ian gently laid Alec down by the hearth and walked over to the monk. Trying not to look too intimidating, he spoke in a hushed tone, "Did ya know what she had planned to do?"

"Nay. I came out just as she was riding across the field. Brave one, that lass. It seems she prevented a great deal of bloodshed."

"Aye. She may think I dinna mean to take her home."

"Why would she think that?" the monk asked, knowing full well that she would be viewed as a traitor and either banished or killed. Brother Douglas didn't believe that Ian would kill her, but being banished would result in the same thing. Without the kindness of strangers, it would not be long before any lass was dead or wishing she were.

"The Sinclair laird has offered her refuge. I told him it wouldnae be necessary. I will take my wife home with me," Ian had a way of saying things that left no room for argument.

But like his wife, the monk would not take the hint. "I will only release her to ya if I am sure ya willnae harm her."

Ian came to stand in front of the monk. His frame was a good foot taller than the monk, but Brother Douglas didn't back down. "Ya dare threaten me?"

"Aye. I know what she did and how most Highlanders would mistake it as treason. I willnae let her go if I think yar only going to punish her for it."

That caused Ian to stop in his tracks. The thought of anyone, especially himself, causing his wife harm was unbearable. He remembered how he felt, watching her ride across that field, especially after she wouldn't stand by him. Even then, he would not have harmed her. The only emotion he felt was the tearing of his heart at the thought of never being with her again.

"Brother Douglas, ya have my word as a Highlander, as Laird and as a McKenna. I willnae ever harm my wife or make her pay for this action. She saved many lives today, maybe my own. My clan... *our* clan owes her a debt, not punishment."

With a sigh of relief, the elderly monk said, "Ya may want to check the room ya had last night. She dinna come in here and there are few other places she would go, save the chapel."

Ian strode from the room, his long legs carrying him quickly as he searched for his wife. He walked quietly down the hallway, not wanting to scare her away. As he approached the door to their room, he noticed it was slightly ajar. Opening the big wooden door, peering inside, he saw her immediately. His wife was laying on the pallet, curled in a ball, fast asleep.

Stepping inside quietly, not wanting her to wake, he stared at his beautiful wife for a moment. Her hair was still braided and wrapped around her neck. He saw smudges of dirt on her face, marring her porcelain complexion. Staring at her face, he noticed how long her lashes were, framing her eyes. Her lips were full and pouty and slightly open as she slept. Her nose, cute and pert, perfectly centered in her heart shaped face. And of course, she shivered slightly. His wife was, once again, cold.

His heart leapt, thinking that this woman was now forever tied to him, would give him sons to carry on his clan and would warm his bed as long as he lived. What had he done to deserve this? Feeling ridiculous at such fancy, he lit a candle and closed the door to the cell. After removing his clothing, he climbed under the blanket and began to seduce his wife.

Ginny dreamt of walking through a snowstorm, blinded by the white. She was frantically searching for something, not being able to see where she was going. Suddenly, she found herself in the eye of the storm. Sunshine, brilliant and yellow, rained down and warmed her body. She stood in a beautiful field of wildflowers, touching the blooms as she walked.

She smiled and sighed, awakening to his touch. Ginny

suddenly realized that she was no longer alone. That someone was beside her, caressing her face, shoulders and back. Without opening her eyes, she knew it was Ian. She could tell by his scent and by the strength of his hands. Turning her face up to his, she opened her mouth and allowed him to invade her.

There was a distinct chill in the room, but it was soon banished by his warm body, wrapped around hers. Ginny used her hands to explore his chest. Running her hands down his body, she realized that he was already naked. "Doesn't seem fair.. you being naked and me not," she said in a raspy voice, caused by sleep and passion.

"Nay, wife, it doesnae. I shall amend that immediately."

His hands slowly lifted her tunic over her head, leaving her only in her chemise. Before Ian could remove it as well, Ginny stood up. Slowly, seductively, she removed her shoes, her hose, and finally, her chemise by lifting it over her head. Ginny was rewarded with a look of awe on her husband's face.

Ian sounded almost tortured when he said, "Och, Ginny. Yar so beautiful. Come back to me, lass. I canna take much more."

Ginny considered asking him what had changed his mind, but didn't want to ruin the moment. She wanted this lovemaking to last, especially if it was to be the last. So she walked to him, lowering herself so she was on top of him, straddling his middle. She could feel his erection rubbing her intimately. In response, she grinded her hips slowly, back and forth, until Ian's face contorted from both pleasure and pain.

His hands reached up and palmed both breasts. Cupping her breast, Ian used his thumbs to rub her nipples, getting them to grow hard. Ginny closed her eyes to the perfection. Reaching down and grabbing his cock, she slowly raised it to her opening, rubbing herself, using him like a toy.

"Please, Ginny. Now, my love."

Suddenly Ginny remembered that he told her he loved her. Before lowering herself on the head of his penis, she looked him in the eye and said, "Ian, now you belong to me. Aye?"

Confusion was written in his perfect features, but then a smile formed on his lips. "Aye. I belong to ya now. Forever." The last word was gruff, mostly from his need for release. With his proclamation, Ginny lowered herself until he was fully inside her. Ian sat up so he could kiss his wife fully. His mouth conquering her, letting her know they belonged to each other.

Ginny wrapped her legs around his middle and reached back with one hand to caress his sack. Her other hand was firmly around his neck, to keep her balance. Ian groaned his approval as he grabbed her hips and began to move her back and forth, in and out. At this angle, Ian's erection was hitting the perfect spot inside Ginny, and soon all thought was gone, only the pleasure of the moment remained. The burning of her orgasm was driving her wild and she began to buck wildly against him, making Ian grit his teeth to hold out, to give her more time.

Almost magically, Ginny was engulfed in all encompassing ecstasy. Like lying on the beach, each wave of her orgasm slammed her body, leaving her spent and fulfilled. Ian, in his own need for release, threw Ginny on her back and continued to pound into her until his orgasm rocked him. Spilling his seed into her, Ian gave a satisfied grunt. He moved to the side, carrying her with him, cradling her in his arms. He kissed her tenderly, but realized that he was already getting hard again. Thinking of his new wife, he pulled the blanket over them and began to rub her back gently.

The room was cool, which for once felt good against Ginny's heated skin. The only sounds were their soft panting, as they tried to regain some control. Ian shifted uncomfortably, as a piece of the straw mattress dug into his back. "Och, sorry, my love." He moved over, carrying her with him, to a more comfortable position.

"Aaah, that is much better. Are ya comfortable?" he asked her, so tenderly it almost made her cry.

Silly, she thought, wondering if she is about to get her period. Hoping she did so she could justify her weepiness and to confirm that she won't be giving birth without an epidural. It occurred to her that he was waiting for an answer to his question. "Aye, I'm comfy." Taking a deep breath and bracing herself for his reply, she finally asked the burning question, "Why did you come back?"

Refusing to look him in the face, she buried herself into his chest. The silence went on too long for good news, she thought. Finally, she looked up to his face, into his beautiful blue eyes. "I dinna think I could live without ya." Well, that explained nothing and Ginny wanted to know what happened after she left.

"What happened?"

"I spoke to the Sinclair. He told me about his father. He and Alec fought alone. Alec could have killed him, but he dinna. There will always be bad blood, but no one was killed today."

Ginny's eyes widened with the shock. Her plan had worked, as convoluted and hastily put together as it was. There had to be a catch. There was no way that she was getting out of this unscathed. "But your clan, they hate me now, don't they?"

"Nay, only Broderick. He may leave when ya return." Ginny's eyes turned sympathetic at this news. Broderick was very important to Ian, as a commander, confidant and friend.

Turning her eyes down, she said softly, "I'm sorry. I would never ask you to choose."

Gently placing his hands under her chin, Ian raised her face back up to his. "I know ya wouldnae ask that of me. I will convince Broderick to stay. Ya may no' want to be around him for a while." He dazzled her with a brilliant smile. She smiled in return, hoping it would all be right in the end. Just like the novels.

"Do you think he'll ever forgive me for taking his horse. Again," Ginny asked, with an innocent smile on her face.

Ian laughed. "I dinna know about that." Becoming serious he said, "I love ya, lass. I need ya with me. After ya look over Alec, we will return home."

"Why am I looking over Alec?"

"He was injured during the fight."

Ginny looked incredulous. "Why are we lying here... or better yet, why did we just... fool around if your brother is hurt?"

Ian smiled again. He loved how indignant she got over silly things. "He isnae hurt so badly. A couple of scratches, maybe a broken rib. He will live."

Pushing away from Ian, Ginny got herself dressed. She skulked around, mumbling to herself about her stupid husband, trying to find her shoes. By the time she'd made herself presentable, Ian was standing there, fully dressed and waiting. She walked past him to leave the room and he grabbed her and kissed her so passionately, she thought that getting dressed was a huge waste of time. At the last moment, he pulled away. "Och, Ginny. Ya make me forget myself. Best get moving before I put ya on yar back and have my way with ya."

"That's what I've been trying to do." Ginny quickly walked up the hallway, knowing it was only a matter of time before he grabbed her again. She almost made it, got all the way to the door of the great room as a matter-of-fact, before Ian had her in his arms again, nuzzling her neck and feeling her up over her clothing.

"Do you want me to look at your brother?"

"Nay, I want ya to look at me."

"No, you want me to do something else to you."

Ian let out a hearty laugh. "Ya may be right. Ya better get in there, Ginny." He leaned closer, mouth against her ear and whispered, "I am already hard for ya. I may take ya against this wall here."

Never one for public displays of affection, or even potential ones, Ginny ran into the great hall.

❖ Chapter 28 ❖

There were few windows in the great hall, so there was little light in the room, save for the candles here and there. In front of the hearth, Ginny saw a few monks crowding around Alec, who was sitting in a chair. As she began to walk over to him, Ginny remembered what he said about her being a traitor. Her steps slowed and become unsure as she wondered if he would even let her near him.

Ian grabbed her arm and dragged her the rest of the way across the room. His lack of sensitivity certainly did speed things up, but did nothing for her fragile self-esteem at that moment. Literally dumping her in front of Alec, Ian announced, "Take a look at him. We need to leave soon." After this, Ian simply left the room, along with every monk who had been attending Alec. They were curiously alone.

" Ian says you're hurt," Ginny stated in a monotone voice while staring at the wall above the hearth. She had to be getting her period, because she could feel the tears forming in her eyes. *Maybe it would be better to get angry*, she thought. Tears made you look weak, and Ginny hated to look weak.

"Ginny..." Alec sounded forlorn. He knew he hurt her earlier, with his unfounded accusations. Truth was, Alec had never admired a woman like he did Ginny. Even his wife, who he loved more than life, had never done the brave things this woman had done. If he didn't know better, he would have bet she was a man.

Hearing his voice, Ginny braved looking at him. His head was in his hands and he was covered in bruises. Without another word, she began to examine his wounds. Nothing serious, a lot of bruises, but no cuts required stitching. Ian did mention his ribs, so she asked, "Does your chest hurt?"

Alec, who had been silent and still during the examination, finally looked her in the eye. "Please forgive me, Ginny. What I said to ya... Yar the bravest lass I have ever known. Thank ya for what ya did for our clan."

The tears fell over and down her cheeks. Until that moment, Ginny hadn't realized how important it was that he believe in her, that he respect her. She smiled and sighed. Maybe this would work out after all. "Your welcome," was all she said.

He stood up and hugged her, like a brother would his sister. As the tears continued to fall, Ginny melted into his arms, enjoying the protection and warmth. Alec gently rubbed her head and back. For whatever reason, she now felt like she might be able to live this life if she had to. She had the love of one man and the respect of his family. What more did she need, besides showers, coffee and Hershey Peanut Butter Cups?

An angry throat clearing came from across the room. "I can see yar well enough to ride home, brother."

Alec laughed as he released Ginny from his bear hug. "Ya got a fine wife here, Laird. I wouldnae do anything stupid to lose her. There are many who would have her," he said, still looking at Ginny and smiling.

"They can try, but they will die trying."

Ginny didn't think she was much into the macho bravado that many men displayed. Somehow, hearing he would kill anyone who touched her kind of turned her on. Of course, in Ian, this wasn't bravado. He would truly hurt another man who came near her. Still, very flattering.

Clearing her throat and wiping the tears from her face, she turned to Ian. She smiled, lifted an eyebrow and looked quite taken by her husband. Ian narrowed his eyes as if understanding what she was telling him with only her eyes. "Alec, go see if the men are prepared to leave. My wife and I will be out in a few minutes." With that, Ian picked her up and carried her back to their little cell.

"What do you mean a few minutes," Ginny asked him as he carried her off. All she could hear was Alec laughing as she left the room.

❖ Chapter 29 ❖

Three Months Later

Ginny couldn't believe it could get much colder. It was summer when she came, so she got a rude wake up call when autumn hit. The temperatures dropped and the wind picked up. The village was preparing for winter, for when there was little to do outside. Ian had told her that they would often host the clan in the great hall, to keep everyone from going crazy from cabin fever.

She sat by the hearth, relishing in the heat. It seemed that like a good Catholic girl, she got pregnant on her wedding night. When her period never came, but the nausea and vomiting did, she was quite certain of her fate. Ian was as giddy as a schoolboy. He was constantly talking about their son and how they would name him after his father. Thankfully his father was named Ronald, so it wasn't as bad as it could have been.

Aileana sat across from her, working on some embroidery. She was quite certain she was having a girl. Since that first awful night when she realized she was pregnant, Aileana had come to find peace. It seemed that this child was the best thing to happen to her, giving her a new lease on life. Aileana needed someone to take care of, and with that care, she could be healed herself. She asked Ginny to be there, for the birth. What could Ginny say? She was beginning to love her new family.

As Ginny came to get used to the way of life here, she depended on Maude much less. It was a good thing, too, since one of the McKenna soldiers, a young man named Timothy, had started courting her. Maude was an expert at casual indifference and was leading the poor man on a merry chase. Ginny had begun to think she was not interested at all when one evening, in a dark corner outside the great hall, she caught them kissing. Both were equally embarrassed, but neither seemed inclined to stop, so Ginny went on her way, leaving the love birds to their moment.

Then, there was Broderick. He made his home, in a newly built hut, outside the walls of the keep. His wife was always so excited to tell everyone about how much she loved her husband. Everyone, except Ginny. Although they decided to stay, they made it very clear that Ginny was not to have anything to do with them. As the Laird's wife, it was sometimes difficult to keep her distance, but Ginny did. It made things easier for her husband.

As Ginny enjoyed her warmth and quiet company with Aileana, Ian strode into the great hall. Without asking, he pulled Ginny from her seat and sat down on the newly vacated chair and placed her on his lap. Aileana smiled, but said nothing, just continued with her embroidery.

Ian leaned in to whisper in his wife's ear, "I thought ya meant to rest more, love."

"I'm just sitting here, Ian. What more can I do?"

"Ya can go lie in my bed and sleep."

Dear God, he did worry about her. He was almost unnervingly affectionate, but Ginny felt they were growing closer. His world did not include using her as a partner in all things, but she'd grown accustomed to taking care of his home. Ginny would often wonder if she would grow tired of the second class citizen feel. When things got bad, Ian would only have to seduce her to make her put her fears aside. Damn, but the sex was still incredible.

As much as she hated to admit it, she was tired all the time. A little nap certainly would do her good and make her husband feel as if he'd taken care of her. Ginny had told him that she loved him, but she still had a level of uncertainty. There were many things about him she loved, even thought she could really mean it eventually, but right now, she just enjoyed their time together.

"Very well, husband. I will take a nap, but only because I know it would make you feel better."

"Aye, wife. It would make me feel better," his smile was genuine, his voice a caress. Ginny could almost feel her loins tighten at the sound. Seeing the look on her face, he added, "Ya better get going before I forget ya need a nap." His eyebrow raised, mocking her. Before she could get up, he leaned in and gently kissed her lips.

Ginny got off his lap and stretched. She reached the door out of the great hall, turned and looked back at him. He was staring at her departure, watching her make her way. Suddenly, Ginny felt dizzy and her vision blurred. Her head began to swim, like after a long night of drinking. Ian must have noticed the funny look on her face, because

the last thing she heard was him say, "Ginny, are ya unwell?"
And then, there was nothing.

Coming Soon

A Lesson in

Forgiveness

Enjoy a sneak preview of Jennifer Connors' next book in the "Ginny" series.

❖ Chapter 1 ❖

Gentle rocking. Back and forth, back and forth. The only sound was the rhythm of the rocking. No smells or tastes or feelings. Only the rocking. It was soothing and relaxing. Mostly, it was hypnotic. No pain, no worries, no anxieties.

Then, it ended, abruptly. The carriage hit a pothole and Ginny was jarred so hard she hit her head against the seat. Her eyes snapped open. She held the carriage seat as if it was a life preserver. That was what it felt like. She was drowning in a sea of mis-comprehension and the feel of the wood and cushion were the only things that kept her afloat.

Her breathing was shallow and sweat began to form on her forehead. The carriage was small and she was not the only occupant. Across from her were two people, a man and a woman, both older, with graying hair and wrinkles around their eyes and mouths. Both were asleep, the man slumped against the carriage and the woman slumped against the man.

Ginny began to examine the rest of the interior. The rocking continued, except now, it wasn't so soothing. There were doors on either side, with small windows that were currently open to allow for air flow. Right beside each door was what looked like an oil lamp, although neither was lit since it was daytime. Everything was a stained dark wood, except for the cushions, which were a lively red velvety material.

Staring out the small windows, Ginny saw a whole lot of nothing, trees and fields along a seemingly never ending dirt road. No highway, no cars, no telephone poles and no houses.

She closed her eyes and took a deep, shaky breath. *Where the hell am I now?* she wondered, keeping her eyes closed against the reality that she was still not home. Ginny had just lived a strange woman's life in medieval times. She was a romance novel heroine, saving the day and winning the hunk. Of course, that wasn't her real life. The life she left behind in 2008, working as a physician's assistant and living the single life of a thirty year old.

The last thing Ginny could remember was walking away from Ian, her mega-hunk, right before she passed out. *Passed out?* she thought disbelievingly. *More like passed to yet another person's life I will have to live.*

Reaching up with both hands, covered in fine, soft gloves, Ginny began to rub her face. *If I keep my eyes closed, maybe it will all go away. I will be back where I'm supposed to be and Lisa and I can have a big laugh over my outrageous dreams.*

It was not to be Ginny's lucky day. Slowly, she opened her eyes to see the two other occupants of the carriage staring at her. The woman had large brown eyes and a stern, down-turned mouth. The man, whose salt and pepper hair was cut very short, had sympathetic green eyes and a kindly face. Ginny had hoped to remember some information on who she was currently occupying before she had to speak, but since it wasn't her lucky day, she wasn't to be disappointed.

"You will not fade in the background here, young lady. It is your responsibility to make a fine marriage and no man wants a woman who cannot hold a conversation," said the stern looking woman. Ginny surmised she was her mother and she was not happy with her.

The man held a hand over the woman's hand and said more gently, "We don't want you to be alone, Bethany. We want you to have a happy life. Your mother and I want to see you settled before..." Her father, she presumed, didn't finish his sentence. It was probably a conversation he'd already had with her on many occasions.

Ginny didn't know what exactly was going on, but she could figure most of it out. "Yes, sir," was all she replied, hoping it would put an end to the conversation and she could sit quietly waiting to find out who she was. Again, she was not so lucky.

"Two seasons! Two! You should be betrothed by now. There were so many fine gentlemen available. If you would just talk to some of them. I can count how many times you danced on one hand. You are such a beautiful girl." Her mother let out an exasperated sigh and turned to look out the carriage window.

"I will try harder, mother," she replied, figuring it was what she was supposed to say. Since the woman continued to stare out the window, Ginny figured it was also the same thing she'd said in the past. Or rather, the same thing Bethany had said. Before she could expound more on a subject she was completely unfamiliar with, there was a knock from above.

"There now, it seems we have almost arrived," her father

iv

smiled openly. "It will be a pleasure to finally meet Lord Whitmore in person. His correspondence has been most helpful."

Ginny had no idea what that meant, so she decided to keep quiet. The carriage turned down a long drive and suddenly her mother looked almost excited.

"There. The house. Oh, my, how beautiful." The woman was practically hanging out the window. "Come, Bethany and look. I do believe that Lord Whitmore is unmarried," she said looking to her husband for confirmation.

"Yes, dear, he is unmarried, but I would not even try to make a match there. I am told he is not interested in marrying."

"He has no heir, therefore, he must be interested in marrying," she stated matter-of-factly.

"There will be enough marriageable men there for our daughter to choose from. Lord Whitmore is our host. Do not disturb him with your plans." Ginny could tell by the look on his face that he meant what he said and he would broach no argument. Apparently, the woman knew this as well.

"Very well, dear. I am told that Lord Clarendon will be in attendance as well. Although his reputation is most disturbing."

The two continued to discuss the possibilities and argue their pros and cons. Ginny, smartly, kept her mouth shut and listened. She had yet to even know who she was, so she wasn't about to offer up any advice. Ginny did want to know what was so disturbing about Lord Clarendon's reputation. It seemed an interesting topic, rather than how much money each unattached man brought to the table.

The feel of the carriage changed suddenly as they approached the house. Instead of the dirt road, they now rode on cobblestones. Ginny wasn't paying much attention, so when the carriage did finally stop, she was nearly thrown forward onto her parent's laps. Her mother gave her another stern look, while her father pretended not to notice. Before anyone could say anything, the door was opened and small steps lowered. Ginny's new father got out first, turning to assist her new mother down the steps. Taking a deep breath to steady herself, Ginny got up to exit as well. Grabbing her new father's hand, Ginny got her first look at the house.

House was not the word she would use. Perhaps, mansion or manor, but definitely not house. The carriage had entered some type of courtyard, with stone steps that led to huge double doors. Her new parents led the way up the stairs into an entrance hall that was probably bigger than Ginny's whole house in her time. The floors were marble tile, alternating black and white. In the center of the room, there was a beautiful inlay of a coat of arms, with dark reds and greens.

There was little furniture in the cavernous hall. Only a few benches and tables, set back against the walls. The grand staircase was in the center of the room, a good thirty feet from the doors. It looked like mahogany, darkly stained and richly ornamented with huge finial balls on either side. Ginny's eyes must have been open wide as she perused the entranceway because her new mother snapped her fan and hit her in the arm.

"Close your gaping mouth," she hissed at her as a man came from behind the stairs and started in their direction.

Her father was the first to speak. "Good afternoon. Lord Whitmore, I presume."

"Indeed. You must be Mr. Hamilton. It is a pleasure to finally meet you in person, sir." Lord Whitmore, Ginny observed, was probably in his early to mid-thirties. His hair was a rich brown color, not at all thinning from the front, and trimmed short. He had almond shaped eyes and a strong jawline. Overall, Ginny would consider him good looking, but not necessarily "mega-hunkish." He was trim, but not overly muscled, which didn't lend to the usual romance hero. *No, Ginny decided, he probably isn't who I'm here to "fall in love with."*

"Please allow me to introduce my wife," new dad turned so Lord Whitmore could kiss her hand.

"It is a pleasure to meet you, Mrs. Hamilton."

"The pleasure is entirely mine, my lord." New mom looked like she just might burst. Ginny felt herself smiling over the thought, as she couldn't quite understand the excitement. He wasn't a rock star after all.

"And of course, our daughter, Bethany," new dad beamed with pride.

Lord Whitmore turned his attention toward Ginny. His eyes, she could now see, were an incredible shade of green. Bright and vibrant, reminding her of Scotland. That thought made her a little sad. "It is a great pleasure to meet you as well, Miss Hamilton."

"You have a beautiful home, Lord Whitmore. I look forward to seeing the rest of it," Ginny stated, not lying. She was really looking forward to seeing more of this house/mansion. "I've heard the gardens are especially lovely this time of year." Ginny heard the words leaving her mouth, but didn't know where they came from. Perhaps a bit of Bethany was popping out.

"Thank you. I am rather fond of my gardens. Perhaps you will permit me to escort you later," he smiled as he took her hand and brushed a light kiss on the backs of her fingers. "Now, please allow my housekeeper to show you to your rooms. I'm sure you are tired after such a long journey." Whitmore turned toward a small, round woman.

"Thank you, my lord. We are most appreciative," her new father said as he took his wife's arm.

"I have a cold luncheon waiting in the dining room when you are refreshed," Whitmore said hospitably.

As he walked away, Ginny noticed his butt. Raising an eyebrow, she thought it looked pretty nice in his tight fitting pants. As a matter of fact, she rather liked the whole outfit, with the coat and boots. She just might like this time period after all.

The housekeeper wasted no time showing them to their rooms. Ginny had her own room, on the second floor with a window facing the infamous gardens. As she looked out her window, she was in awe. They really were beautiful. The housekeeper noticed her attention and said, "Lord Whitmore is famous for his gardens you know. He employs twenty gardeners to maintain it."

"I can tell. They look outstanding. I'm happy to have a room with a view of them."

"Your maid arrived before you and has everything put away. Do you wish me to call her up?" the housekeeper asked. The woman was a bundle of energy, not able to stop moving for even a moment. Her face was round and her eyes were kind.

"Thank you," was all Ginny said, wondering what her maid would do to her.

"Very good, miss," the housekeeper said as she flitted from the room. For the first time since popping into another life, Ginny was alone. She wondered if she would remember some details of her new life before having to play the part. She also wondered if she would ever see her real home again.

CPSIA information can be obtained at www.ICGtesting.com
Printed in the USA
LVOW041817060512

280557LV00002B/208/P